AFRICAN WRITERS SERIES

206

The Journey Within

The Journey Within

I. N. C. ANIEBO

LONDON

HEINEMANN

IBADAN · NAIROBI · LUSAKA

Heinemann Educational Books Ltd
48 Charles Street, London W1X 8AH
P.M.B. 5205 Ibadan · P.O. Box 45314 Nairobi
P.O. Box 3966 Lusaka

EDINBURGH MELBOURNE TORONTO AUCKLAND
SINGAPORE HONG KONG KUALA LUMPUR
NEW DELHI KINGSTON

ISBN 0 435 90206 7

Set in Linotype 10/11pt Pilgrim
Printed in Great Britain by Cox & Wyman Ltd
London, Fakenham and Reading

To my parents:

Monica Chiji Aniebo
Augustine Nwafor Aniebo

At the time I was born
The earth did not exist
And when my parents died
I buried them in my head.

> 'The Hornbill'
> (Igbo Folk Ballad)

And the way up is the way down, the way forward is the
  way back.
You cannot face it steadily, but this thing is sure,
That time is no healer: the patient is no longer here.

> T. S. Eliot:
> 'The Dry Salvages':
> *Four Quartets*

End/Begin

'Young people of these days do things the other way round,'
Nelson said. He took a sip of his palm wine and went on. 'If you
tell them to jump, they sit. If you tell them to sit, they run. How
can a wife leave her husband and not say when she will return?
I miss my grandson. You should not have let her leave with him.'

'Papa, she is his mother,' Okechukwu said. 'It wouldn't be fair
to deprive John of his mother.'

'I never allowed your mother to take you to *visit* your grand-
parents after we quarrelled. Not even when she left me to stay
with them because I married Josephine without telling her.'

'*Agu*, you did things!' Ibealọ said. Holding out his cup to
Okechukwu he added, 'Fill my cup, my son.' He rubbed his bare,
thin chest as he accepted the full cup. 'You know my son, you
should have consulted your father on this matter. Now that your
wife has little John, she will stay away as long as she wants.
Why should she return early when you do not speak to each
other? Little John would have brought her back to you.'

'Things have changed,' Okechukwu said.

'The only things that have changed are that we lost the war
and you are no longer in the army,' Nelson said.

'And that it has never rained as much as it is doing now,'
Ibealọ added quickly.

'Ibealọ is there a time when you won't joke about serious
matters? Okechukwu my son, refill my cup.'

'I was not joking,' Ibealọ said. 'In the old days this type of
rain was a harbinger of bad news.'

'I did not know that.'

'You have lived most of your life abroad, so how would you
know?'

'How would I know?' Nelson repeated incredulously. To stop himself from making a disrespectful comment he drank half the contents of his cup, and rubbed his paunch with satisfaction. Suddenly there were sharp, staccato reports of rifle fire and a heavy explosion that made Ibealọ jump. Nelson and Okechukwu laughed.

'The war is over, uncle,' Okechukwu said.

'Nothing is ever over,' Ibealọ said.

'You must go tomorrow and get my grandson back,' Nelson said. 'In this type of weather a boy should be with his father and not a bunch of women.'

'Papa, John is only six months old. He needs his mother more than he needs me. He should not suffer because of me.'

'It is not a question of suffering. John is too young to know what suffering is. What is important now is your relationship with your wife. I know you are as soft-hearted as your mother, but you must not let your wife know that or she will climb on top of you and dance all over you. So you must show your wife you are tough and you are her master. Marriage is not a game, it is hard work. Never show a woman your armpit. It is the most vulnerable part of your body.'

'It looks like we are going to have a visitor,' Ibealọ said, peering through the pseudo-French windows into the rain-splashed evening.

'In this rain?' Nelson asked. 'Ha, I know it must be one of those young boys. Nothing frightens them any more. What have they not seen?'

A young man came in from the rain on to the veranda and lowered the large umbrella that shielded him.

'It's Onyeama's son,' Okechukwu said.

'Come in, my son,' Nelson called out to the young man. 'What drove you out into this rain? Is it all right?'

The young man did not answer. He folded the umbrella and stood it up where the rain-water would run off it into the gutter. He was barefoot, and his calf-length trousers were wet almost up to the waist. His cheap, black polo-necked singlet contrasted sharply with his fair, self-indulgent looking face as he came into the sitting-room trailing water.

'I have come to tell you that my father is dead,' he said in a flat voice.

'*Ewuo-o!*' cried Ibealo.

'When?' Nelson asked.

'This afternoon,' Onyeama's son said. 'Just before the rain started.'

'*Ewuo-o* my son,' Ibealo cried again. 'I said this rain is not a good rain. It is not the type of rain that comes empty-handed.'

'Sit down, my son,' Nelson said in a sorrowful voice. 'Okechukwu, give him wine to drink. It will help him bear the pain. Oh my poor Onyeama! Is this how a man goes? Without warning? Without farewells? *Chukwunna, onwu gbara ndu anyi gburugburu.* Okechukwu, have you given him the wine? Good. Drink it down my son, drink it! It will brace you up. I am glad you are taking it like a man. *Ewuo-o*, what will your poor mother do now? How did it happen? In the house or in the hospital?'

'At home,' Onyeama's son said slowly. 'He had gone to the backhouse just as the rain was threatening. Then I thought I heard someone shout. I ran out to see. Then I heard someone whimper. It was my father. He had fallen on his excrement and could not get up. I could not lift him. I shouted for help and people helped me to carry him to the house. After we washed him, we sent for Ndubia. By the time Ndubia came my father was already dead.'

'*Ewuo-o*, how terrible!' exclaimed Ibealo, his old wrinkled face crumpling in anguish.

'Ejiaka! Ejiaka! Ejiaka!' shouted Nelson, 'Okechukwu go and call your mother. She must be in the kitchen. And call Josephine too!'

Nelson gulped down air to calm his racing heart. What a horrible death? Just as bad as Christian's. No, worse! *Nshi nwanyi* had made Christian insane, so he did not know what he was doing when he ran out naked and was struck by a car. His death had been swift; so had that of his only heir, blown up in an air-raid. But Onyeama, oh, my little boy Onyeama, what a fate your *chi* reserved for you. To fall in, to lie in . . . God, did he deserve that?

Okechukwu had not been gone long when Ejiaka's wails broke

out from the kitchen. They cut across the drumming of the rain on the corrugated iron roofing of the house.

She rushed into the sitting-room crying, '*Ewuo-o*, my child!' She stood in front of Onyeama's son, wringing her hands. 'My child, my child, what will you do? Chukwunna, how can this thing happen? And to such a young man? Onyeama! Onyeama! *Ewuo-o*! To go like this! What shall I do? What shall we do? I said what shall we do?'

'It is enough Ejiaka,' Nelson said, feeling the prickling of tears at the back of his eyes. 'It is enough. He is dead! There is nothing we can do now except look after his family and help them as much as we can. It is enough. Don't make the young man cry.'

'*Nnamu-ukwu*, let him cry,' Ejiaka cried, almost beside herself with grief. She wanted so much to hug Onyeama's son whose face now glistened with tears. She wanted to make him feel her grief, its depth, in a way that would limit her descent into despair. 'Let him cry,' she said, almost unintelligibly. 'It will do him good. Crying doesn't kill. It has never killed anyone.'

'Ejiaka, it is enough,' Nelson said. In one of his rare moments of feeling his wife's needs, he went to her. 'It is a great loss, we know. But it is not helping the young man to see you cry like this. You should be consoling him. Come, let's go into your room. Come! Do you hear? Josephine! Come and take your mistress to her room. Don't stand there like a stranger.'

Ejiaka let herself be led to her room crying bitterly all the way. As Nelson returned to the sitting-room her keening voice rushed out, over and ahead of him, asking: 'Is this the way a man should go?'

PART ONE

Chapter One

1 ❀ The ticking of the Smith alarm clock was magnified in the early morning silence. It sounded to Nelson like the clanking of a locomotive returning from a long haul. Nelson stirred restlessly in his high-backed wooden chair. A loud, protesting creak made his lean dog, curled up on a new mat in the far corner of the room, get up and walk over to him. Its head was hung low in affected sympathy. Nelson did not look at the dog but turned to Okoro and asked:

'How long will it take?'

'How long will it take?' Okoro repeated, startled out of sleep. He blinked rapidly to shake off the sleep and said in a thickened voice, 'Perhaps five, perhaps fifty minutes. Sometimes three hours or even days. You are never sure, never sure about these things. You just have to wait.'

Nelson stood up almost stumbling against the dog now curled at his feet. He stepped over it to pace around the room.

'I know how you feel Nelson,' Okoro said, now wide awake. 'Try not to worry. It will be all right. My wife will take good care of her. She has never lost a baby. No, never. Not even once.'

'I know,' Nelson said. A car bumped its way loudly down the deep ruts of Aggrey Road. His tone lightened as he continued, 'You know Ejiaka is still a child. 'I can not help but worry about her.'

'How old is she?'

'Eighteen.'

'My wife had her second child at eighteen and she had no trouble.'

Nelson said nothing. What could he really say? Okoro could never be made to realize that he should not compare his mannish wife to Ejiaka. Their *chi* were not the same. They were never

3

the same for any two people, not even blood relations! But Okoro would not understand that! He had been away from home for too long, away from the customs, beliefs and traditions. His black skin was now just an accident. He had become a white man. His aloofness and arrogance enhanced by suits ordered from London set him apart. Watching him walk down the street, suited and tied, disdainful of the hot, scorching sun, impressed you with the fact that here was a black man whose roots were no longer in the soil he so impatiently trod on.

Nelson stopped at the small centre table. His pacing had dissipated part of his frustration. He picked up the smoking lantern and shook it close to his ear. The kerosene in the tank gave a slushing sound.

'I should have cleaned this thing this morning,' he muttered. He put the lantern back on the table and resumed his pacing.

'You really should not worry so,' Okoro said. 'Ejiaka is in very experienced hands. You know that Janet has delivered European women?'

Nelson grunted. That was indeed a formidable qualification, the ultimate in midwifery—to deliver European women.

But he did not care much for that type of qualification. European women were not Igbo women as their men were not Igbo men.

Just last week a friend told him that pregnant European women had to be put to sleep to deliver a child. Otherwise they would refuse to deliver the child or even kill it as soon as it was born. In fact, the urge to kill was so strong in these unnatural mothers, their children were never allowed near them until three days afterwards. The information confirmed what Nelson had always thought. People who were as white as ghosts behaved like them.

And the other day, the night-soil man of the European quarter had said European excreta were watery, never solid. Which again was nuderstandable, as they never ate solid food. Vegetables made up their main diet, and so like goats they excreted hard droplets swamped in watery waste. One saving grace, the night-soil man had added, was that their bucket latrines were neither heavy nor offensively odorous. In the past six years

4

the night-soil man had bribed the foreman so as to remain in the European quarter.

And now Okoro uses the fact that Janet has successfully delivered European women to console me. But then, what alternative do I have? If Janet had not come, Ejiaka would have had to go to the filthy maternity hospital where girl-nurses would jeer if she so much as groaned in labour, or make crude jokes about paying for those nights of enjoyment.

The most annoying part was that Janet who worked at the maternity hospital would not have been able to attend to Ejiaka. Only high government officials (senior service) and rich traders could afford personalized service. Her present call was costing Nelson all of five pounds!

Is it worth it?

Nelson halted in mid-stride as he became aware of voices, one soothing, the other edged with pain, coming through the closed door of the bedroom. Ejiaka was in pain! He made to go to the door, but Okoro's voice stopped him.

'No, no, do not go in there. It won't be long now. Just be patient.'

'But Okoro,' Nelson said turning, 'she is in so much pain. There must be something I can do to help her.'

'All you can do is sit down and wait quietly.'

It is easy for you to say that, Nelson thought. Your wife is not the one in pain. Nelson resumed his pacing around the small room, slowing down each time he heard a cry from the bedroom.

He had heard of labours lasting a whole day, even a week; of the most notorious killer, the afterbirth, nicknamed *our great mother*; of still-births and operations. Women never really trusted those operations. They were risky. Besides women considered it presumptuous for doctors, though they were white and allied to ghosts, to assume the power belonging only to God, and to cut and sew up human beings as though they were pieces of cloth. Although very few recovered, cutting and sewing was a religion to these doctors. Probably a periodic sacrifice of human beings was part of their pact with the devil. It was comforting. Ejiaka would not be one of the victims. It was definitely worth five pounds to be saved that anxiety.

5

Suddenly a drawn out cry came from the bedroom. Nelson rushed to the door. 'Ejiaka, Ejiaka, are you all right? Are you all right?'

Before he could push the door open, Okoro grabbed him with a strength Nelson had not suspected in his small frame.

'No, no, don't do that. The end is almost near. That cry is a warning signal that the new traveller is on his way. I know.'

Okoro's statement acted like magic on Nelson. He stopped struggling. His breathing steamed in the early morning air.

Ejiaka's cries came at shorter intervals. Would she be all right? Would the baby be born alive? Janet had better make sure it was—they had agreed at the outset, that if the baby died at birth, his payment would be refunded.

'Let me sit down,' he mumbled.

Okoro led him to a chair. Sweat streamed down his face, down in rivulets on to the collar of his white American shirt, down his back giving him goose pimples. He shivered, too weary to wipe off the sweat. It would soon dry up. The harmattan would see to it.

A high-pitched, querulous cry burst from the bedroom.

'Congratulations, congratulations.' Okoro gripped Nelson's hand. 'You are a father now.'

'Yes?' Nelson said. Then it hit him. I *am* a father now. And that cry, lusty and angry, is that of my child? My first child. Is it a boy or a girl? Is Ejiaka alive and well?

Nelson was filled with prideful warmth as he sat down again. It seemed hours before Janet came out of the bedroom smiling.

'Is Ejiaka all right?' he asked.

'Yes, she is. And your son too!'

Nelson rushed into the bedroom. He stood a few feet from the bed and looked at the small cloth-wrapped bundle in the crook of Ejiaka's arm. His tongue was like sandpaper, his throat dry. All the things he had planned to say in the past six months ran away from his groping brain.

'Isn't he handsome?' Ejiaka asked with a smile.

Nelson nodded.

'You blew him from your nose,' Ejiaka said.

Her voice was full of pride and satisfaction, he thought. 'No,' he said, 'he looks more like you.'

6

'That is bad,' Ejiaka said and laughed softly. 'We do not want a man that looks like a woman, do we?'

'No,' Nelson said, 'but it does not really matter.' Then with the tension gone, he laughed.

'Has he touched his son yet?' Janet asked from behind.

'No,' Ejiaka answered.

'Nelson, what are you waiting for?' Janet asked. 'He won't bite. He has no teeth yet.'

Nelson bent slowly to hide his embarrassment and touched the little, pink hand that lay on the small chest. The skin was delicate as though it would crumple under the slightest pressure. This little thing with the squeezed up, oldish face will grow to become a big, strong man. Nelson felt elated and filled with wonder.

Janet pushed Nelson aside.

'You men behave like women at the wrong times,' she said, and folding over some pound notes into the baby's hand added, 'Here, my little one, this is to start you off properly on life's long journey.'

'You should not have done that,' Ejiaka protested weakly.

'Yes, you should not,' Nelson said surprised. Janet was not one to present a gift spontaneously. Perhaps the strain had been too much for her. She had come to the house from the hospital and had not had a moment's rest before the delivery. But she was smiling, her eyes steady.

'Okoro, please tell Janet she cannot do this,' Nelson said turning to Okoro standing at the door like an intruder.

'Why not?' asked Janet. 'It's done now anyway.'

'Yes, it is done,' Okoro said. He came into the bedroom. 'Janet always does what she sets her mind to do.' He picked up the pound notes that had fallen on the cemented floor and handed them over to Nelson.

'I really don't think I should accept this money,' Nelson said.

'Why don't you let the baby decide when he grows up?' said Janet laughing. 'What name are you going to give him?'

'Today is *afor*, isn't it?' Nelson asked Ejiaka.

'Yes.'

'Then he is Nwafor.'

7

'What name do you want for him?' Janet asked Ejiaka.

'I have not thought of one,' Ejiaka said.

'That's not true. You had nine months to think of one.'

Nelson caught Ejiaka's look of appeal, but he too wanted to know the name she would give their child, so he ignored it.

A faraway look came over her face, and after a while she asked, 'What do you think of Okechukwu?'

Nelson nodded. It was a good name. *God's creation.* She said the name over and over, gently and lovingly, testing it to be certain it really was the right one.

'Okechukwu,' Janet said. 'That is a pretty name. Nelson, you had better start learning how to carry your son.'

'There is nothing for me to learn,' Nelson said pocketing the baby's money. 'You forget I took care of my master's children at Ndi-okoroji.'

'That was long ago. I am sure you have forgotten all you knew then.'

'Watch me.' Nelson picked up Okechukwu gently. The baby gave a lusty cry. He rocked him to and fro, but it only increased the baby's crying. Janet and Okoro laughed.

'I warned you,' Ejiaka said. 'Now he will wake up the neighbourhood.'

Nelson quickly handed over the child, a sheepish grin on his face. 'I used to be the best baby-sitter when I was small. Imagine my own child rejecting me.'

'Tch, tch, now Okechukwu,' said Ejiaka. 'Be quiet. Mother is carrying you. Yes, that is it. No need to cry now.'

The baby stopped crying.

'He already recognizes your voice?' Nelson asked.

'He must have or he would not stop crying,' Ejiaka replied.

'I don't believe it,' Nelson said. But in reality he did. He had always felt there was a special bond between mothers and their children.

'Of course you won't,' Janet said. 'Men are not believers. It is their duty to ask questions, to doubt, so we can look for new ways of doing things. Christian, don't you think we should leave the new parents and go home?'

'I am waiting for you,' Okoro said.

'Why didn't you tell me? We could have left sooner.'

'You did not seem ready to go.'

'Now I am. Nelson you better go to bed. Tomorrow will be a busy day, shopping for Ejiaka and Okechukwu.'

'Why don't you two sleep here? It's past three o'clock. I don't think it is safe to go home at this hour.'

'What do you say?' Janet asked her husband.

'Whatever you say,' Okoro said.

'Well, it will soon be morning, and I have to go shopping with Nelson early. We might as well stay.'

'I just remembered that today is pay-day. I have to be at the pay table first thing tomorrow morning. I'll be back late in the afternoon though. Can we do the shopping then?'

'Of course,' Janet said. 'Lucky man. No need to borrow money to look after your son. He must have known today is pay-day. He does not want to go hungry. I tell you that child came with a purpose. But let's all go to bed now. Don't forget to tell Onyeama to wake you or you will be late for your pay. Good night.'

'Till day breaks, Ejiaka,' Nelson said, and led Okoro to the sitting-room. 'I am sorry I don't have a second bed,' he said.

'We will manage with the new mat, that is, if your dog will let us. It is only for two hours. Don't forget to tell the servant to wake you in time.'

Nelson nodded and went to the next room which served as a pantry-store as well as Onyeama's bedroom. Onyeama lay curled on an old mat. As usual, waking him was difficult, but when he did wake up Nelson was sure he would be woken at six o'clock. Okoro was already snoring stretched out on the new mat when Nelson returned.

Nelson took off his white shirt, turned down the light, and stretched out beside Okoro. His dog came over but he pushed him away. Now sleep seemed far away but he did not mind. Thoughts whirled in his head. Turning his head he noticed that the bedroom door had no chinks of light. Ejiaka and Janet must be asleep already. They deserved all the rest they could get.

Ejiaka! How the time had passed away. It seemed only yesterday he had asked for her hand in marriage.

'And where will you be living with my daughter?' her mother

had asked him in a falsely disinterested voice, while her gnarled long fingers deftly squashed tobacco leaves into her blackened clay pipe.

The room they were sitting in lacked furniture like most homes in the village. A new mat, made by Ejiaka, was laid on the *ngidi* he sat on. On the opposite bed, covered with an old mat, sat her mother. Between them the hearth fire glowed, the pungent smoke getting into his eyes, making them water. He regretted having put on his best outfit—white shirt, khaki shorts, white hose in black Oxford shoes. He had wanted to create a favourable impression on his prospective mother-in-law but now he felt he had not succeeded, and would only leave smelling of wood smoke.

'At Port Harcourt, mother,' he had answered carefully. 'It is a big, beautiful town. It has water taps and big zinc-roofed houses built with cement. People wear beautiful clothes there, all the time.'

He glanced towards the door to the kitchen hoping Ejiaka was there listening to his words. She was. The two red strings of beads on her slim waist set off her brown, clear skin so well. She had not acquired the luscious, ripe palm-fruit colour of maturity yet and was still sharply cornered like the houses at Port Harcourt, not rounded like those in the village.

Ejiaka's mother cleared her throat loudly and he looked away quickly, pretending to be fascinated by the glazed clay plates, the hand mirror with the carved handle, and the small four-legged stool on the wall above Ejiaka's head.

'Potakot,' the old woman said tentatively. 'Potakot,' she repeated, piercing him with her eyes.

There was so much menace in the look he was sure he would be driven out of the house. To his surprise she asked in a bored voice, 'And where is that?'

'Over there,' he said, pointing vaguely to where he thought the west lay. 'Many miles away.'

'How far is that?' she asked, her tone sharp and accusing. 'How long will it take me to walk there if my child is taken sick?'

'You go by motor,' he said slowly. He felt uneasy as she deftly lit her ugly, clay pipe with a smouldering wood.

'By motor?' she asked as soon as her pipe caught.

'Yes. It is a two-day journey. Three days during the rainy season.'

His uneasiness turned to dismay when she got up abruptly, with an agility he did not suspect in the stocky legs and pot-like body.

'You are not taking my child there!' she said. 'It is too far. I don't like to travel by motor. It makes me very sick. I want to see my child when I want, be with her when she delivers a child, and take care of her when she is sick. I cannot do all that if I let you take her to that foreign place.'

'But, mother, I will send Ejiaka home if she falls sick.'

'And if she dies on the way what am I to do? My daughter was not born a slave. There are no slaves in our family tree. Only slaves die alone, with no relatives by their deathbed. If you want to marry my daughter you had better live where I can walk to in a day. If you insist on living far away, then you do not really want to marry her. I am not in a hurry to marry her off. She is still young and can wait for better suitors.'

Nelson had never seen an old woman's face set so hard. And that infernal pipe made her look mannish. A quick glance at the kitchen door told him that Ejiaka (so unlike her mother it was incredible) was no longer there. Her disappearance was a let down. He stood up feeling hollow in the stomach and weak in the limbs. He had expected to be welcomed if not with outright joy, at least with open arms. Instead he was being turned away as though he were a night-soil man.

He walked out of the round hut without a word. He was a man. Men do not cringe, not to women. Moonlight and the cool air soon dissipated his anger. He was in a better frame of mind as he let himself out of the compound. The shouts and the singing of children came from a distance. They enveloped him with warmth and nostalgia that softened his present disappointment. He was no longer annoyed with the old woman. After all Ejiaka was her youngest daughter. It would indeed be unfair to carry her off to a distant, unknown place.

His kinsmen were to blame. Why had they chosen a girl who was the sole companion of a mother without a son? They should have known better.

Nelson had not gone more than a few hundred yards down the path leading to his village when he heard running feet behind him. Probably some child returning from the moonlit games. He heard his name whispered. He turned around.

It was Ejiaka. She stopped a few feet from him, and as soon as she had controlled her breathing, she said, 'I . . . I just wanted to tell you . . .'

'What?' Nelson prompted her, hoping her mother had changed her mind and told Ejiaka to call him back. But Ejiaka remained silent so he asked impatiently, 'Did your mother send you?'

'No,' she said quickly. 'She does not know. I just wanted to tell you we will be married soon.' Then she ran back to her house.

How she had overcome her mother's reluctance Nelson had never been able to find out. For there was no doubt in his mind that *she* did it, despite his kinsmen taking the credit.

Nelson slowly turned over on his stomach. Morning sounds invaded the room, competing vainly with Okoro's snores.

Nelson yawned. Maybe he should not sleep at all. Would Onyeama wake him if he did? He yawned again and instantly fell asleep.

2 ⁂ Nelson willed the railway Pay Clerk to speed up the payments. But the man would not be hurried. First, the painstaking check of credentials, then the slow search for the worker's name on the rolls although the shouting of the name from the same rolls was what brought the worker to the pay table in the first place. Finally, the careful counting of the money, handing it over, then the signature-squiggle, scribble or thumbprint of the worker as proof he had received his wages for the month.

It was past morning and rushing into afternoon. The thrill of seeing so much money was losing out to the boredom of waiting. Earlier, Nelson swore at the Pay Clerk for being so slow. Now he cursed the stack of money for not diminishing more quickly.

He and his co-workers of the same shift sat, gathered, on the slag heap behind the loco' shed. It provided a vantage point from which to see the pay line, table and wagon, and hear their names when called. At the beginning of the pay-day, seven o'clock sharp, Nelson and his 'work-shift' had chattered and laughed like people about to embark on a long journey. Later the talking had become desultory. Although his announcement of having become the father of a son that very morning had kept the talk going longer than usual, it died away as each person retreated into himself.

For a while Nelson toyed with the thought of how easy it would be to steal the workers' wages if he were the Pay Clerk. But then he remembered that the Pay Clerk slept with the rolls and the officer with the money. It would be something to own all that money though. Five thousand pounds! *Nnu kwuru nnu!*

What would he do with it? Buy a gramophone first, and hundreds of new records. Then get a brand new Raleigh bicycle? No, have the bicycle first, then the HMV gramophone. A Vono bed with cotton mattress would be next. Cushion chairs, tables and, those beautiful white enamel plates from Japan. What about getting some small and large iron pots for Ejiaka?

Ah yes, what would Ejiaka and the baby be doing now? Sleeping? Bathing? Probably just resting? Or perhaps preparing the evening meal? Oh no, it was too early for that.

He smiled remembering the short conversation he had had with Ejiaka before leaving for work that morning. Dressed for work he tiptoed into the bedroom to have a peek at his son again and was surprised to find his wife awake.

'Did I wake you?' he whispered so as not to wake Janet still asleep in the far corner.

'No,' she said.

'Did you sleep at all?'

'No.'

'Why?'

'Sleep refused to come.'

She looked rested, and very much herself. Nelson bent down to look at their son. His puckered face was young-old in the morning light, not old-young like the night before. He wanted to touch the cheeks but was afraid to wake him. He smiled, filled with the pride of achievement more than ever before.

'I hope he grows up as tall as you,' Ejiaka said.

His smile broadened. He hoped so too. Ejiaka was of average

13

height for a woman but some of her sisters were quite tall, almost as tall as he. With above-average-height people on both sides of the family, Okechukwu would not lose out completely. Height mattered a great deal for on it depended one's view of the world. It made the difference between having to fight daily or simply sailing through life like a *through* train.

'When is Mgbeke coming?' Ejiaka asked. 'And my mother?'

'Are those the things that kept you awake all night?'

'Some of them.'

'What else?' He sat gently on the bed.

'Oh many things that I cannot tell you now, or you will be late for your pay, and that will be terrible.'

'You spoke the truth.' He got up reluctantly. She was right. Anyone not present when his name was called had to wait two weeks to get his money. The white heads of the railways had made the rule that everyone in the railway system was to be paid and when a surplus was declared then anyone who claimed he had not received his salary would be paid.

'I'd better be going.'

'What of Mgbeke and my mother?' Ejiaka asked again.

'Mgbeke cannot come. She is very sick. As for your mother, as soon as I get my pay, I will tell the motor-driver to see her. You know she hates motor-journeys. If she agrees to come, she should be here in a week's time.'

'Then I won't wait after *imacha omugwo* to do housework. I should be cooking as soon as possible.'

'No, no, Onyeama and I will take care of things. You just rest.'

'Much good your cooking will do me. You will over-salt the food, or Onyeama will over-cook the yam as Mgbeke used to do. I am not going to let your good intentions kill me. In three days I will be strong enough to prepare my own food. I may even get up before then. I cannot just lie here doing nothing.'

'You say that because you have not felt your feet on the ground yet. You will find your legs are not as strong as you think. Remember you have just come back from a long journey.'

'You may be right, but I do not feel that tired. Go. You are going to be late.'

Nelson left, running part of the way to the loco' shed. He was beginning to realize how lucky he had been to have married Ejiaka.

Thinking about it he was indeed lucky.

With his first wife, Mgbeke, it was otherwise. His father died soon after paying Mgbeke's bride-price. Then Mgbeke could not be made pregnant. And she blamed him for it, stressing the difference in their ages, which was a mere four years, claiming him to be inexperienced and incapable of making her pregnant. But then she had refused to see a European doctor with him. He had gone alone and was reassured of his virility. He decided then to look for a second wife.

Mgbeke became ill after he told her about his plan. She still refused to see a European-trained doctor, instead she went to every *dibia* she knew or had heard of, returning with jars, bottles and leaf-packets of concoctions of all sorts. Their apartment began to look like the storeroom of an unsuccessful *dibia*. Her illness worsened despite the growing stock of medicinal herbs, roots, and other mixtures. Never following through any course of treatment did not make things better for her either.

Nelson sent her home to her relations when she began to put on weight and exude an offensive odour. He had hoped they would be able to persuade her to see a trained doctor. Luckily, Ejiaka came to him a week after, so he did not feel alone. He was happy to see Mgbeke go. During their last weeks together, she had become as reticent as she had grown enormously fat.

Ejiaka dispersed the air of bad luck hanging round the house like a new broom making clean a dirty compound. They moved to Aggrey Road where the houses were bigger, newer and built with cement instead of mud, making the clean sweep permanent. Everything was definitely looking up.

Even his job responded to the changes in his fortune. The senior fitter no longer criticized him as much as before. The other day, the Chargeman had actually congratulated him for completing on time a piece of work to which he had been assigned late. His heart had beat excitedly when the Chargeman, an Urobo man, said he would mention his name to the white foreman. The rest of the day flowed like a laughing mountain stream.

The shift preceding Nelson's was now called to the pay table. Nelson stood up and stretched. He could see the whole shed, and the haze of the rising heat made things shimmer. Oiled parts of engines looked wet and dripping.

Nelson loved working in the railways. The engines were human to him. They possessed limbs, bellies, eyes and hissing life. They could speak and once one was attuned to them, learnt and understood their language, they gave a great deal of information about themselves, their drivers and the journey they had just made. It was easy to tell when they were feeling robust— their hissing was lively, full-blooded and defiant. One felt their eagerness to go, impatient with the vigour of youth on a leash, steaming vitality bursting from every pore, and glowing with the oil of health.

He often felt sad on pay-days, because the shed always looked deserted and forlorn. The engines . . . they stood with their limbs strewn all over the place. At times it reminded him of the scene of a massacre, at other times a desecrated graveyard. The engines with cylindrical boilers opened from one end looked disembowelled. More affecting were the ones that hissed their annoyance at the neglect they experienced on those days. They reminded him of children crying for their mothers.

Close to where the pay table was set up, but outside the shed proper, was a collection of orphaned engines. They were half clean, half-dirty as though the cleaners had died suddenly, or perhaps been chased away since no bodies in grimy, blue overalls lay around. As soon as payments were over, however, those engines would be reclaimed by their parents. They would be fussed over, clothed and fed, till they shone, sighing with joy and happiness.

From the shed, a long line of men in overalls came out headed for the pay table. Nelson recognized the men from the electrical sections not only because his shift was usually paid just before they were, but they stood out like rail tracks under a hot sun. When he joined the railways he had envied their ever-clean overalls, shiny tools—screwdrivers, tiny hammers, pliers, wrenches, calibrated metal rulers, and writing equipment—and the special treatment they received. Their salary payments were timed efficiently. One had the feeling that if they were kept waiting even for a second more than necessary, all the electrically powered equipment would revolt.

For a time Nelson had toyed with the idea of joining them after his apprenticeship, but then he fell in love with the engines. One could never compare *chukwu* with *egbe igwe*. The latter though awesome, was a manifestation of the former. But the glamour of the electricians!

The cloth of ignorance over his eyes came undone a week after he was promoted to Fitter Grade Three. He had assisted a Fitter Grade One on some complicated and long drawn-out work on a *garratt* engine, the one with two heads! The poor engine had been in the shed for repair for months, and Nelson had come in towards the end. Actually he only helped with the tightening of the last bolts and nuts of the drive wheels and oil-waste boxes, but he felt as if he was in on the resurrection.

With the steam up, the tender filled with coal and water, the body cleaned and gleaming, he had felt a lump in his throat as he watched the *garratt*, engine number 39, driven out of the shed by the shunter. He had worked through the rest of the day feeling the power of a god. He had raised a giant from the dead, brought light and power where there had been none before.

And what had the electricians done? Nothing! Well, not exactly nothing, but in terms of breathing life into the mass of steel, nothing. They only checked the wiring of the engine, cut holes in pieces of cast-iron sent over from Ikeja, Lagos, and filed down joints to the allowable tolerance. That was all. They were like those European-trained doctors whose religion was cutting up people. People in the business of taking things apart rarely see the magnificence of the whole.

'Nelson, it is our turn,' a member of his shift said.

Nelson led the way down the slag heap to the pay table. He was first on the rolls.

'Tally number 1314, Nelson Achu!' the Pay Clerk shouted, his mouth a cavernous hole in a small, fired-black face.

'Sir!'

'Five pounds.'

Nelson watched the Pay Clerk count out the notes in his deliberate, finger-wetting way. He wanted to snatch the notes out of his fat hands, but suppressed the urge. But soon, he was holding the money himself and counting it carefully. It was all in new notes and he prayed that the Pay Clerk had made a mistake and given him one, or maybe two more in excess of his pay. Such mistakes did occur.

No, the beast of the forest had not made a mistake. It was exactly five pounds. The latest increment of ten shillings brought it up to that amount.

'Is it complete?' the Pay Clerk asked smiling.

Nelson smiled briefly and turned away. He pocketed the money hastily, his eyes darting from side to side. The Pay Clerk's remark had made him very self-conscious. He felt all eyes were on him and among them those who wanted to see where he put the money so they could take it away from him. It had happened to other people before, although he had assumed the victims had been too careless or stupid. But then, his pay had not been worth worrying about at the time.

Things were different now. A penny was worth a hundred times more. Not to attract any more attention, he kept his hand in his pocket as he walked away slowly. But his legs would not let him walk slowly. They assumed a life of their own, carrying him away from the vicinity of his co-workers almost at a run.

'Nelson, you are running like a thief,' Ume said from the tail-end of the line. 'Didn't you earn your money?'

Nelson stopped. He covered his embarrassment with a smile as usual.

'Don't mind me,' Ume assured him quickly. 'Run on home. I am sure the little man will need all the money you can bring home. I'll drop by soon. Isn't it a good thing the boy came when we have no legitimate excuse not to buy him a present?'

Ume was a wonderful friend and Nelson thanked him for coming always to his rescue. Nelson disliked to be ridiculed. He assiduously avoided situations that would put him in positions of prominence, but of late the harder he tried to remain inconspicuous the more he became involved in scenes that called attention to himself. Ridicule was the shadow of prominence.

As he walked away down the ash slope, he could feel the mocking smile of the other grimy workers. Their smile stayed with him, prolonging his feeling of unease till he reached the path that led to the town.

The regular fixtures of pay-day were there all right. They lined the road on both sides, their robes uniform in a dirt-brown colour of white, the dirt ingrained in the material. They were so sure of being given alms that only a few of them were actually begging. The rest simply made their sore-encrusted presence felt by exhorting the passers-by or singing in disharmony.

Nelson usually rushed by them, his eyes fixed at a point in the horizon. His heart susceptible, it beat faster with guilt at his determination to ignore human misery. On the other hand he hated to feel he was being taken advantage of. From the day when Obi, whose attitude of superiority and air of sophistication sprouted from Onitsha's smelly crooked streets, had told him, 'Never give those beggars anything,' it had become easier.

'And why not?' he had asked.

'If you give them a penny, they'll praise you there, invoke all their Allahs and Mohammeds to keep and preserve you. You go away thinking you have won everlasting life. But do you know what they do when they get home? They pray for forgiveness.'

'For forgiveness? Why?'

'Ah, I see you don't know. Of course you are new in the town. They pray to Allah to forgive them for having received something from a heretic, an infidel.'

'That is hard to believe. I mean their invocation of blessings sounds so sincere.'

'Of course, it is their business to sound sincere. They have been practising it for a long time. But you don't go home with them so how will you know what they do there?'

'How did you know what they did in their homes?'

'It is common knowledge. Only you new people do not know about it. But don't worry, there are many things you will have to learn if you want to survive in this town.'

Nelson could not and did not want to hurry past the beggars today. At the end of the long line, as though he was not one of them, a small boy stood. His glazed, sightless eyes turned in the direction of those approaching. The fixed stare that showed its open-eyed blindness in the way the shaven head jumped at sounds made by passers-by was touching. Nelson thought the stare was specially for him until he noticed the jerky movements of the head. When he stood in front of the boy holding out a penny he realized the stare was for everybody.

Things were rarely what they seemed in this place! Nelson searched his pockets for another penny. He found one, coughed, and placed the pennies in the dirty, calloused hand that automatically shot out at his cough. Nelson's smile and cheerfulness returned as he walked away from the shrill voice that was thanking and praising him. The boy would be sure of food for at least one day.

Nelson had heard that beggars always spent what they made in one day. They did not believe in keeping anything for the next day. It was against their religion. *Allah zai kawo*, they were said to reply when asked why they did not put something aside. It was a faith that required an inordinate amount of belief in God's infallibility. God would provide indeed.

But the point was He did not always provide. If He failed what could one do then? Beg again? Could that be the reason so many of them begged? Or could they be simply lazy?

At home begging was a sign of laziness. One had to wrest sustenance from the earth to survive. It was the basic principle for all living things. Plants, trees, ants, animals, all had to work to stay alive. It did not matter how little they worked, it was still work. Why should human beings be different? Mother Earth worked too. The heat she maintained inside her was proof. And the way she broke things up and changed them into other things, was that not work? One would have thought that since she owned everything she did not have to work at all. But that was not the case.

Nelson was certain it was plain idleness that made the beggars not work or plan for the next day. Unless . . . unless their religion did not want them to work so that only a few could compete for the possession of material wealth and land? No one would fight to own land he thought was useless. To go and live in the north would be interesting. There must be large tracts of unused land there. One could farm and farm till one got tired of farming. And the land would be fertile too. Perhaps one could even buy land cheaply there?

My God, it would be something to own land that stretched as far as the eye could see, as far as one could walk in four days.

That would be a great deal of land . . . a great deal of land . . . big enough for a large family to inherit. There was nothing like land. Where would anyone be without it? Perhaps he should work towards being transferred to the north in three years' time, or at least by 1944. Okechukwu would be five by then and ready for elementary school. They had very good schools up north.

Chapter Two

The post-noon sun lay in shimmering strips on the parlour's cement floor. The centre table was pushed against one wall, and in the vacant space Janet was giving Okechukwu a bath. Seated on a low stool, she had him face downwards across her bare thighs resting on a new, white enamel bowl. Her multi-coloured *lappa* was rolled up and tucked in at her crotch so as not to get it wet.

'He will grow up like his father,' she said as she poured luke-warm water with a cup on Okechukwu. The water ran off his back, down and between her legs into the enamel bowl. Scooping up some water from a smaller, enamel bowl by her side, she splashed it on his back and turned him over gently. 'There are the makings of shaggy eyebrows and a rather large nose,' she went on as though she had never stopped. 'Even the mouth is large. How about shaving his face? There is so much hair on it.' Not hearing any response she looked up.

Ejiaka, lying on the new mat a few feet away from her murmured something drowsily.

'What did you say?' Janet asked.

Ejiaka's eyes were startled open, and a guilty smile spread on her face, apologetic and captivating:

'I did not hear what you said. I was at home.'

Janet smiled. What a shy but stubborn girl! 'I told you to stay in bed. I wish you were in the maternity hospital.'

21

'I feel guilty lying in bed,' Ejiaka said.

'And you don't mind lying on the floor?'

'No,' Ejiaka said, looking serious. 'I did not intend to fall asleep.'

'I see.' Janet smiled but suddenly feeling self-conscious at smiling so often turned back to bathing Okechukwu. 'What about shaving his face?' she asked, and in her embarrassment splashed the baby with more water than was necessary.

Okechukwu let out a lusty cry, showing his delicate pink tongue and throat.

'That's enough, that's enough,' Janet cooed, lifting him up by the armpits and rocking him gently from side to side. That's enough now. We know we have a man in the house. That's enough. We have heard your command loud and clear. That's enough.'

Okechukwu fell silent as suddenly as he had cried. Except for the sound of a lorry rumbling down Aggrey Road, it was as though everything was still.

'That's my man,' Janet said laying him gently on her thighs. 'I like a man who knows when to stop,' she said as she tested the temperature of the water in a small drinking bowl with the little finger of her right hand. 'Too hot,' she muttered, and mixed it with some cold water from a bottle until she was satisfied.

'I don't think we should shave his face just yet,' Ejiaka said.

Janet had forgotten that she had asked the question—she was absorbed in what she was doing.

'All right,' she said, 'we will wait. I would have suggested we shave it now. What do you think, Okechukwu?' she asked the baby, making faces at him. 'We are not a monkey now, are we?'

Okechukwu cried loudly again. His face squeezed up as if in anger.

'That's right,' Janet said with satisfaction. Smiling, she poured a teaspoonful of water from the drinking bowl into his throat, effectively choking back his cry. She then shook him gently, humming soothingly all the time. 'You really feel strongly about being called a monkey,' she said drying him with a soft towel. 'Don't worry. Since we now know how you feel about it, we won't call you that again.'

22

After she had dried him completely, she rubbed talcum powder all over him, her fingers moving gently and slowly over his body. It was more of a caress, her touch sensitive and light on the soft-textured skin, the newness of it, unmuscled and velvety. Her face softened, remembering the children she had bathed— her own. How many were there? Five . . . Five . . .

Ejiaka turning over on the mat brought Janet back to the present. She glanced up to see if Ejiaka had been watching her. No, Ejiaka was fast asleep. Okechukwu had dozed off too under the soothing massage.

'Gently now,' Janet told herself as she turned Okechukwu on his back. He did not waken. She applied coconut-oil to his navel using a large chicken feather plucked to form a painting brush, as an applicator.

The cord would soon shrivel and fall off. She regarded the falling off as the true birth, the real beginning of the new life. The new person, self-contained, set up his own house to which he held the only key. All one could do from then on was guess at what went on in the house, unless one was invited in.

Even then how could one ever know? How could one ever tell what was going on beneath the smooth skin? It was almost impossible even when the baby was still in the womb. The warning often came late. Only mothers whose *chi* were watchful were not dragged to the other world with the baby. And when it was born, how could one tell what was going on beneath that new-old skin after the connection was broken and speech, its replacement, not yet taken root?

Janet carried Okechukwu into the bedroom and laid him gently in the centre of the bed. He did not stir. She walked back to the parlour. For a while she was unsure what to do. She adjusted and retied her *lappa* so that the hem now rested on her bare feet.

She wondered when Onyeama was going to return from the market. Young boys these days were so unreliable. Sending them on errands was like throwing a bone to a dog. As the dog made off with the bone, so boys seized the opportunity to play around.

Remembering Ejiaka, Janet turned and saw her still lost to the world, the tiredness gone from her face smoothed out by the giant but gentle hands of sleep. A slight smile was on Ejiaka's lips, a smile that said many things and perhaps nothing at the same time. Some time ago Janet had noticed there was a difference between the smile of new mothers of male heirs and those of first daughters. The smiles of the latter often came and went like the sun during the rainy season.

Lucky Ejiaka!

Nelson would soon come to her, vibrating with the happiness new fathers always had, looking every inch like a returning conqueror. Yet he had had little to do with the birth of the baby. He experienced little of the pain and the weariness of bringing forth new life. Nor did he know of the fear, the impotence, the disappointment, and the deep-down feeling of worthlessness that was the lot of a woman whose child was born dead.

Worthlessness was a feeling Janet knew well. It had coloured her outlook to such an extent that rejoicing fathers reminded her of green-bottle flies dancing noisily on top of a mound of excreta.

Janet drew one of the high-backed chairs to the open, uncurtained but barred window. The crisp, harmattan morning had gone completely, soaked into staleness by the overcharged heat of the sun. The wide sandy street looked hard. The surface reflected and intensified the heat. The zinc roofs expanded and crackled as if children were throwing stones at them. A few yards away, children were playing loudly and energetically with a small, india-rubber ball.

Children! They were like God. They behaved like Him too, coming and going as they pleased, doing what they felt like doing.

The doctor was surprised when she asked for a day off. To him she was a child and her requests were always a surprise as if she could not plan ahead.

'Anything wrong?' he had asked, peering at her like an owl. She never looked him in the eye when he had his ridiculous glasses on. They made her want to laugh but she had discovered a long time ago whites did not like to be laughed at.

'No, sir. Nothing is wrong.'

She took a quick look at his face when he remained silent for so long. His lips were pursed and looked like a small piece of red meat. Silently he wrote in the log-book. He was giving her his silence trick. Not all of us feel uneasy in front of white people, she wanted to tell him. But then she knew he would not change his method. It had worked well for him so he would continue to use it.

She had her own method to counter it however. She studied the patterns of dust on the cement floor, and the flies that ran about, alighting in slivers of sunlight, washing their hands as if they had just eaten, and taking off again in curved swoops. She settled her body on her sandalled feet, prepared for a long wait. When he cleared his throat, she knew she had won.

'Did you speak with Mr. Alagoa?'

'Yes, sir,' she answered without looking up.

'Is it all right with him?'

'He said I should ask you, sir.'

Things were following their usual pattern.

'That's right,' the doctor said after scribbling a couple more lines. 'You are the best midwife here.'

Janet smiled. When a white man praised you he made it sound like a statement of fact.

'You'll be away for only a day?'

'Yes, sir.'

He stood up, small and white coated.

'All right. Only for a day, remember?'

'Yes, sir. Thank you, sir.'

Janet walked out of the office into the cramped but familiar and alive waiting-room.

It was while passing through the waiting-room a few months ago that she noticed Ejiaka. They liked each other instantly, which surprised her. They talked briefly and discovered they were both from Awka district. It was Ejiaka's first prenatal visit and Janet made her promise to visit the hospital every week.

Not long after they began to see each other frequently, they brought Okoro and Nelson together.

As Janet got to know Ejiaka her affection for her grew. There was an openness and forthrightness in her that Janet found appealing. She now became the younger sister Janet had often wished for. It was to Ejiaka she had turned when a woman in labour bit her right index-finger to the bone. The solicitation and help she had received from Ejiaka surpassed her expectations. In an outpouring of gratitude Janet promised that Ejiaka should have her baby at home, since the prenatal check-ups showed that everything seemed normal.

And delivery was easy. The labour was short for a first baby. Ejiaka was lucky to have a wide pelvis which allowed the baby's big head to come through easily without tearing the vagina.

Janet hoped the ease with which things were happening would not make Ejiaka think that that was how life went on. Not that she wished ill to the poor girl but she longed to shake her out of that dream world of a doting husband and freedom from want. When one became aware of life with the constant changes that made it what it was, much of the merriment drained out of one's face like the high tide running back into the depths of the ocean. A doting husband would eventually cease to be so. Necessities would catch up and finally outstrip resources.

Janet shook her head as the feeling of impotence she thought she had under control threatened to swamp her. She got up quickly and went to the small kitchen in the backyard that served the six families in the building. On her way there she looked in at Okechukwu. He was still fast asleep.

Concentrating on the task at hand, she made fire and placed an iron pot above it. She was glad it was between meal-times and she had the kitchen to herself. She would not be comfortable cooking in such a cramped space if she had to share it with five others. She had just restoked the fire to bring the water to boil quicker when Onyeama appeared at the door of the kitchen.

'Uh huh, there you are,' she said stepping out of the kitchen, rubbing her smoke-filled eyes with the bottom edge of her *lappa*. The railway depot running shed steam siren hooted two o'clock in the distance. 'What were you doing in the market that took you so long?'

'Good afternoon, ma,' Onyeama said.

Janet blinked a number of times before replying grudgingly, 'Good afternoon. Let me see what you bought.'

'There was no meat in the market, ma,' Onyeama said, handing over the market basket.

'No meat?' she exclaimed as she rummaged in the basket, frowning heavily. She found a package of meat wrapped in fresh leaves at the bottom. Her frown was taking on the hard lines

26

of anger when she looked up and saw Onyeama smiling and tugging nervously at his khaki jumper. 'You naughty boy,' she said, her voice more censorious than she intended. She quickly lightened this by adding, 'You nearly made my heart jump out of my mouth.'

Onyeama's smile widened. 'My Hausa friend rescued me today. He always reserves meat for me whenever he kills a cow.'

'Ye-es. And he sells it to you at a higher price?'

'No, ma,' Onyeama said, his voice going up an octave. 'Hausas don't behave like that. Once you become their friend, they never try to cheat you. They are very trustworthy. They only cheat bad people.'

'That is what you say. But you are too young to know anything different.' Janet turned back to the kitchen. 'Now, let us get to work. We'll cook the yam for your mistress first. We have to hurry. Make another fire in that cooking place. Put a pot there.'

'Mrs. Okafor won't like it, ma. The last time I used her fireplace, she beat me, and called me names.'

'You mean you allowed a woman to beat you without fighting back?'

'Yes, ma. She was old enough to be my mother.'

'I see.' Sitting on the kitchen stool Janet looked up at Onyeama. 'You must have messed up her fireplace when you used it.'

'No, ma.'

'Or perhaps you broke her hearth-stones.'

'I was very careful, ma. No one is allowed to play with Mrs. Okafor's belongings. Not even her children.'

'And this fierce woman has children?' Janet asked, convinced Onyeama was telling the truth. She had not really doubted him, but something in her made her fight his apparent look of trustworthiness.

'Yes, ma. Four girls.'

'No wonder!' Janet transferred the things from the shopping basket to the wooden mortar near by. 'Did you report her to your master?'

'No, ma.'

Aha, here it is Janet thought. 'Why not?' she asked, looking

27

at him fixedly. At the boy's hesitation a triumphant smile lifted the right edge of her lips.

'My master would have beaten her.' Onyeama finally said.

'Put that basket away,' Janet said turning once more to the things in the mortar. 'And start peeling the yam. A big one. Your master will soon be home.'

'Yes, ma.'

Taking water from the big water-pot set under the eaves of the kitchen, Janet washed the meat Onyeama had bought. It was of high quality and would not shrink much upon cooking. It was probably cut from the hump of the cow, and the pieces were large, bloody-red and fresh. Thirty pieces in all, for one shilling! It was a bargain, in fact a steal.

Janet decided to quarter-boil the meat before putting it into the *awa*. That would ensure it would be well done and tender by the time the yam was cooked. Port Harcourt yams cooked very quickly, melting in the water to become yam porridge instead of *awa*.

Onyeama had bought the right amount of small red peppers. Janet tentatively bit into one. It stung her tongue like an *agbisi*. Good, that was exactly what Ejiaka needed. You fight the devil with its own power. Raw pepper neutralizes the rawness of the womb. Janet debated whether to cook the family's food in one pot or to do Nelson's separately, but decided she was not going to let him off that lightly. He took part in the enjoyment, let him partake of the treatment too! Janet beat *all* the pepper in a small mortar.

Chapter Three

1 ✂ 'I want ciga,' a reedy voice called to Christian Okoro.

He turned from his image in the mirror and walked up to the counter to see who it was. Christian took the money gingerly between his index and forefinger. It must be past three o'clock

28

judging by the boy's arrival. He knew the boy and his family. His father was an ash-pan man in the railways who smoked like the chimneys he cleaned out daily.

Christian took out five white sticks of Craven A cigarettes carefully wrapping them in a piece of paper. The boy took the small package with both hands but did not leave. He stood looking at it as if he expected something more to be given to him, although Christian could not see how he would be able to hold anything else.

Then he remembered what the boy was waiting for.

'I do not have an empty tin today,' he said slowly. 'Tell your father. Perhaps next time.'

The boy stood there for a while longer and just when Christian was about to repeat his statement, turned and padded away out into the afternoon sun that beat upon his skinny back mercilessly.

Christian watched him go. Poor little devil! Not fed and clothed properly yet his father smokes the most expensive cigarettes. Once again Christian thanked his stars that none of his children had survived. Life would have been hell if any one had lived. Having children changed Janet. They turned her into a hard-driving, over-ambitious woman. And jealous to boot. Without children, living with her was at least tolerable.

Christian turned back to the mirror in which he had been examining his face. The little sleep he had the night before had left its mark. His eyes, always sensitive, were puffed. He would tell Janet to apply cold compresses to them as soon as he got home. But would she be home? Perhaps it would be better to check at Nelson's house before going home, if only to see Ejiaka.

Christian smiled. That had slipped into his thoughts. He smiled again, liking the way his eyes crinkled at the corners, covering over the fine lines that had taken up residence there. They were one of the reasons he smiled often. The other was his perfect teeth. He stroked his long chin, glad his face was small and fairer than the rest of his body. Janet had commented on it. She had thought he used powder. He stroked his slender neck, pressing the base gently. Even his Adam's apple was not very visible. He flicked off invisible specks of dust from the broad lapels of his coat, loving the smooth feel of the material.

29

Today had been a really busy day, he told the mirror. Yes, he had been right to let his hair grow. Its shiny blackness looked more natural now than when he had it short. It lent more weight to his figure and his suit. It also made him look more authoritative, less easy-going.

He squared his shoulders, and stuck out his chin. Yes, it had been a busy day. All through the morning he had been trying to convince some government officials to order suits through him. Today being their pay-day accounted for his success with three of them. That was one of the first things he had learnt when he became the sole agent of Johnson Drapers & Co. of London and Liverpool—you can only get government officials to buy things, particularly expensive suits, on their pay-day or up to three days afterwards. Going at any other time was like trying to squeeze out milk from an old woman's breasts.

It was a good thing the end of the month fell on a Tuesday. He still had three active days to get in more orders. Last month had not been too bad, but it was the Christmas month and he would have jumped into the Lagoon if he had not made that many sales. He had received fifteen orders and everyone paid a sizeable deposit. This month he did not think he would equal that, but he would surely try and try and try.

Christian came away from the mirror humming a song to himself. Carefully he leaned his elbows on the counter and stared out into the paved street. The evening flow of people was beginning. Railway workers coming off the afternoon shift stood out like black crabs on a sandy beach. Traders from the hinterland walked by with their little tin boxes tucked lightly under their arms, the rest of their bodies in dreamland. Now and then one that had finally integrated Port Harcourt into his reality would hurry by, purposeful and singleminded, the complete story of his life—his constant chase after pennies, shillings and a few pounds—written on his oily, lined face.

Christian was reminded of Angela by a lovely woman passing by, her *lappa* tight but covering her to her ankles.

When is that stupid boy coming back? he wondered. It was a good thing he did not have to be at Angela's house by a definite time. It was already well past the hour her husband was to leave for Enugu, so it did not matter now when he got there.

The coast was clear. Christian felt a pleasurable tingle of excitement start up in the pit of his stomach. He pushed himself away from the counter and rubbed his stomach with his right hand.

I have not eaten all day, he thought. But he was not really hungry for food. That hollow feeling at the bottom of his stomach was not for food, although eating could fill it up.

'I want sugar,' a girl said, suddenly appearing at the door of the shop, her shadow huge.

'How much?' Christian asked, glancing swiftly at the large breasts that pushed out her print blouse.

She held out a penny. Her fingers were dirty and the coin was almost worn smooth.

'That na good money?' Christian asked, eyeing the coin and seizing the opportunity to appraise the girl's breasts. Why must young people always have old money? And she was new in the neighbourhood. He would never have failed to notice that lively, young face and those breasts.

'Yes,' she said glumly, her face closing up either from anger at her money being doubted or . . . Christian turned to where the sugar was kept and brought an opened packet to the counter on which the girl had now placed the coin.

He counted out fourteen white cubes of sugar.

'I want paper,' the girl said.

Christian agreed. Her dirty hand would make the sugar look like pieces of charcoal by the time she got home. He tore off a large sheet from one of the old newspapers he kept as wrappers and wrapped up the sugar. He did not want her hands to touch his so he left it on the counter. The girl picked it up and quickly walked away.

'Servant girl,' Christian said to himself. She had been barefoot. 'Probably from the Rivers. Too grown to be Igbo.'

After dropping the penny into the cigarette-tin money-container, he paced around his store. It was only a small one, ten by eight feet, filled with goods that sold quickly to back up his main business of ordering suits from the U.K. There were a few bundles of white shirting, green U.A.C. khaki, baft and other gaily coloured cloths. The khaki and shirting sold like brush fire before and after Christmas. Railways workers, school-children and their teachers needed them, and even the local traders, especially those who travelled into the hinterland and riverain areas, now preferred khaki outfits to others. Christian made sure he never ran out of khaki, stocking up in the mid-year when the demand was lowest and he could buy at a profit.

Over the months he had also added a few dozen tins of tea and coffee, cigarettes, sardines, corned beef, and a dozen large matchets to his stock. Because they sold well he had added other things people often bought singly—sugar, soap, vaseline, sponges, biscuits and so on—and then sent for his young cousin, Vitus, to mind the store and perhaps pick up a few skills in merchandising.

His cousin's arrival convinced Janet that he was determined to be his own master. He had always hated serving under anybody, whether in the government or in the merchant house; but he had been able to control his aversion until something happened soon after he and Janet were married.

As a clerk in the Public Works Department with a Standard Two pass, he was slated to become the Chief Clerk eventually. The white engineer liked him, treating him as a special assistant. The Sierra-Leonean Chief Clerk did not like this, and made sure Christian knew it.

Christian and the white engineer had gone on a certain day to inspect the new construction going on at the wharf, when Janet visited the main P.W.D. office to tell him she was pregnant. According to witnesses, some of the men had whistled at her—so beautiful did she look in her white uniform.

Again, according to eye-witnesses, the Chief Clerk on learning who Janet was, had behaved like a man possessed. Insisting on sitting her in his office, he sent for biscuits, oranges and sweets and generally made himself obnoxious with unwanted attention. Janet became so uncomfortable she went home rather than wait till Christian returned. Those who watched her leave said she had left the P.W.D. compound as if a masquerade was after her.

All this and more, Christian was told on his return. It acted like the small amount of water with which a smith wets a grinding stone. Earlier, the white engineer had told him of the Chief Clerk's complaints about his work—so the man was not only trying to get him kicked out of the P.W.D. but to take his wife away from him as well! He had wasted no time in confronting the Chief Clerk with all that he had heard. Although the man denied having any designs on Janet, Christian had cursed and threatened him in front of the workers.

A week later, Christian had received a termination notice. To give Janet the impression that he minded being sacked, he went to the white engineer who promised to do something about it. The termination became effective a week after and Christian was banned from entering the P.W.D. compound under any circumstances. Janet did not give up, but Christian knew she would not succeed in changing anything. The P.W.D. threw workers out periodically, no matter how long they had served, and the Chief Clerks used this to get rid of those they did not like.

Christian had opened his agency business with Janet's savings a month later. At last he was free. He became his own master and no one was there to tell him to control his temper. And his agency did very well. He modelled the suits as he sold them. Janet's savings had gone mostly into buying the first suits. It was one thing to show a customer the picture of a white man in a suit—suits *were* made for white men—and another for the customer to actually see it on a fellow black man. In fact, most of his sales did not need any sales pitch. The way the suits looked on him, coupled with his reputation for prompt deliveries, made them very saleable.

His success had, of course, made him a few enemies; but all they could do was to make dissatisfied customers unnecessarily difficult. There was the fat Chief from Abonnema—Chief Briggs—who complained about the fitting of his suit. He not only wanted his money back but also demanded compensation. It was a hard case because the Chief threatened to run Christian out of Port Harcourt. Christian could not therefore use his standard argument:

'Look, British tailors are the best in the world. They never make mistakes. You are not made for suits. That's why yours doesn't fit well. Look at me. Now, if you were to eat less, and drink less, that stomach would lessen and be like mine.'

No, he would not use such an argument with the Chief who could reduce Christian's body to food for the fishes. Port Harcourt waters were notorious for never giving up a body they had taken in until it was a mere skeleton. Christian was forced to refund the Chief's money and as compensation Janet delivered three of his wives free of charge.

But Christian did not lose in the transaction. A few days after the suit was returned he was able to sell it at twice the price. Also the fact that he had returned the Chief's money reinforced his integrity.

'Good evening, sir.'

'Vitus! where have you been?'

'Nowhere, sir. I was cooking at home.'

'Were you cooking for the whole of Port Harcourt? I have been waiting for you for three hours. I have an important appointment, but of course you were at home gorging yourself with food.'

'No, sir, you told me to take my time so that you . . .'

'Shut up! If I said you should take your time did I mean you should go to bed?'

Vitus silently raised the drop-leaf of the counter, walked through and let it down gently. He stood, awkward and embarrassed, while Christian looked him over. He had on a clean, well-pressed pair of khaki shorts and a sleeveless white singlet. He was barefoot, his feet covered with a fine layer of reddish dust. He was still an adolescent, but already close to manhood. His sharp features were a leaner version of Christian's.

'So you had time to bathe, pomade and change your clothing,' Christian said, his anger mounting. 'Look at me when I am talking to you. Have you eaten?'

'No, sir.'

'Good! I suppose you were too busy combing your hair to remember food? I am going to see a customer in the European quarter. Don't close the store till I am back.'

'Yes, sir.'

Christian picked up his small, black leather handbag of samples and walked out into the cooling day. He gave his dark coat an adjusting pull, felt it settle on his shoulders, and without a backward glance headed for Nelson's house. He had to know where Janet was before he went to his appointment.

As he walked into Angela's house he knew she was about to call the whole thing off, but his knock came in time. The tension in the air reminded him of the night before when he and Nelson had waited for Ejiaka to return from a long journey.

For a while Christian stood irresolute in the centre of the sitting-room pretending to be fascinated by his reflection on the highly polished wooden floor. That floor was one of the things that made him extremely careful whenever he visited Angela. The day he had come to show her husband sample suitings, he slipped nearly breaking his neck. He had learnt since then to walk like an *ogwumagada*.

Angela still did not say a word, but he could feel her eyes on him. It effectively broke the intimacy between them and kept him standing there like a naughty schoolboy in disgrace. She knew it made him acutely conscious of his height which made him angry. She delighted in seeing him angry, but he was determined not to oblige her. Resolutely, he kept his eyes on the floor. One should always try to remain in control when confronting women who had power over one, whether that power was one of pain or delight. And Angela was a dangerous woman. She was used to having her way—her husband being a doting old man who pandered to the huge difference in their ages.

Christian looked up when he heard her get up. She walked off through the door that led to the kitchen. Suddenly alarmed, he turned around slowly, searching for the cause with narrowed eyes. From the kitchen came the sound of voices, subdued and deferential. He was about to retrace his steps to the door when she returned.

For the first time Christian realized how vulnerable he was. No man was expected to spit out sugar placed in his mouth, but to snatch it from someone else's mouth or table was something else. And that was what he was about to do.

'Everything is all right,' she said in her lilting voice. 'Why did you come so late? You had another assignation I suppose?' She threw herself into her favourite chair, a huge wooden affair with deep cushions covered in a dark-blue cotton material which Christian had supplied. The whole sitting-room was furnished with heavy government furniture. The blue of the cushions joined with the brown of the wood to give off a warm, mysterious air in the evening light.

'No, no assignations,' Christian said coolly. 'Business kept me. You know today is pay-day.' Now he smiled. He could feel the tension running out of the room.

'I know,' Angela said, flipping one edge of her *lappa* open and shut and squirming deeper into the cushions, her legs spread out as though for inspection. 'It is the pay-day that made it possible for you to be here! Are you going to stand there all day?'

'No,' Christian said, and walked slowly to the chair next to her. 'You looked as if you didn't want me here when you opened the door. I have been expecting you to ask me to leave.'

Angela smiled, her brilliant teeth breaking the mammy-water image her long dark hair and oval face created. She put her hand on Christian's arm, her eyes twinkling. 'We know each other too well for that. But you're right. I was mad at you for being late. You looked so calm that I felt you had been with another woman.'

'You know that can not be, Angela. Since you have allowed me to visit you, no other woman interests me.'

'Except your wife,' she said.

'Not even my wife.'

'You don't need to lie to me, Christian.'

Christian looked into her serious face. 'I know. That's why I tell you only the truth. I haven't touched my wife for months now. Truly.'

Angela said nothing but slowly got up, still keeping hold of his hand. Christian got the message and stood up too. As always, he was surprised at her height. In the chair she looked small and voluptuous. Standing, she was a head taller, her legs seemingly elongated. It gave him a thrill to look directly at her breasts and picture them uncovered.

She let go of his hand and turned towards the bedroom, her slightly swaying walk accentuating the rhythm of her full buttocks, each half rising and falling in alternating time. He followed her, the hollow feeling he had felt earlier was now a desire. His senses, as keen but more discriminating than when they had come together the first time, noted the dry scent of the evening, the blaze of red, rust, brown and gold covering the

36

sky beyond the wide, mosquito-meshed windows, and the tight-bloused, tight-lappa'ed woman in front of him.

The bedroom was as it always was—clean, wide and airy. The bed dominated the room, the canopy of white mosquito-netting turning it into a carriage of the gods. The fact that the bedroom was a floor above ground level accentuated the feeling of being in some alien yet familiar and intensely erotic abode near the sky.

Gently she took his handbag of samples and placed it on the dressing-table. When he made no move to undress, she stood looking at him, her eyes seemingly dilated. A chill finger traced his body from the feet up as he saw she was as moved as he. It was not the first time they had made love in the daytime. She always said there were certain things people did not expect to happen at certain times, and to her, making love in the day was one of them. She also insisted on leaving the windows wide open. Given what they were doing, a closed window attracted more attention than an open one. Besides it was easier and quicker to escape through an open window.

Now she came to him, touched his face briefly and went to lock the door.

His mind latched on to the open door as the reason for his excited state, but acknowledging this did not in any way slow down his heartbeat. His hand trembled as he untied the King Edward knot and pulled the tie from around his neck. She took it from him before he could lay it on the bed, and soon divested him of his coat. He felt like a young boy being undressed by a woman for the first time as she unbuttoned his white shirt and with gentle tugs pulled it off him. His polo-necked singlet came off in the same way. Leaving him to take off the rest of his clothes, she placed a straight-backed chair beside the bed and began to lay those he had taken off neatly on it.

Christian sat on the edge of the bed and unlaced his shoes. Folding his grey wool socks in such a way that the ankles were turned inside out and over the heels and feet, he placed them across the shoes. She took his pants and underwear from him and put them with the other clothes. Then she sat on his lap and his heart beat faster as his hands told him what he should have thought of earlier—she was naked under her blouse and *lappa*.

He clasped her to him with such strength she gasped and pulled away. Gently disengaging herself she stood up, cold air rushing in to touch the places her warmth had been. He wondered what type of powder she had on, it smelt so good. He watched her remove her blouse, his passion rising.

Her breasts cascaded once they were set free, their dark aureoles and erect nipples accentuating their fairness. He always marvelled at her fairness, a light golden complexion with the creaminess of a plucked, plump chicken.

Before she could untie the cord that held her *lappa* he grabbed hold of her waist, pulled her legs astride his lap—she helping by gathering and lifting the bottom of the *lappa*—and lowered her on to himself, her wet heat warming and burning down to the root, her hands now clasped at the back of his head pressing his face into her scented, cushiony breasts, his hands seeking more of her and finding more than a handful under her *lappa*, holding on, hanging on as she bucked and twisted and slid up and down, impressing her softness and heat on him, on his senses, on his brain, on his imagination till he lost control.

He could have groaned with despair, but it came out as a grunt. It had been too fast. Oh my God, it had been too fast!

Already the heat ebbed like a tide, and rivulets of warm sweat trickled down his sides, leaving a crawly wake behind that made him break out in goose-pimples. And she was wet too, through and through, the top of her *lappa* damming the flow on the outside. Her steam filled his nostrils and he flared them and got the taste of it too, a tangy sweet taste, richly erotic yet fresh.

'Christian, Christian!' There was a break in her voice, and she squirmed as though to dislodge what ever had caught in her throat. 'Christian,' she began again, her Owerri Igbo a sensuous scream, 'You will kill me!'

Again she squirmed and to his dismay he felt himself subsiding. Oh God, not now, not now, he screamed silently. An emptiness was manifesting itself at the bottom of his stomach and he tried desperately to gather together his mental powers to pump it full again with *okwute*. But they had been scattered to the winds and were floating like rice-chaff. Suddenly he was raven-hungry, and his hands relaxed under her buttocks.

She must have sensed the change in his thoughts for she stood

38

up quickly, bunching up her *lappa* to catch any overflow. Christian lay back pillowing his head on his hands. His whole body was falling apart and he watched her hoping her nakedness would knit him back together.

She took off the *lappa* so fast he did not have time to concentrate on her body. She was soon by his side.

'Wouldn't you like to get into bed?' she asked.

Christian sat up and she stood up as though she had read his mind.

She was beautiful. Her pubic hair, charcoal black and carefully trimmed glistened with moisture, little stars that scintillated having drawn all the light they could from the fading evening light. Her thighs, rounded and firm, tapered off to incredibly long legs on which were a light covering of hair. She came in between his knees. He held her hips and nuzzled his face in her small belly, her deep, deep navel, gulping in great draughts the intoxicating scent of her womanhood.

'Do you want to get into bed?' she asked again, running her hand over his hair, caressing his forehead.

'Yes,' he said against her belly. Thank God his body was knitting together and filling up once more. 'You make me feel so very young.'

'Lie down on your back,' she said, pushing him gently.

He looked up quickly into her smiling face.

'Angela,' he said.

'Don't worry, we have time to try everything. You can leave as late as you want. No one will disturb us tonight.'

They had planned this for so long that now he could not believe it was all coming to pass. Thank God Janet was sleeping over at Nelson's. Thank God Angela's husband had travelled to Enugu. Thank God!

He did as he was told, glad she was part of his destiny. She lay on top of him and slowly, tantalizingly, drew up her legs till they were one.

2 ✂ 'Now, drink it all up. You should be used to it by now. Besides it is very good medicine for you. It will keep your stomach in place.'

'Yes, you have told me that many times before, but it is very hot. Truly it is and the pepper is too much.'

'I did not add as much as I did yesterday, and you drank that without complaining.'

'I did not want you to think I am a constant complainer. I have complained from the first day. Today I thought I would not feel it so much. But it does not seem as if one can ever get used to it. Each day it hurts like a fresh burn. Can't you reduce the amount of pepper, Janet?'

'Well, since you feel it that much! You know, without the pepper it will be useless, it won't do what it is supposed to do. I will lessen it next time.'

'Thank you.' Ejiaka took a tentative sip of the steaming, rich palm-oil broth. The heat and pepperiness burnt their way down her gullet and into her stomach. She breathed through her mouth to cool it down. Tears started down her cheeks. It felt cool and seemed to help dampen the burning in her mouth. 'You know, Janet,' she said as soon as she could close her mouth, 'my stomach has been running since Wednesday.'

'That is good. That is one of the things the broth is supposed to do for you. With your stomach always open you will continue to have a good appetite and eat well. Don't forget you are now eating for two. If your stomach is not open you will become constipated.'

Ejiaka thought that made sense. She had to remember little Okechukwu depended on her for his own nourishment. It would take her a little more time to remember that automatically. She had just become used to hearing him cry and having to care for him all the time. She was almost at the stage where she could anticipate his cry, often getting to him just as he squeezed his beautiful face to let out one of his piercing screams. His wide-eyed surprised look when she picked him up, thus aborting his summons, was comical. And when she laughed at him, he would join in with a wide, toothless grin that made Ejiaka catch her breath at the beauty of it all. His eyes filled to the brim so that they twinkled like drops of rain on *mpoto ede*.

Ejiaka took another sip of the broth. With its decreasing heat she could now gulp down a couple of spoonfuls before her mouth felt as if live coals were in it. She stole a look at Janet who had gone back to staring out through the window. Ejiaka rested her spoon on the edge of the enamel bowl. She took a piece of yam and ate it slowly. It was not that hot, so she added a piece of the dried fish that looked like dried strips of chicken. She had never eaten anything so delicious. It tasted better than fresh meat. She wondered if it was from Onitsha.

'Where did you buy the fish from, Janet?' she asked.

'Uhh?'

Ejiaka repeated the question, picking up her spoon at the same time.

'Here. Do you like it?'

'I have never tasted anything so good. I think it is what I shall buy when I start going to the market again.'

Janet laughed and Ejiaka was glad. Laughter seemed the only thing that could disperse her gloom.

'You know this type of dried fish is more expensive than meat. It is called *oku azu* and it comes from Onitsha. I don't think Nelson will give you enough food money to buy it every time.'

Ejiaka took some more spoonfuls of the broth. She was beginning to taste it now.

'Do you think this pepper will get into my milk?'

Again Janet laughed. 'I hope not; if it does Okechukwu will let us know. You ask such queer questions, but I don't blame you. When you do something every day you tend to take it all for granted. You reopen my eyes to many things, which is why I enjoy coming here every day.'

'I enjoy your being here, too,' Ejiaka said. 'With you around all the time I feel as if my mother were here with me. You make everything so easy for me.'

'Eeyah, look who is talking. I haven't told you how wonderful you were during the delivery. You behaved like one who has had many babies before.'

Ejiaka smiled embarrassed. She did not know how to take compliments. Her mother had not been one to hand them out, and on the rare occasions when she did, she always took them back with the admonition not to let them make one's head as big as a ripe *isi ukwu* which would fall *nnkwapi* and embed itself in the earth.

Ejiaka attacked her food with renewed vigour to keep Janet

41

from paying her any more compliments, but at the same time kept watch to know when to stop. The opportunity came sooner than she expected. Something in the patch of a dappled, reddish, evening horizon visible through the window kept attracting Janet's attention.

Ejiaka took a big piece of fish and nibbled at it. Recalling what Janet had said, she did not think she had behaved well during labour. In the beginning she had wanted to impress Janet, but that resolution soon disappeared when actual labour started. The long prelude to the main event had been tiring, but underlying this tiredness was a feeling of relief that the baby was at last on its way. To hear Nelson's voice from the sitting-room was comforting. Although it sounded far away it was quite distinct, possessing the startling clarity of a dream. She believed she had smiled then for Janet had said, 'That's my child,' over and over again in a soothing voice.

Then the contractions began causing hard, strong pains across her back that travelled slowly around to the front. She began to toss and turn, lying first on one side, then the other. She did not know if she groaned—she wanted not to—but Janet told her to take it easy, that she was here to help and make everything easier. Yes, she clearly remembered Janet saying that because it was soon after that she felt her back being rubbed gently but firmly in slowly widening circles. The resultant relief was such she became lucid enough to smile and laugh at herself.

But her awareness of the funny side of her behaviour did not last long, neither did her lucidity. She lapsed into a special kind of twlight, or pre-dawn when one could see hazily if one did not stare. It was like those moments when she was on the edge of sleep, teetering there, now almost in, now almost out. Janet had continued to talk to her gently, reassuring her that although it might seem bad it was in fact very good; and praising her for her courage and strength.

Soon Janet stopped rubbing her back to dry her forehead or simply place a cool, broad hand on it. It felt good and when the contractions hit with a strong thumping pain across the small of her back it was what kept her from crying out aloud.

And then for a moment she felt fear. The pain became a steady drumming and she did not think she could stand it much longer.

She wished she could stop the whole thing, give herself a respite during which she could reassemble her depleted strength. Suddenly, out there, Janet's voice sounded urgent. Ejiaka strained to hear what she was saying:

'Bear down, Ejiaka. Bear down, bear down!'

Ejiaka's near panic disappeared and joyfully she bore down hard the way Janet had taught her. As the contraction came, she took a deep breath, held it and bore down. She got into the rhythm of it and simultaneously the pain across her back disappeared completely. With each push she gave, she felt the baby slide down and back.

It was hard work and it got even harder as time went on. Then unthinkingly she began to grunt and groan. Embarrassed, she stopped but Janet told her to continue grunting if it helped her. It did. It made it easier to bear down and expel air. Just when she thought she would not make it, Janet said, 'Good girl, keep doing it. The baby is here!'

The joy that suffused her whole being when she heard the baby cry could never be equalled. She felt an intense relief that it was all over. Then it struck her that she had given birth to a living being, and to her feelings of wonder were added those of power and exhilaration. Then Janet had crowned it all by saying:

'You have a son, Ejiaka, a man to lead the way.'

'Thank God!'

'What did you say?' Janet asked turning from the window.

'Nothing,' Ejiaka said, quickly finishing off her meal.

'You said "Thank God," ' Janet said laughing.

'I thought you didn't hear what I said?'

'You can be cunning at times.'

Ejiaka did not see what was amusing Janet. She got up, retied her loose *lappa* and picked up her two empty dishes. She had thought she could eat only a third of the food. It reminded her of the story of two Umueji men who visited their in-law and protested strongly at the size of the pounded yam placed before them. Their in-law knew how light and savoury the yam was and urged them to eat as much as they could. Whatever was left would not be regarded as a sign of their dissatisfaction with the food. The men set to, and to their mortification emptied the plates of yam and soup. Shamefaced they slunk away before their in-law could check on their progress.

On her way to the kitchen Ejiaka looked in at the sleeping Okechukwu. He had wet his bedclothes and she debated whether to risk waking him to change them. He was a beautiful baby and already so big. Only four days old and he showed some of his father's impatience at feeding times. Ejiaka subdued the temptation to pick him up and hug him, and quickly moved to the kitchen. Onyeama was washing plates and pots, whistling to himself. She gave him hers and washed her hands with some of the water he was using.

'Have you eaten?' she asked as she straightened up and dried her hands on her *lappa*.

'Yes. Janet gave me food when she finished cooking. She is a very good person.'

The yard was waking up after its afternoon slumber. Three children were playing hop, skip and jump near the gate. Servants were preparing ingredients for the evening meal. Round Mrs. Ajimoke was collecting her line of washing.

'Ah, Ejiaka, how you dey?' Mrs. Ajimoke cried.

'I dey well, ma,' Ejiaka said, the words heavy and foreign on her tongue. 'What about you?'

'We thank God. Nelson never come back from work?'

'No, ma.' Ejiaka wanted to run back into the house. She always felt this way when she had to speak in English. But Mrs. Ajimoke stood there, her arms full of dry washing, blinking in the setting sun as though she could not see clearly. She rarely came out of the house during the day.

'Ah, you dey well true true. I go come thank Nelson some time. E dey look after you well well.'

'Yes, ma.'

Okechukwu's cry came to Ejiaka's rescue.

'Master dey call,' Mrs. Ajimoke cried. 'Make you run-oh.'

'Yes, ma,' Ejiaka said, going quickly to the bedroom door.

Janet had already picked him up and was trying to quiet him.

'He's wet,' she said.

Ejiaka nodded and took him over. '*Odunma, odunma*,' she said, 'You have told us you are awake. No need to shout so loud any

44

more. I am here. You don't recognize your mother?' Ejiaka asked, smiling at Okechukwu who now stared at her silently. He looked clear-eyed, as though he had been awake for some time. She put her mouth against his chest and made a buzzing noise at him. He grinned.

'That's better,' Ejiaka said, turning to the bed only to find that Janet had already stripped off the wet bedding, and was now replacing it with dry things. 'Shall we bathe him?'

'No,' Janet said. 'It is too early. You may try feeding him.'

They went back to the sitting-room. Ejiaka sat on the mat on the floor while Janet went back to her chair by the window.

'Where is your dog?' she asked.

'Oh, that dog,' Ejiaka said, pulling her right breast from under her loose blouse. 'It comes home when *nnamu-ukwu* returns from work. I don't think it likes to stay with us.'

'Hm.'

'It is a queer dog. Things here are so different from those at home.' Ejiaka stretched out her legs, cradled Okechukwu more comfortably and guided her nipple into his mouth.

'You mean dogs in your village are different from those here?' Janet asked incredulously.

'Yes, they are. A dog in my village is only partial to the person who feeds it most of the time. It is, however, friendly with every member of the household. But this queer dog likes *nnamu-ukwu* so much that it goes out when he does and returns when he does, although we feed it all the time. *Nnamu-ukwu* has no time for it, and the dog becomes wary and as soon as it sees a chance, escapes. It is unhealthy and suspicious.'

'Perhaps it behaves like that because you met it here. It still regards you as a stranger.'

'What of Onyeama? He was here before me.'

'Perhaps Onyeama maltreated it at the times Nelson was away. What I am saying,' Janet said as Ejiaka shook her head, 'is that a dog grows the way it is treated. Just like children. A change in treatment does not often destroy the effects of earlier mistreatment.'

'I don't know, Janet. There are times when I feel the dog does not like me, that it preferred Mgbeke to me.'

'No, I don't agree.'

'Well, it makes me uneasy. I wish my master would sell it to the butchers and buy a young one that I can train myself.'

'Have you asked him to?'

'No, but I will some day. Heh you,' she said to Okechukwu who had stopped sucking and was staring at her, 'if you have finished eating let us know.'

'How?' Janet asked laughing.

Ejiaka laughed and tucked away her breast. 'We will soon see,' she said. Okechukwu continued to stare at her. 'It looks like he is full. Or perhaps he was not hungry. He did not eat much.'

'That is what you say,' Janet said. 'You know he eats as fast as twenty men. Burp him.'

Ejiaka put him over her left shoulder and tapped him gently on the back. He did not burp. 'You see, I told you he did not eat much. Did you my small man?' She put him on her lap again, sitting him astride facing her.

'Will Nelson go to the service tomorrow?' Janet asked.

'He doesn't go to church.'

'What do you do on Sundays then?'

'You know railway people don't have Sundays. They work every day, even on Christmas day. If he is on morning duty, I stay at home and prepare food and then visit our neighbours afterwards. If he is on evening or night duty, we just stay at home and play games or tell stories. Sometimes he invites some people or some come to see how we are. Sunday is a good day for visiting. Most people are at home.'

'Why doesn't he go to church?'

'I don't know,' Ejiaka said, turning Okechukwu round to face Janet. 'He was not going to church when I first came here so I assumed he did not like to go. I never thought of asking him why. You know, when my father—he and his fellow spirits—was alive, I used to accompany him to church. He was a very important person in the church, and when he died the Christians and the others buried him. I will never forget the wonderful songs the Christians sang at his burial. They made me cry and cry and even now, nine years after, whenever I remember any of those songs tears come to my eyes.' Ejiaka wiped her eyes with the back of her hand.

46

'The Christians made me realize I had lost my father,' she continued struggling to keep the tears from her voice. 'Since then I have not been inside a church. My mother doesn't like Christians. To her, going to a church is a waste of time and money. She said what the Christians really worship are cowries. I did not mind not going because the church always reminded me of my father. If I cry when I remember the songs they sang, what will I do when I go into the church itself?'

Ejiaka wiped her eyes again, this time using the edge of her *lappa*. Afterwards she tried to smile through her tears. To get her mind off the Christian songs she lifted Okechukwu and turned him round towards her. As though sensing her distress Okechukwu let out a cry that was painless in its cadence. Ejiaka put him in the crook of her left arm and rocked him, while smiling at Janet.

'You must have loved your father very much,' Janet said.

Ejiaka nodded, not trusting herself to speak. Finally her smile won and her eyes ceased refracting the light.

From the street came the sound of children's voices raised in argument. They must be returning from a game because the words 'goals', 'stud', 'foul' and 'replay' detached themselves from their shrill unintelligible sounds. Twilight had set in and a cock in the distance crowed, setting off a short-lived chorus. A dog barked twice and discouraged fell silent.

Ejiaka stopped rocking Okechukwu. Before many years had run their course she would be sitting here or in some other town waiting for him to come back from a game, or probably hoping he had not hurt himself. Judging from his size now there was no doubt he would be a very energetic and playful child. He had the big bones of his father, a rabble rouser in his youth if there ever was one. For a fleeting second Ejiaka wished Okechukwu would remain little for a long time to come. She quickly unwished it by saying to herself: '*Ngele-oji* will not permit it.'

Janet suddenly stood up. 'It's time for me to go,' she said. 'I think it's time to bathe him.'

'Onyeama!' Ejiaka called, in soft but distinct tones so as not to startle Okechukwu who stared at her fascinated.

'Ma?' Onyeama said, appearing at the door panting.

47

'Bring the things for bathing Okechukwu. Do you have any water on the fire?'

'Yes, ma.'

'Bring it too.'

Onyeama went back to the kitchen.

Janet carried Okechukwu so Ejiaka could get up. 'Cover him up with something if you are going to come with me.'

Ejiaka brought a small jumper from the bedroom and dressed Okechukwu. They all went out to the street, Ejiaka struck by the width of it as always, and by the number of people virtually rushing past in opposite directions. It was a beautiful twilight, cool yet not cold, with the colours of the setting sun dressing everything in the primary tones of life and the smooth ones of nostalgia.

'You should try to talk Nelson into going to church,' Janet said.

'He will not agree.'

'But you said you had not spoken to him about it?'

'Yes, but I have heard him say bad things about the church, so I know he will not agree to go.'

'Try anyway. It is important.'

'Really?'

'Yes. If he wants to do well here, he must become a Christian. The white men in the railways are all Christians. Do you think they will promote someone who is a pagan? Also, it would be good if Okechukwu could be baptized in the church now. It will help him a great deal when he starts going to school. You want him to go to school?'

'Yes, oh yes he will.'

'Well, it will be easier for him to be admitted if his parents are Christians.'

'Nnamu-ukwu is not someone you can easily talk to about things concerning himself. When he wants to discuss a personal thing with me he lets me know, and I can tell when he wants to just by looking at him. You know how stubborn he is.'

'Yes, but you won't lose anything by trying to tell him how important it is for him to become a Christian. You can say I told you to tell him.'

'Then he will ask why you did not tell him yourself. No, if I

48

am going to tell him I will not mention you at all. He does not like unnecessary talking between husband and wife and I can see his point. He says that people talk when they do not really understand each other, and they understand each other less when they do talk. There is an Itsekiri husband and wife in our yard who quarrel most of the time. You should hear them talk. And they have been married for more than ten years! *Nnamu-ukwu* says they have merely been living together and are not really married. Real husbands and wives can easily communicate with each other without words, like they do at home. There, they don't have the time and strength to talk all the time. After working on the farm all day who wants to sit around and talk? Talking won't bring in food or prepare it. Don't you agree?' Ejiaka broke off when she realized she had been talking for a long time.

'I agree with Nelson, but I still think you should try to make him start going to church. Let him try it for a while at least. You can go to church without becoming a Christian. If he does not like it, then there is nothing lost.'

'All right, I will try. Perhaps he will bring it up himself.'

'Here take him. You have gone with me far enough. If we go any further, then I will have to walk you back.'

'And I will go with you again,' said Ejiaka laughing.

'And we will go on and on till one of us drops dead,' Janet said, joining in the laughter. 'May the day dawn, Ejiaka.'

'May the day dawn, Janet. Greet your master for me.'

'All right. I will see you tomorrow evening.'

'All right.'

Ejiaka started back, carrying Okechukwu at her side, her right arm crooked to form a chair he half sat on. Janet was right about talking Nelson into going to church. If he did not like it, then no harm was done; but if he did, Sundays would be days to look forward to. It would be fun to dress up for church, with Nelson walking by her side and one of them carrying Okechukwu dressed in those beautiful baby clothes she saw in the market. She wondered whether they sang the same church songs they sang at home. She was not sure how she would react if she heard those songs again. But she need not worry about it now since

49

she could not go to the church until after *imacha ọmugwọ* which was twenty-three days away.

And she remembered she should not have actually left the house, she should not be seen outside before *imacho ọmugwọ* She had forgotten all about it and Janet was not one to have reminded her since she was against it. She said a week or at the most two weeks was enough for a woman to recuperate from childbirth. After that the woman should go to the church, give thanks to God and then go about her normal wifely duties.

Ejiaka was glad it was getting dark. But she did not want to give anyone who knew her the chance to see her so she lengthened her stride. Silently she prayed she would reach home without running into anyone she knew. She got home almost out of breath. Onyeama had lit the lamps and got ready the bathwater for Okechukwu. Ejiaka was already seated on a stool when Onyeama came in from the kitchen.

'Onyeama, don't ever tell my master that I walked Janet home tonight, you hear?'

Onyeama smiled. 'I won't ever tell him,' he said reassuringly.

Ejiaka tested the bathwater by pouring a little on one of her bare thighs. It was a little colder than she liked.

'Get me some more hot water.'

'Yes, ma.'

Chapter Four

1 ✂ It was four days now since the traditional birth-feast had been held welcoming Okechukwu to the world. Ejiaka was still trying to sort out the plates, glasses and cutlery they had borrowed from neighbours for the feast. The neighbours had been surprisingly helpful; perhaps, as Nelson thought, fully aware they stood to gain from the quality and/or quantity of their generosity.

The grumblings he heard from those who felt they had not been amply rewarded for their munificence, confirmed Nelson's cynical thought. Nwankwo said he had given a large quantity of cutlery but had received less meat than Okoye who had given only one plate. Okafor complained that he not only gave money but also raw rice, yet Okonkwo who had given a small sum had received a plate of cooked rice more.

None of the complaints were delivered first-hand. They came through various routes, some through three or four people. This Monday morning he felt he deserved the peace with which he was eating his breakfast of roasted yams and *ukpaka* stew.

It was a good thing Ejiaka was up and about. Although he tried to dissuade her from taking on the household chores so soon after the delivery—only twelve days—he was pleased she had argued with him over it. He knew she was strong enough to do anything the second day after the baby was born.

Nelson chewed a piece of yam he had dipped in the stew slowly and with relish. Ejiaka was a good cook. From where he sat he could see her giving Okechukwu his regular morning bath in the bedroom. With her *lappa* rolled up to the upper part of her thighs, she splashed water over him the way she said Janet had taught her. Okechukwu made no sounds of protest, unlike some children who screamed their heads off at the mere touch of water.

And the way Ejiaka handled him, one would find it hard to believe he was her first child. Even her fast recovery was remarkable. Her skin had tautened once again over the bones. She was too restless to grow fat, and Nelson was grateful for that. There was nothing more irritating than overblown wives. Their ugliness inhibited the natural desire for children a husband should have, and Nelson planned to have many. Okechukwu must have brothers and sisters to keep him company. He must not suffer as he had, orphaned at an early age, left alone in the world with no one to call brother or sister, no one to guide or counsel him.

Nelson washed his hands in the small wash-basin on the floor, moved the dining-table back, and went to Ejiaka. She was putting powder over Okechukwu and gently rubbing it into the dimples of his joints.

'I have never seen a baby who enjoys a bath so much,' Nelson said squatting on his heels.

'He really loves it. It is second only to his food. Yesterday I had to bathe him three times before he would go to sleep.'

Ejiaka turned Okechukwu over on his back and applied heated palm-oil with a small chicken feather to the shrivelling navel.

'This is healing well too,' she said, standing the baby up.

'Yes. You know, he is going to have your long neck. And look, that mole on your forehead is on his too. And his eyes are like yours as well. Now, I really see you did not give me a chance! He is all yours. You spat him.'

Ejiaka smiled. She knew Nelson was only teasing her. If their son resembled one of them, it was more likely to be him.

As she played with Okechukwu she threw smiling glances at Nelson, squatting like a huge child, his *lappa* bunched between his big legs, his bare, hairy chest looking broader than it actually was. She said silent thanks to *Ngele-oji* for having given her such a good husband and blessed their union with a male off-spring.

'Hold him, while I throw the water away,' Ejiaka said, handing Okechukwu over. 'Don't pinch him.'

'You mean he should not cry,' Nelson said, carefully placing Okechukwu on his left knee. 'Do you know who I am?' Nelson asked him. 'Did your mother tell you that you have a father?'

'Don't make that child cry,' Ejiaka said coming back with the empty basin. She was laughing as she continued, 'That is how you men are. You talk to children when they cannot talk, but as soon as they start talking, you won't have any time for them.'

'That is not true and you know it. You have never seen me with children so how do you know I will behave that way?'

'I know you will so I am preparing myself for it.'

Ejiaka took the small basin and the drinking bowl. Nelson stood up carrying Okechukwu with him to the parlour. Expecting the baby to cry at any moment he was no longer as relaxed as he had been earlier. He pulled up one of the chairs to the window and sat down. The baby seemed to follow every movement he made.

'Do you know that tomorrow you will be circumcised?'

Nelson asked him. 'Yes, tomorrow you'll join your people. At the moment you look like something from the compost heap.'

Nelson laughed gently at his own joke. 1939 was going to be a fateful year. It had started off remarkably well and he hoped it would go on like that.

'Ejiaka!' he called, 'what of getting my man his dress?'

'I am coming,' Ejiaka said. 'Is he cold?'

'No, I don't think so.'

'Let me find one of his light dresses.'

A boy running hard and looking back frequently although no pursuer was in sight caught Nelson's eye. Was the boy running from his shadow? It was Onyeama! What had he done? Had he got into a fight or insulted some older person? Nelson stood up abruptly and Okechukwu let out a scream of protest.

'Is everything all right?' Ejiaka asked from the bedroom.

'Yes,' Nelson said, rocking the baby. 'Nothing is the matter. I moved suddenly.'

'I will soon come and carry him.'

'Are you still looking for his dress?'

'I found that long ago. I am putting away the things that litter this place.'

Onyeama ran up to the house, panting.

'What have you done?' Nelson asked. 'Why are you running when no one is pursuing you? Have you been fighting?'

Onyeama regained his breath with an effort. Beads of perspiration covered his forehead. Shamefaced he tugged at the hem of his jumper.

'Speak my man! What have you done? Are you deaf?'

Okechukwu started crying.

'Ejiaka, come and take this child,' Nelson said angrily. As soon as Ejiaka took the baby he shouted at Onyeama, 'You, come into the house, and tell me what you have been up to. And if you won't I shall beat it out of you.'

By the time Onyeama came into the house, Nelson had got the cane out of its hiding-place.

Boys from home had to be taught things the hard way. Their heads were like a basket, porous to the finer grains of truth and common sense, but able to retain boulders of stupidity, lies and disobedience.

'How many times have I told you not to get into fights?' Nelson said. 'This is not our home town where you can knock any one down. Do you want to go to prison?'

'I did not fight anybody,' Onyeama said half reproachful, half fearful.

'Look at me if you are going to tell me lies. If you did not fight what did you do then? Do you want me to worm it out of you? Say something, you are not dumb.'

'I went to the shed,' Onyeama said. He seemed to hesitate for a minute and then he looked Nelson full in the face. 'I wanted some oily waste with which to make fire this afternoon, but the engine cleaners wouldn't give me any.'

'Why should they when they don't know you? So, when they refused what did you do next?'

'I went to the workshop and got some from the spoilt engine.'

'Go on,' Nelson urged him. 'Go on, what . . . ?' But Nelson did not complete his question. The full significance of what Onyeama had done hit him. 'You mean . . . ' he began slowly, trying to control his anger, 'what you are trying to tell me is that you opened the axle-box of an engine and removed the oily waste from it?'

Onyeama was silent. Then as if time were running out he began to speak very fast: 'Many boys do it. They say there is no harm if the waste is taken from an engine under repair. Yesterday I even saw a loco' shed man open and take the waste out of the axle-boxes of four wagons, put it in his basket and cover it all up with coal. I saw it all.'

'You fool!' Nelson shouted. 'Do you know what will happen to you if you are caught taking or carrying the waste. You will be put in prison and I will be sacked from my job. I see now that telling you not to do something is a waste of time. You never listen. It enters one ear and leaves through the other. But I will teach you. Don't move,' Nelson said, as Onyeama backed away a few steps. 'I don't want to go chasing after you. And don't disgrace yourself by crying like a woman either. Just stand still and take what you deserve like a man.'

Nelson belaboured Onyeama with the cane. Before long Onyeama was whimpering like a frightened and wounded dog, and then bellowing like a cow. Ejiaka was the first to come to

54

his rescue, followed closely by two or three neighbours. They upbraided Nelson for meting out such a heavy punishment, and dragged Onyeama away with them.

Appeased, Nelson put away the cane. He was sure Onyeama would think twice before committing the same offence. Corporal punishment was a great cure for wayward behaviour. While Ejiaka fed the baby, Nelson explained to her the gravity of what Onyeama had done.

'The police might search this house one day. Just like that. And if they find oily waste, I will be accused of having stolen all that has been missed. Oh yes, we were warned about it. Do you know that without oily waste in the axle-boxes, there will be so much friction in the wheels that the coaches will catch fire? It is a very serious thing! And you can't trust your neighbours not to talk, especially someone like Mrs. Okafor. It makes me angry to think she has watched Onyeama use oily waste all these days. I wouldn't be surprised if her husband reports me to the Chargeman now we are running for the same promotion.'

'Where is Mr. Okafor from?'

'From Arochukwu, the most cunning people in Igboland. Make sure Onyeama never brings oily waste into this house again.'

'I think we have a visitor,' Ejiaka said, rushing into the bedroom with the baby.

'Bring me my singlet,' Nelson called after her. The visitor knocked at the door as Ejiaka brought his singlet. He struggled into it and opened the door immediately afterwards.

'Theodore my man,' Nelson shouted with surprise. 'It has been a long time since we saw you in this area.'

'Four days only,' Theodore said, shaking Nelson's proffered hand gravely. His voice was loud, a necessary peculiarity for anyone who had to talk above the din of the railway running shed.

'Four days seems a long time ago,' Nelson said laughing. 'Please take a seat. Your coming has made my day beautiful once more.'

'You don't look like someone who expects visitors today,' Theodore said sitting down slowly.

'Why do you say that?'

'You are wearing your singlet back to front.'

'*Imakwa na idi* right,' Nelson said, pulling down the front of his singlet to look at it. 'You are the only one who would notice such a thing as soon as he walks into a house.' Nelson put the singlet on correctly. 'Ejiaka!' he called. 'Ejiaka, kola.'

'It is coming,' Ejiaka answered from the bedroom.

Nelson pulled up a chair near Theodore. He was smiling as he asked, 'Now Theo, what brought you out here? If I know you, you don't go to a place without thinking hard about it beforehand. What I am trying to say,' Nelson continued softly, deference and admiration creeping into his voice, 'is that you are too great a man to go visiting a small person like me without reason.'

Theodore smiled, his perfect set of rat-like teeth gleaming for an instant. He placed a small effeminate hand on Nelson's knee. 'Are you trying to tell me something you are ashamed of?'

Nelson burst into nervous, protective laughter. He had great respect for men of learning, and when they were small-statured and older he regarded them with awe. 'No, no, it is not like that,' he said quickly, trying to stop laughing and failing. The more he tried, the more helpless he became. Finally he gave in and let the laughter laugh itself out. 'You know that is not true,' he said afterwards.

'I know,' Theodore said gravely and then smiled, destroying the credibility of what he had just said.

There was something in his face Nelson could never fully fathom. Maybe it was the shape of his nose like a proboscis, or his mouth that was small and yet full, but Nelson always felt that he was looking at someone who had seen it all, and passed judgement. That impression was especially strong when Theo was behind his huge Chief Clerk's desk trying to decide if a railwayman was lying or telling the truth.

'I am sure you have something important to discuss with me,' Nelson said seriously.

'Yes, otherwise, as you said, I wouldn't be here.'

'Forgive me for having said that.'

'You have done nothing wrong to ask for forgiveness. Your statement has shown me something important. I thank you for

56

that. But you are right, I have something to discuss with you. I have a message from home for you.'

Just then Ejiaka brought in the kola in a small enamel plate. 'Good morning, sir,' she greeted Theodore.

'Morning missis. How is our young man?'

'He is asleep.'

'Lucky children. Sometimes I wish I could go back to my mother's womb to be born again. I wouldn't grow up. I would just eat and sleep, wake up, eat and sleep.'

'That wouldn't make your mother happy,' Ejiaka said.

'You are right. My poor mother (she and her fellow spirits) was not a very cheerful person. Well, here's the kola and we are behaving like children. Nelson, this is a good kola.' Theodore split it in half. 'Thanks to him that brought the kola. It is always a thing of joy. And may God grant ample replacements where this came from.'

'*Ise*,' Nelson and Ejiaka said in unplanned unison. They looked at each other in surprise and smiled.

'There is nothing like a new wife,' Theodore said, busy breaking the kola into five pieces. 'She brings sunshine and laughter into the house.'

Ejiaka embarrassed, made to go back to the bedroom but Theodore stopped her.

'Wait for your own share.'

Before putting the five pieces in the plate, Theodore touched his forehead, stomach and shoulders in the sign of the cross. Then he took one piece and passed the plate to Nelson, who did the same. Ejiaka retreated to the bedroom with the plate.

Now, Nelson thought, he knew why Theodore rarely smiled. He had inherited his mother's sombreness. Perhaps that had helped him to get as far as he had in the railways. White men regard those that laugh often as immature. Nelson for his part preferred some laughter. It was what had attracted him to Ejiaka in the first place. Just as Theodore's gravity robbed the morning of its light and freshness, Ejiaka's laughter added to it.

Theodore crossed his lean, white-hosed feet and said gently, 'The driver of "No Telephone to Heaven", says your mother-in-law cannot come to Port Harcourt. You know she vomits whenever she travels by lorry. I suppose it is the petrol fumes and the dust. Some people's stomachs cannot stand it.'

'Ejiaka will not be happy to hear that,' Nelson said unhappily. 'She has been looking forward to her mother's coming.'

'Why don't you send Ejiaka home? You do not really need her here right now. Besides, the longer she stays at home the better for you. Her mother will feed her, or even if she cannot, you will only have to send her a small amount monthly. Things are much cheaper back home. You should consider it.'

'I have thought of nothing else for the past few days. Having a child eats up your money. The month has not reached twenty-hungry yet, and I am already broke. But one thing keeps me from sending Ejiaka home . . . water. It is hard to get water at home. The spring is over a mile away and I do not expect my mother-in-law to help fetch water. So in the long run Ejiaka will work harder than she is doing here and that is not what I want. Another thing is I do not want anything to happen to my child. Here, we are near a hospital. At home, the nearest one is over twenty miles away and lorries do not go that way daily. If Okechukwu falls sick, how will they get him to the hospital? Walk?'

'You have really thought of everything. You are right about her having to work harder at home than here. I am glad you give a great deal of thought to the things you do. You have really matured.'

'Ah Theo, what can I give you? You walked in after we had finished eating breakfast. Will you stay for lunch? No? And you don't drink!'

'Don't worry, you have already done a great deal. You know whenever I belch I can still taste the feast of four days ago.'

Nelson laughed. 'You must be joking,' he said.

Suddenly he felt as though a weight had been lifted from his shoulders. So his mother-in-law would not be coming? It was just as well. In the past few days he had wondered whether he would be able to stay in the same house with the tough-minded old woman.

'There is one thing I have been waiting to talk to you about,' Theodore said suddenly.

'Oh-o?'

58

'It means a great deal to me and I want you to promise that you will at least consider it.'

'Theo, you know I will do anything you ask me. A chicken never forgets the person that pulls its tail feathers during the rainy season. And a dog,' Nelson added as his dog walked up to him looking somewhat shame-faced, 'does not forget the person that feeds it.'

Nelson leaned sideways and awkwardly patted the dog on the head. Theodore had helped him a great deal during his first weeks at work. But for him, Nelson would have fought the Time-Keeper who tried to cheat him of some hours of work, probably losing the job and his pair of shorts. It was Theodore who told him to give the Time-Keeper a bottle of schnapps. After that, he began to receive pay for overtime he had not really done.

'Thank you for saying what you did. I shall always remember it even if you decide not to accept what I am going to suggest.'

'I am not that old that I won't consider suggestions from my elders.'

'Nelson, I know you are a very ambitious person, and you want to go far in the railways. Am I right?'

'Yes, Theo.'

'What I am going to suggest is something that I think will help you achieve your aim. You do not know this, but when white men consider people for promotion they usually try to find out from their friends, enemies and *oga* the type of people they are. Do you know that a large number of people are not promoted because of what they do, or what their friends and enemies say they do after work?'

'Truly?'

'Yes, truly.'

'White people always do things differently.'

'You are right. So, what a man does after work is as important as how well he does his work.'

'But why?'

'How can I explain it to you? All right, let us say a farmer stays up half the night drinking and then goes home and fucks his wife till the first cock crows. That farmer will not be able to do much work the next day; do you agree?'

59

'Yes, and the same applies to a railwayman.'

'Yes. Now you see why white men want to know what a person does after work and why those people who do certain things are not trusted. I hear you do not go to church on Sundays?'

'Yes.'

'Why?'

'It is foreign and most of the people who go there are pretenders.'

'Does that include me?'

'*Hewu-o* Theo, you know it does not.'

'All right. Do you want to tell me that all those who offer sacrifices to the gods at home are good people?'

'No.'

'Then why should you condemn the church because some of its members are hypocrites, and not condemn home religions that have the same type of membership?'

Nelson did not know how to answer that question. He had not really thought out his objections to the church nor his reasons for disliking it. He had always had vague feelings of discomfort at the idea of dressing up and going to sit for hours listening to some white man, or black-white man say things in a language he did not understand. He had also seen marriages break up as the result of a wife attending church services too regularly. The dressing up not only made women look more desirable but attracted the dogs that crowded the church. Going to church was a handy excuse for wives who wanted to betray their husbands. After spending some time with their boyfriends, they claimed afterwards they had been in church all along. There was no doubt many women were first seduced in churches, and Nelson did not want to expose Ejiaka to that.

'I hope you know that when I speak of the church, I mean the Roman Catholic Church, the only true church?' Theodore asked. 'You do? Good. Well, white men regard people who go to church as responsible and trustworthy, and those who don't as pagans.'

'I don't know,' Nelson said, and patted his dog for want of something better to say. 'I will have to think about all that you said.'

'I will be the first to suggest that you do. I know what I am asking you to do is not a small thing, but think of all that you will gain from it.'

And all that I may lose, Nelson said to himself. But he was prepared to give Christianity a try since Theodore praised it so much. If he found it as bad as people said, he would simply withdraw. The experience would arm him with good arguments to keep future crusaders at bay. At the moment he had nothing with which to counter Theodore's statements.

'I will remember,' Nelson said with a half-smile. 'There are two problems, I think, that will be hard for me to solve. I don't have any good clothes to wear to church and no prayer books to use when I get there.'

'Clothes you have to get for yourself. I will get you a missal tomorrow.'

'A what?'

'A missal, you know, the Catholic prayer book.'

'Oh! The other problem is I won't be able to follow the service. I mean, if you go to a priest of Ajala and ask him to offer prayers for you, you will understand what he is saying. That way you know you are not being cursed. With a Roman Catholic priest you are never sure what is going on. I am afraid I will feel lost during the service.'

'Don't worry about that. The missal has the mass in English translation. You will be able to follow the service quite easily. You know you should not compare a priest of God with a pagan priest of Ajala. The former is the servant of God while the latter serves the Devil. If you are going to join the true church you must not make such comparisons or you will be committing a mortal sin.'

Nelson could not stop himself from laughing, and the harder he tried the more he laughed. Because of Theodore's uncomprehending stare he suddenly felt foolish laughing so much.

'What have I said that is so amusing?'

'I just recalled something very amusing,' Nelson said between laughs. 'Forgive me. I understand what you said but I do not agree that Ajala's priest serves the Devil. Ajala is God's greatest creation and no one can equate her with the Devil. But don't let us argue. I respect your deep knowledge of the Catholic church and I will consider all that you have told me this morning. No man can go into things affecting his destiny without communing in thought with his *chi*. I will talk it over with Ejiaka also. If I go to church I want my family to go with me.'

'I am glad to hear that. One thing you can be sure of is you will not lose anything if you join the church. Tomorrow I will bring you a missal. Tell Ejiaka I am leaving.'

Nelson was relieved the conversation was over. He shouted to Ejiaka and she came hurrying into the room.

'Theodore says he is leaving,' Nelson said.

'Yes Ejiaka, I have stayed longer than I planned.'

'But I was just beginning to cook lunch. Won't you stay?'

'No, I am sorry I cannot.' Theodore stood up. 'Since you were only just beginning to cook, it is not too late to reduce the quantity. Thank you so much for the kola.'

'It pains me you are not staying for lunch,' Ejiaka said.

'It pains me more. I know I am missing a great meal. Don't worry, another time when I don't have other engagements I will not only stay to lunch but dinner also. What about Okechukwu?'

'He is still asleep.'

'Here,' Theodore said, dipping his hand in his pocket and bringing out some coins that he gave to Ejiaka. 'Buy soap and powder for him.'

'Hiya!' exclaimed Nelson, 'we were just talking about all that you have done already and you are doing more.'

'The child deserves it,' Theodore said shaking hands with Nelson and Ejiaka. 'I will see you all tomorrow.'

'I will see you out,' Nelson said, and as he followed Theodore, Ejiaka held out three of her fingers to indicate that Theodore had given her three shillings.

2 ✄ Nelson was already looking forward to going home—he had been working since three in the afternoon—when he was told to report to the office of Chargeman Grade One immediately. The summons was a surprise and he was apprehensive as he cleaned himself up a little. He had never been summoned by any railway official before. And no one he knew had ever come from such a summons with a happy story.

'Hurry up, Nelson,' James, his co-fitter, urged him. 'The Chargeman is as impatient as *nmanwu ojo*. He'll soon come running here.'

'I wonder what he wants,' Nelson said, running his hand over his hair. Sometimes he found gobs of grease stuck in the tight coils of his hair.

'To promote you,' James said laughing.

'This is no time to joke,' Nelson said angrily. James's humour often turned dark with the night. On day shifts he was sensible and understanding, but evening and night shifts made him undergo a radical change. 'What time is it?'

'I will tell you when I buy a watch,' James answered. Nelson did not say another word but hurried off to the Chargeman's office, picking his way carefully through the inadequately lit running shed, sensing rather than seeing the yawning examining pits, pools of oil, heavy iron limbs and flitting shadows that materialized into human beings. The closer he got to the offices, the faster his heart beat and the more certain he was that the summons did not augur well.

What if he was going to be sacked? For what? Who knows! For a while he did not know whether to pray to the Christian God or his *chi*. His uncertainty lasted only a short time, however. No, he had done nothing wrong to deserve the sack, he reassured himself. His *chi* was not asleep and would not permit him to be sacked when his son was barely three weeks old.

The Chargeman was at his desk in a corner of the large room. The electric light shone on his polished dome. He glanced briefly at Nelson, his bulging eyes resembling those of a large, dead fish sold at the creek. His desk was high and only his white-shirted, barrel chest was visible. Nelson looked at the wall clock and noted that his tour of duty would end in twenty minutes. He stood ill at ease, wondering if everything would be over in that time. He should reconcile himself to going home late, perhaps very late.

Why hadn't the Chargeman spoken to him? The silence in the office isolated by the surrounding noises of the running shed, was very disturbing. It made him feel hot and fidgety and he cracked his knuckles gently, rubbing his hands together. His hands were clammy and in an attempt to dry them on his overalls, he got them greasy. Suddenly a hot band of air hit him and he looked round to see if the windows were closed. They were open. The sweat that had built up on the back of his neck, trickled down towards his buttocks.

Then two strange men came in, whispered to the Chargeman and positioned themselves on either side of him. The Chargeman lit a cigarette and fixed his eyes on Nelson who promptly looked away. Those eyes always made him feel queasy.

'Do you know why you are here?' the Chargeman finally asked, in a surprisingly pleasant voice.

'No, sir,' Nelson said, trying but not succeeding to avoid looking at the moustache-heavy lips and the sweeping Yoruba facial marks.

'Why did you do it?'

Nelson was not sure he heard correctly. 'Why did he do what?' he wanted to ask but the Chargeman's face did not encourage questions. What was he supposed to have done? He looked away towards the windows and felt the cool, night sea breeze send a chill down his spine. So he was going to be dismissed after all. His *chi* was asleep. The realization made him acutely aware of the sounds floating in through the windows. A large frog croaked nearby and an engine about to leave the running shed whistled thrice. Iron clanged against iron, and soon subsided in the distance.

The Chargeman cleared his throat and asked impatiently: 'Did you hear my question? Why did you do it?'

'Do what sir?' Nelson asked automatically.

'Why did you steal the waste?'

'Steal the waste?' Nelson asked. 'Steal which waste, sir?'

'Now look here Mr. Achu, stop behaving like a fool. You are in serious trouble and if you are not going to co-operate I will turn you over to the police. I know you understand me perfectly. Your file here says you passed Standard Two and can write English. Now, will you tell me why you stole the waste?'

'I never stole any waste,' Nelson shouted angrily. 'Who says I steal waste?'

The Chargeman glared at him silently. Suddenly Nelson was beset with doubts. Had that stupid Onyeama been caught stealing waste despite the beating he received?

'Ajala don't agree!' Nelson said to himself. 'I will certainly kill the idiot this time. To lose one's job because of mere waste! That is the trouble with having a relation as a servant. You can't punish him as much as he deserves.'

'Mr. Achu, listen to me carefully,' the Chargeman said. 'You have a clean record and I wouldn't like to see it soiled because of your obstinacy. I have also heard you have a reputation for honesty and trustworthiness, so I am prepared to give you the benefit of the doubt. Just confess and I will settle the whole matter here.'

'I do not know what you are talking about, sir,' Nelson said. He was no longer angry. The Chargeman's reasonable tone made him feel he had actually stolen the waste. 'Since I joined the railway, I have never taken more than my week's share of waste. Everybody knows it is not big enough for us but I will not steal some because of that. Even my wife have baby boy few weeks ago and we need more waste, but I will not steal. No sir, I will not steal ordinary waste.'

'Call Mr. Igwe,' the Chargeman said abruptly.

One of the men standing by the side of the Chargeman's chair, went out.

Mr. Igwe? It sounded familiar. Nelson tried to remember the face to which the name belonged. It was not one of his fellow-workers. Probably a cleaner or an ash-pan man. Mr. Igwe? He was saved further effort when the door opened and a small man sidled into the room accompanied by the man who had gone out a moment before.

Oh no, not that rat! Nelson knew him well but he did not know his name was Igwe. They called him *nkekwu*, derived from his size and his name, Okeke. The oldest member of the ash-pan gang and the most untrustworthy, he had been in the railways for years but never promoted. He was bitter against young men he thought were doing too well. He had been heard to say that all promotions came through bribery or having the right connections.

A short while ago he had intentionally, Nelson thought, left hot coals in an examining pit in which Nelson was going to examine a *garratt* engine. Nelson had not been burned, but had lost a pair of good work-shoes. *Nkekwu* had claimed it was all a mistake. Because Nelson had earlier tried to befriend *nkekwu*, his work-mates made fun of the hot coal incident for days. Play with a chicken, they said, and you get chicken shit on your hands.

'Mr. Igwe, you said Mr. Achu gave you some waste to take to his wife. Tell us how it happened.'

'Yes, sir.' Igwe licked his lips and his overhanging moustache. 'It was before five o'clock and Nelson called me. He ask me if I take permission to go home. I say yes, and he beg me to take something home for him. I ask him to tell me what the thing he want me to take home for him is. He say not to worry about that. Then he give me an old salt bag and tell me not to let people see it because it be special present from his Chargeman. Since he be my friend I take it. I no worry. As I dey go home I think I must know what in the bag. I open the bag and see plenty waste inside.'

'What did you do then?'

'I stop where I open the bag,' Igwe went on after running his tongue over his lips. 'Then as I stand dey think what to do two men meet me and ask me what dey inside the bag. They look like loco' people so I tell them everything. They take the bag and bring me here.'

'Is that all?'

Nelson jumped at Igwe before he could answer, but was restrained by one of the Chargeman's men.

'You are a liar,' Nelson shouted in Igbo struggling to free himself. 'You know you are lying. What have I done to you that you want me to be sacked from my job? Tell me, what have I done to you?'

'Shut up, Mr. Achu,' the Chargeman ordered.

Nelson obeyed. Now he wished he had beaten the *nkekwu* up long ago. Igwe! What a waste of a good name.

'Did anyone else see Mr. Achu give you the bag, Mr. Igwe?'

'Yes, sir.'

'You sure?'

'Yes, sir.'

'Tell me who they are so my men can go and get them.'

'I no know whether they still dey for work, sir. Make I go for them house call them, sir?'

'No! Tell me their names and where they live and we will call them.'

There was silence. Igwe's eyes seemed to move of their own volition, from Nelson to the open window, from the Chargeman and his men and back to Nelson. Then Igwe's intent to make a break for it, as tangible as a spoken word, could be felt in the room.

'Well?' said the Chargeman. 'We cannot wait all night, you know.' Then turning abruptly to one of his men he added, 'Tell us what you discovered during your investigations, Paul.'

'Yes, sir. I spoke to Chargeman Grade Three Ikime, Mr. Achu's immediate head, and he said he did not give Mr. Achu any presents. He also said he had not let Mr. Achu and the other fitters out of his sight since four o'clock this afternoon. They had all been working on Engine 602. Under-Fitter Grade One Jonathan said Mr. Achu never left his side. The other fitters who worked with Mr. Achu on Engine 602 said the same thing too. And when Mr. Achu was called to come before you, he was still working on the said engine.'

'What do you say to that, Mr. Igwe?'

'All na lie. They plan against me.'

'How?'

Igwe remained silent. Nelson watched him, and it seemed to him the man was shrinking, merging with his dirty, ash-coloured overall, turning into the dried-up branch of a tree that would soon drop off and disappear in the undergrowth.

'There is no point wasting our time any more,' the Chargeman said. 'Igwe, your friends reported you and I am glad we caught you red-handed. You have been stealing waste for a long time and getting away with it. This time your luck ran out, so you tried to incriminate Mr. Achu. I am glad it did not work. Paul take him to the police right away. Mr. Achu, go home to your family. So you have a baby boy?'

'Yes, sir,' Nelson said, taking a deep breath and letting it out slowly.

'When?'

'Three weeks ago, sir.'

'Congratulations. Is it your first?'

'Yes, sir.'

'Hm, you worked like a man.'

Nelson smiled for the first time. 'Thank you sir for helping me.'

'Well, just be careful. We make many enemies we do not know about.'

Nelson was about to add that what one did not know would not kill him, but remembered that the Chargeman was not an Igbo. So he said, 'Yes, sir,' and 'Goodnight, sir,' and went back to the shed to put away his tools.

Although Under-Fitter Grade One, Jonathan, had done it for him, Nelson checked them again to assure himself they were complete. They were expensive tools housed in heavy, iron-bound, tool boxes with massive keys. The railway authorities provided each fitter with a complete set of tools and a tool box. The cost of missing tools was deducted from the pay cheques of the owner in monthly instalments.

His co-workers waited for him near the showers. They wanted to hear all that had happened. He tried to make his ordeal sound like a fairy tale but they would not let him. Their quick sympathy made telling the whole thing worthwhile. At the end everyone agreed small men could not be trusted.

Nelson felt like singing as he showered. The cascading, almost limitless quantity of water always made him take his time at the shower. Afterwards he was glad to slip into his ordinary clothes and hang up his overalls, which were not dirty enough to be taken home for washing, in his locker.

He and Jonathan walked home together by the light of his carbide lamp. They did not, as was their wont, talk much on the way. Nelson felt drained of speech, although he bubbled with an inner excitement.

'Goodnight, sir,' Jonathan said as they parted.

'Goodnight,' Nelson said, rather briefly, but added: 'Come and taste some fresh palm wine when you wake up.'

'Yes, sir.' Jonathan took the branch path that led to his home about a quarter of a mile away.

One moment we are here and the next we are not, Nelson thought as Jonathan was quickly engulfed by the darkness. He had often wondered what happened to the space one vacated. Was there an imprint, permanent and unerasable, left by our corporeal presence, that waited for us to rediscover it when we passed that way again? Or if we did not pass that way, waited for a kindred spirit to find and bear witness to our having been there? As in the ruins of a dwelling, one can easily tell if human beings have lived there, and can even reconstruct their lives if one has knowledge enough. If, however, we do not leave an imprint, and our absence is surrounded by emptiness, why bother to make noise, to assert our existence, to pit our puny strength against oblivion? Why bother to struggle between right and wrong, to amass properties and wealth, to torment ourselves over our prospects for the future? Why bother to do all those things and more when in the long run everything will be as it has always been and silence will reclaim its peace?

And not even the air we have pushed around so violently can testify we have been there?

Ejiaka opened the door for him, her worried face breaking into a smile. 'Ilọ,' she said. 'I thought you had gone to raise a derailed train again.'

'No,' Nelson said, sitting down and unlacing his boots. 'I would have sent a message earlier if that was the case. I was delayed at work. Where is Onyeama?'

'I told him to go to sleep.'

'Is Okechukwu all right?'

'Yes, he has been a very good boy today. He went to sleep immediately after I fed him.'

It was good to be home again. Nelson no longer felt drained of speech. He could, if need be, talk till dawn. He put his boots aside and stuffed his socks into them. Then he sat back, but could not find a more relaxing and comfortable position in the straight-backed chair. Pushing the dog away he sat on the mat. The dog licked his hand.

'No!' Nelson said sharply, snatching his hand away.

'What did you say?' Ejiaka asked, coming back from the pantry-store carrying a small bucket of water.

'Nothing. I was talking to the dog.'

Ejiaka put the bucket down by his side.

'I am not hungry,' Nelson said.

'Are you well?' Ejiaka asked in alarm.

'So if I am not hungry, I am sick?'

'No, but it is not often that you are not hungry after a hard day's work.'

'I am well, but I am not hungry.'

'Did something bad happen at work?'

'Speak softly, we don't want to wake the neighbours up. Yes, something happened, but it was not bad.'

'Tell me,' Ejiaka said sitting down on the mat.

Nelson felt her eyes embrace his face, absorbing everything he said, ejaculating at intervals, her tone ranging from horror to surprise. At times he felt he was talking to himself. Although she sat some feet away she seemed to have fused with him.

When he had talked himself dry, she relaxed and said, 'No wonder you are not hungry.'

'What did you prepare?' he asked.

'Your favourite—*onugbu* and pounded yam.'

'I think I will eat after all. It is not good to let the pounded yam go to waste.'

'You don't have to do that. Onyeama can eat it in the morning and I will make another one for you.'

'You women, one can never understand you. When I said earlier I was not hungry, you said I was sick. Now I say I want to eat, you try to put me off.'

Ejiaka laughed softly as she retied her *lappa* over her breasts. 'I just want to be sure you really want to eat.'

'You don't need to warm up the soup. It is too late in the night.'

'I already have it on the fire. I hope it is not burnt.'

Nelson watched her hurry away but deliberately refrained from dwelling on the sensuous bounce of her buttocks. That would be self-punishment. Picking up his boots and the lantern he went into the bedroom. Okechukwu slept peacefully like the child he was, and looked small and defenceless in the huge bed.

Nelson changed quickly into his *lappa*, leaving his singlet on to keep off the insipient cold air. Settled on the mat once more, his back against the wall, he thought it was time he bought two comfortable armchairs with cushions. He could save money by ordering them together instead of one at a time. Carpenters often tried to make huge profits on single orders.

The meal was delicious. He cleaned the plates joking that he had saved Onyeama the extra work of eating the left-overs before washing the plates in the morning.

As he picked his teeth with a tooth-pick Ejiaka had carved out of firewood, she said:

'Your dog is useless. I wish we could get a young one that we can train the way dogs are trained at home.'

Nelson belched. 'Did he destroy anything?' he asked.

'No. He is rarely at home to do that. Once you leave for work we don't see him until it is almost time for you to return. I have washed him many times with Izal but he always comes home from wherever he has been full of new ticks. We are wasting good food on him.'

'He probably has a wife somewhere that keeps him away,' Nelson said and laughed. 'I don't blame him though. Home is where the wife is.'

'I don't think that is why he stays away. He does not like us. You are the only one he likes.'

'*Ibia kwa*! He is only a dog. How can he not like the people that feed him?'

'Let me show you. Touch him and see how he reacts.'

Nelson patted the dog, it raised its head, wagged its tail and made as if to turn over on its back. Nelson withdrew his hand quickly before it could lick it, one thing he never allowed it to do since he discovered that its breath stank.

'He behaved like a dog,' Nelson said.

'All right, watch me touch him.'

Ejiaka walked over to the dog but before her outstretched hand touched its head, it stood up, its neck stretched out, and its tail and hindlegs stiff. The dog remained stiff and tense even when Ejiaka touched its head.

'You see what I mean?' Ejiaka said, going back to her place on the mat.

'Yes,' Nelson said, surprised that a dog should be so discriminatory. 'Does he do the same with Onyeama?'

'Yes,' Ejiaka said.

'Hm,' Nelson grunted. He would be sorry to see the dog go. It was his last link with his first wife. But if it was going to be antisocial, it was best to get rid of it. Seeing it lie there, its head pillowed on its forelegs, its brown coat full of white patches acquired in numerous fights and skirmishes, one would have thought it was a normal dog.

'I am worried that it may not like Okechukwu,' Ejiaka said. 'The child will soon start crawling all over the place and will try to play with it, and I don't know what will happen. The dog may bite him. One thing I am sure of is that the dog will not help me to keep Okechukwu clean.'

'We will know what to do with it soon,' Nelson said. 'We can sell it to the market people.'

As though sensing that its fate was being discussed, the dog got up and walked slowly to the far corner of the room where it curled up. Nelson and Ejiaka exchanged glances.

'We had better discuss this another time,' Nelson said. He yawned prodigiously, feeling tiredness all over his body.

Ejiaka got up too and adjusted her *lappa*. Her bare shoulders had a rich-brown glow as though she had applied vaseline to them a moment ago.

Nelson checked the doors and windows to keep his mind off Ejiaka.

'The time for sleep has come,' he said, heading straight for the bedroom.

Ejiaka followed with the lantern, which she placed on a small stool by the head of the bed. Gently, so as not to wake Okechukwu, she climbed into the bed and lay down, her back against the wall, her left arm across Okechukwu's feet.

Nelson shook the lantern. The kerosene in the tank would last the night. He turned down the light and eased himself into the bed, leaving enough space between him and Okechukwu. When they had first started sleeping in the same bed, he had feared he would wake up one morning to find Okechukwu's lifeless body smothered under him. That fear was gone now for he no longer thrashed around in his sleep because Ejiaka had complained before Okechukwu was born.

'May the day break,' Ejiaka said.

'May the day break,' Nelson replied, consciously relaxing every limb, every muscle in his body. He closed his eyes.

The next time he opened them, God had drawn back the curtain of darkness, Ejiaka was no longer in bed, and the whole yard was establishing its noisy presence. He lay on his back for a while relishing the deep sleep he had had, then he turned to Okechukwu. The baby's bright, brown eyes seemed to quiver in the hard morning light.

Nelson smiled. 'They deserted us didn't they?' he said.

Okechukwu responded with a cry.

The new day had really begun.

3 ✂ Janet woke early as she always did on Sunday mornings, but did not get out of bed immediately. She had decided to try once again to get Christian to make her pregnant. She lay still wondering what time it was, how she was going to get to the bathroom, and how loudly he snored.

His snores sounded bad. They started off like a tubercular wheeze, checked and then ended with a sound equal to that of a double-charged dane-gun. Janet would normally have woken him to correct the position of his neck and reduce the sound, but she could not afford his waking up in a bad mood. She had to discuss an important matter with him, so it was best he woke up on his own.

But when would he wake up? The first thing she did on waking up each morning was to go to the bathroom. Now she couldn't. She lay still, her legs together, staring up at the top of the mosquito netting that covered the bed. Taking her mind off her need, she became absorbed in observing the huge, bloated mosquitoes, resting there.

Who knows which poor person they had sucked last night. Most probably Vitus who slept in the sitting-room. She would get him to brew and drink some malaria medicine before he had another of his attacks. Better still she would buy him a small mosquito net for his bed. Prevention is better than cure as they say.

She would like to reach up there and squash those overfed mosquitoes. But not today. She did not want to have to take down the net to wash off the red splotches they would leave behind.

Did those wicked things feel pain when squashed? One would never know. But it would be wonderful if there was a way to find out. Make the bastards feel the pain they give us, and perhaps, fear us as a result. There is no satisfaction in causing pain if your victim does not show he feels it.

So, how would one go about making the mosquitoes feel pain? Crushing them to death was such a futile act. The more you destroyed the more you were attacked. If only there was a way that the ones you crushed could send messages back to the others, so that fear of what could happen to them would keep them away. Unfortunately there was none. So they kept coming and you kept crushing them until those that have escaped make you and yours so ill that you are all in turn crushed. And this goes on for ever, world without end. God, it is insane.

A twinge of pain reminded Janet that her bladder was still full. She shifted cautiously. The pain gradually went away. Then the funny side of what she was doing struck her. Ordinarily she would jump off the bed without caring whether she woke Christian or not. But now here she was going through so much pain only on the faint hope he would wake up soon. She was amused initially, but then cynical. Was there no other way of getting pregnant? Really, why should she subject herself to this charade? Her cynicism did not last long, however. She was horrified that she had ever thought of the possibility of there being another way. She would never bring herself to commit adultery.

But, oh God, I want a baby badly.

If only she could get Christian to make love to her! She would do all the work, cause him to have an erection, guide him into her, do all the movement. All he had to do was ejaculate inside her, impregnate her and she would never bother him again. Somehow she was convinced that her sixth baby would be destined to live, to survive. It had to be. But Christian would not give her the chance to demonstrate this. He always reminded her that during the past twelve years, she had said the same thing about their third, fourth and fifth children that did not survive.

Oh God, if there was a way to take his penis, arouse it without waking him, stroke it until it was about to pump out semen, then push it into her . . . how she would love to present him with an accomplished fact! Just to see his debonair face naked and open with surprise!

The pain came on fast and unthinking now. Janet slid off

the bed grabbing her *lappa* as she went to the door. She struggled with the door bolt. It used to slide out easily, but now seemed possessed of a life of its own. She would not panic. It was the quickest way to wet herself. She stood perfectly still and soon the pain passed. She tied her *lappa* properly above her breasts, picked out a blouse from the top of her box of clothes and put it on. The bolt slid out easily.

Christian had not woken; if anything his snoring was heavier.

Janet slipped on a pair of brown-strapped slippers and walked out of the bedroom closing the door gently behind her. She stood by the door for a while to get her eyes used to the brilliance of the Sunday morning. In the kitchen Vitus sat in front of the fire on which the kettle was boiling—the steam, wispy white above its heavy blackness. He seemed engrossed in the patterns the fire was making around the kettle.

The bathroom smelt fresh with Izal disinfectant. Good boy, Janet thought, he had already cleaned up the place. She took a deep fold of her *lappa* around her thighs, raised it, and squatted. A smarting pain shot across her stomach and the downpour started, emptying it. Back in the yard, she asked Vitus to get her a small bucket of warm water, the soap container and a towel. She washed herself in the bathroom, giving her pubic hair that was overdue for trimming a special cleaning. Long pubic hair made her feel uncomfortable, but she had not had time to trim it recently. After washing she did not wipe herself totally dry. A little wetness would help her plan with Christian to succeed. Some time ago, she had noticed that he lost his erection at the least resistance to his entry.

Christian was wide awake when she got back to the bedroom. Ignoring the question in his eyes she removed her blouse, kicked off her slippers and got into bed. She loosened the top of her *lappa*, her legs slightly spread, a feeling of clean femininity rising in her.

'What time is it?' Christian asked.

'Nine o'clock,' Janet said, turning on her left side to look at his profile and the few ringlets of grey hair in his side-burns. She waited for him to ask why she was still in bed, but he did not. She placed her right hand on his hairy chest that always fascinated her—such a small man with so much hair on his chest. He cringed under her touch, slowly picked up her hand with his left hand and placed it between them.

'Your hand is cold,' he said.

'I did not know.'

She slipped her hands between her thighs to warm them. They were cold. The harmattan wind had sucked up all the moisture.

'You are not going to church today?' he asked.

'No.'

But he did not ask why. He just lay there, unmoving, his eyes staring up at the netting.

Her hands warmed up, Janet started playing with Christian's hairy chest again. Christian invariably made her feel like a young girl, unsure of herself. While with others she could be domineering, acerbic and mannish, with him she was once again the unlovely little girl he had blessed with his attentions. She had been seduced by his charms. There was a pointedness in his looks that rarely failed to stab her between her legs. The rare times it was blunted, she was merely testing her ability to resist sexual advances. She had believed at the time he was the only safe person to test her strength with. Surrounded by the *tigers* of the hospital, she had to find out very quickly how strong she was, how much she could withstand.

Now she knew.

'I did not hear you when you returned last night,' Janet said, to distract his attention from her hand working its way down his body.

'You were asleep,' he said, crossing his legs.

Undaunted Janet continued her exploration. The change in temperature was striking when she went under his *lappa*. His pubic hair, all she could touch because of his crossed legs, was as luxuriant as usual. She stroked his thighs gently, their hairlessness making for better tactile contact.

'Why did you decide not to go to church today?' Christian asked.

'There are things I wanted us to discuss,' Janet said without slowing down her stroking action.

'Is that what we are doing now?'

'No, we are just beginning.'

'I have to go and urinate.'

76

Janet withdrew her hand and held him round the waist.

'You will come back to bed? Please, there is a very important thing I want to ask you.'

'All right. I will come back.'

He parted the side of the netting and swung out of bed. For a brief moment he was naked as he tried to grab hold of his falling *lappa*. Janet was not surprised to see he was still flaccid although she had hoped he would be otherwise. How was she going to turn him on? It had not been a problem in the early years of their marriage. He had even been too ready at times, and she often had to plead tiredness to get some sleep. But now, he pleaded tiredness.

If she came out with what was on her mind without trying to arouse him, would he understand her position? Did it mean she could no longer excite him sexually? Was she really no longer appealing? If it were not for the fact that she often had to fight off interested men at the hospital, she would have said she was.

It was getting warm. She was not used to lying in bed so late. What was he doing out there anyway? His bladder did not contain gallons of water. If he did not come back to bed, what would she do?

The bedroom door suddenly opened and Christian came in. Janet turned on her left side as he got into bed.

'Please lock the door,' she said.

He hesitated and then did so.

'What did you want to discuss?' he asked, as he settled in the bed. His tone, no longer as neutral as before, had taken on an edge of impatience.

'Christian,' she said placing her hand on his chest, 'I have been thinking.'

He remained silent and still.

'I am hot,' Janet said, pushing the top of her *lappa* down to her hips. 'What of you?'

Again he was silent.

'Why don't you want to fuck me any more?'

The question hung in the air like a vulture, heavy, obscene and revolting. Janet could not believe she had asked it. Yet those very words had been in her brain for so long. They had seemed so innocuous and appropriate there.

'What did you say?' Christian asked, turning towards her.

Janet held him and burst into tears and in between sobs she said over and over again, 'I want a baby, Christian. Please, I want a baby.'

Later, Janet could never fully explain to herself why she had cried, her first tears since her beloved grandfather had died years ago. Maybe it was the shock of the words she had spoken? Or its effect on Christian who had sounded surprised and shocked? Or perhaps it was the culmination of emotions that had been building up in her for some time? Initially her crying was painful and rending, but when Christian held her, it became an emptying that at the end left her hollow.

'We have lost so many children already,' Christian was saying, 'it is futile to keep on trying.'

'Let's try just this once,' she said, as soon as she could control herself. 'I am sure this one will survive.'

'You said that many times before but none survived.'

'I know I said so before, but this time it is different. I can feel it in my womb.'

'You have always been an obstinate woman,' Christian said.

Sensing him weakening, Janet gently removed his *lappa*, and then her own. His body was warm and alkali-scented. She could feel herself getting really wet and, oh God, he too was becoming aroused. She embraced him harder shifting her body in such a way as to convey the message that she wanted him to get on top of her.

He did not respond and she held herself from lifting him over her. He had complained about that before and she did not want to give him any excuse to withdraw now. But she could not stop herself from feeling him with her free hand, just to be certain he was aroused. Throwing her right leg over his slim hips she brought him into contact.

It was done. He was in, warm and filling. She started to move slowly, trying, with each move, to get him farther in. But it seemed he was holding back although she did not feel any pressure on her arms.

Then he was out. At first she thought he had merely slipped out, but when she explored with her hand she found he had gone slack. Nothing she did now aroused him again, and she tried all that she knew, cursing him under her breath, her *chi*, and the creator who had made it impossible for a woman to be pregnant without the acquiescence of a man.

'Christian, what have I done to you?' she asked, filled with defeat and despair.

'You cannot decide everything alone,' he said.

'But why don't you want a child?'

'I do. You are the one who does not.'

Janet pulled back to look at his face. His eyes were cool, his small lips lifted in a slight smile. She felt like hitting him, shoving him out of the bed, sending him out of her life.

'Did you say it was I that didn't want a baby?'

'Yes,' Christian said. 'There is something unhealthy in your womb that kills those babies even before they are born.'

Janet was shocked into silence.

'Go and have your womb examined,' Christian continued. 'You are killing your children without knowing it. We will try again after your examination.'

Janet did not try to stop him as he got out of bed.

Husband? Is he my husband truly? Am I the killer of my children, children I wanted so badly? Nonsense. I gave them birth didn't I? They were not stillborn were they? Oh my God, help me.

And a small voice said:

'But none lived longer than six years.'

Tears filled her eyes and ran down her nose and on to the pillow.

Chapter Five

1 ✄ 'Only twenty-eight days,' Ejiaka said to herself as she dressed carefully. 'It seemed so many years.'

She had waited and chafed for this day and now it had arrived she was in no hurry to rush out, to taste her freedom. Like a bird caged for too long she experienced a momentary fear of the outside world. What was she afraid of? She knew what to expect and Janet had kept her up to date with the current gossips so that she knew what questions to ask and what not to mention at all.

She put on the new white blouse Janet had bought her. It was a bit tight and seemed to show too much of her breasts. She looked at her bosom from many angles in the hand mirror. It was big, almost as large as small heads of coconuts.

'What shall I do?' she wondered. 'Cover it up? With what?'

The blouse was beautiful and the material looked expensive and delicate. It would be a shame to cover it up. One good thing about it was that it would be easier to breast-feed Okechukwu if he got hungry during the excursion. She decided not to cover the blouse up, and hoped that no one would make a silly comment about it.

That decided, she draped the large reddish-brown *lappa* round her waist, her legs slightly apart to get the tension that would hold up the cloth right. For added security she tied the top part of the *lappa* with a cloth-string and folded down what was above the string. Next she wrapped a second, smaller *lappa* round the first one leaving it loose and looking bulky. Stepping into her new sandals and tying a multicoloured silken head-tie, completed her dressing. She closed her wooden clothes-box and turned to Okechukwu. He was still asleep. Should she wake him? The outing was as much his as hers and it would be much easier to carry him if he were awake.

Ejiaka sat down hard on the edge of the bed. He did not waken. Bathing and feeding him earlier than usual, and the quietness of the house must have sent him off into a deep sleep. Nelson was on his troublesome morning shift, and Onyeama at school to repeat Standard Three for the third time and probably fail again at the end of the year. The boy was a school dunce. Nelson should take him out of school, but would rather Onyeama made that decision himself. Ejiaka could not see the logic of it. Onyeama was not the one that decided to go to school, so why should he be the one to decide not to continue? It simply did not make sense. But then neither did many things Nelson did these days, especially his frustrating, periodic bouts of inaction.

'Time to get up, my child,' Ejiaka said turning once more to Okechukwu. He was getting beautifully plump. His circumcision had healed perfectly and his navel did not protrude.

'The product of my womb,' Ejiaka thought, lifting him from the bed and carrying him into the parlour.

Janet would be surprised to see the three, cushioned armchairs, the polished centre table and the massive cupboard that filled the room transforming it into a clean-looking modern place. Even Ejiaka was still not used to it for she sat gingerly on one of the armchairs as though expecting someone to ask her to get up.

It would take some time for her to really feel at home in the chairs, just as it would be some time before she would be used to the change Nelson had undergone since he had received his promotion to Fitter Grade Two. The letter, in an official-looking long, brown envelope arrived the day after he was falsely accused of stealing waste. Its coming must have been engineered by the gods. Total vindication of a person was rarely so complete.

Nelson's joy was boundless, like a child's. She did not blame him. As he explained, he had been promoted above many other equally deserving and experienced people. For many days the house was filled with joy, wine, food and people. It was during this time that Nelson bought the new furniture without even discussing it beforehand.

She should have read the signs—or had they always been there?—of Nelson's new-born arrogance and reticence. Whereas previously he had requested things, he now ordered her to get them. And new things started appearing in the house. Admittedly they were things they needed—teacups and saucers, glasses, spoons, knives and forks—but the way they appeared in large numbers, was disturbing. Each time she saw something and asked where they came from, Onyeama gave the classic answer:

'*Oga*'s apprentice fitter brought it last night.'

There was no doubt Nelson was being cheated by whoever was selling the things to him. Ejiaka once asked Janet to check the price of a set of drinking glasses and as she expected it was twice that which obtained in the markets.

As though that was not disturbing enough, he had become

81

obsessed with the Christian church. Ejiaka had nothing against Christianity, but she did not like the Roman Catholic version. Those who belonged to it were often fanatical, clannish, inconsiderate and arrogant, just like the members of a powerful, secret cult. Really it should not matter what version of Christianity one practised, in the same way that it did not matter whether one prayed to God through *Ngele-oji*, *Ajala*, *Ubahaudo* or *Izo*.

The important thing should be the type of life one leads. Everything else is merely the husk of the fruit, and not all husks of the same type of fruits are the same size and shape. But it apparently means a great deal to the Romans whether you belong to them or not.

'Ah, my child, you are awake,' Ejiaka said. Okechukwu looked so bright-eyed and knowing one would think he understood all that was said to him. 'Did you sleep well? Why don't you say something?' She lifted him up by the armpits and stood him on her thighs. She shook her head rapidly, smiling all the time. His smile came, slow but sure. 'That's more like it,' she said. 'Now, we had better get dressed before Janet arrives.'

She went into the bedroom and dressed him quickly in a loose-fitting dress.

'You look like a girl,' she said after they were back in the sitting-room. 'I can see a great number of people asking, "left or right?" before rushing off to buy you a gift.'

That was the way it often went. Women would cluster around the mother and child extolling the beauty of the baby, and afterwards rush off to buy the appropriate presents for a girl if the answer was 'left', or a boy if the answer was 'right'.

Rich women, close friends or relatives would buy things for the mother as well, congratulating her on her healthy looks, thanking God for a safe climb down from the high mountain that was pregnancy. They would escort her round the market urging her to point out what she needed for making soup during the coming week.

Finally one woman would volunteer to carry all the presents to the new mother's home. It was all done in a spirit of *umunne* and friendliness. Although the more people the new mother knew the more gifts she received, often more gifts came from strangers than acquaintances.

'Where are the people that live here?' Janet asked, as soon as her face appeared at the door, but she stopped at the threshold to survey the room. 'Nelson *ngbọ*!' she said. 'I knew he would do something like this before long. Or did you put him up to it, Ejiaka?'

Ejiaka stood up with happy laughter. 'I did not even know he was going to do it,' she said. 'One afternoon, Onyeama ran to me in the kitchen to say there were people outside who wanted to put chairs, a table and a huge cupboard in the sitting-room. I did not believe him till I saw with my own eyes. The people said *nnamu-ukwu* had bought the furniture on his way to work. So I let them bring the things in.'

'Sounds like Nelson all right. Well, enjoy it all while you can. Men like to act the strong, silent role of gods. Are we ready?'

'Yes.'

'You look wonderful. That dress has made you look like a new bride. Who made it for you? She must be a very good seamstress.'

'Mrs. Obiekwe made it. You know, the one that lives at number ten, Hospital Road. I made the *lappas*.'

'I didn't know you have a sewing-machine?'

'I don't,' Ejiaka said. She hoisted Okechukwu on to her back. 'We don't print money in this house. I used Mrs. Obiekwe's sewing-machine. She has two. She is a very kind and honest woman.'

'You must take me to her. I have been searching for a good seamstress for a long time. I have an Ikwere man now but he steals half the material I send to him.'

'You mean a man makes your dresses?' Ejiaka asked. She had never heard of a man knowing how to, let alone setting up shop as a seamstress. How would he take the measurements of his female customers?'

'Yes. There are many of them here and they are good.'

'Do they take measurements themselves?'

'Yes. That and cutting the material are the most important things in making a dress. A good tailor will never allow his apprentices to do those things for him. Mistakes made in measurements or in cutting cannot be repaired easily.'

Ejiaka did not think she would ever let a man make her a

dress. It would give him the licence to touch her under the guise of taking her measurements. She did not say so, however, but briskly tied the second *lappa* round and under Okechukwu and over her first *lappa*. Janet helped straighten it out over the baby's back and buttocks.

'Let's get going before the sun climbs to the top of the heavens,' Janet said. 'You have an umbrella don't you? Get it to shade the baby. Where is the shopping bag? Yes, here it is.'

By the time Ejiaka returned with the umbrella, Janet was at the door peering out to left and right as though she expected someone. Ejiaka had never seen her so restless. Usually collected and somewhat aloof, her strong face dared one to break in on its repose. Now it was open, inviting intrusion.

Ejiaka stepped to her side and asked, 'Are you expecting someone?'

'Me?' she looked startled but did her best to hide it. 'No,' she said, 'I was just waiting for you. It took you long to find the umbrella.'

'No, it did not,' Ejiaka said. She closed and locked the door.

'I thought it did,' Janet insisted. Then she added quickly, 'But it doesn't matter.'

They walked down the street towards the market. The morning rush over, there were few people in the streets. Children too young for school or playing truant had taken over the wide spaces and turned them into a vast playground. All they had to contend with were an occasional car or truck, and a few passers-by.

Ejiaka, mindful of the baby on her back, dodged not only the children rushing around recklessly, but also their india-rubber balls that could hurt like stones. But not so Janet. She was oblivious to her surroundings. More than once, her *lappa* enfolded a ball which she extricated with strong admonitions to the players.

And how she talked, worse than an *asha*. She commented on everything in a strident voice. She teased Ejiaka about the few men that looked their way. She said men did not look at her when she was alone, so it must be Ejiaka who attracted them. And to keep time with her chatter, she untied and retied her large blue-black *lappa*, touched her piled-up hair every now and then, and shifted the shopping bag from the left to the right hand and back again.

They had been walking fairly fast. At the outskirts of the market they stopped to rest.

'Is anything wrong, Janet?' Ejiaka asked as soon as Janet gave her the chance. Watching Janet's face intently, she saw a momentary flash of anguish come and go quickly.

'No-o,' Janet said, her smile small and tight. 'Do I look ill?'

'No,' Ejiaka answered softly, afraid to overstep the bounds of their friendship. She had always felt that Janet was one of those who preferred to be needed.

Trying to decide whether to challenge Janet further, Ejiaka looked up into the mango tree. A huge vulture landing on one of the top branches set it shaking. Had she been making a sacrifice to the gods, its arrival would have been a good omen. Well, in a way she was going to do just that.

'Janet, you know from the time you walked into my house today you have not been yourself,' Ejiaka said slowly.

'Who told you that?'

'Someone doesn't have to tell me what I can see with my own eyes. I know it is hard to tell someone what is worrying you, but there are times when you have to. Silence is not always the solution. In the beginning perhaps, but things sometimes go beyond that and one has to talk. You have been very good to me. You have helped me through my delivery, treated me like your own sister. Now, all I ask is that you let me help you. There is something worrying you that you have been trying to keep to yourself, but it won't let you. Why don't you let me share it with you? It will be one of the few ways I can show you how grateful I am for all you have done for me and Nelson. Please give me the chance. Please!'

Ejiaka stopped and waited. Janet's eyes were fixed on a group of chattering people coming towards them. Would Janet start talking before they drew closer? Ejiaka searched in her mind for some key words that would start Janet talking. But none came quickly. Perhaps this was the time for silence and waiting.

Janet's face looked gaunt and old in profile. She squinted and her eyes were furrowed; the gloom-lines at the side of her mouth were more pronounced. Saddened, Ejiaka looked away towards

85

the market. People were concentrated mostly at the meat stalls, making the market seem empty. Soon they would spread to other areas. Turning to the chattering group on which Janet's eyes were still focused, she saw them go into a house.

'Janet,' Ejiaka said hesitantly.

'Ejiaka, how can I . . .?' Janet began, blinking rapidly to keep back the tears that had suddenly filled her eyes. Failing, she dabbed them with the top edge of her blue *lappa*. 'Why did you do this to me?' she asked.

Ejiaka did not know what to say.

'How can I begin to tell you what I have been going through?' Janet asked.

'Just any way, any way will do,' Ejiaka said with certainty.

'You are right. Christian said I kill my children in my womb before I even deliver them.'

'God forbid!'

'He may be right. You know none of my children lived to be ten. What am I saying? Five.'

'But that is not your fault. You are not their *chi*.'

'Christian thinks I am, so he says we will have no more children till I have done something to my womb.'

'Is he serious?'

'You don't know Christian. When he says something he means it. Two days ago, the white doctor examined me thoroughly and he said nothing was wrong with me or my womb. But I know Christian will say I am telling lies if I tell him what the doctor said. He won't even believe that I had a medical examination. He does not trust hospitals and those who work in them. Now I don't know what to do. I want a child so badly I'd give anything to have one.'

For a while all Ejiaka could think of was how unfair and cruel the world was. Here was a woman who had helped many to deliver their babies safely unable now to have one of her own! How could God allow such a thing to happen?

'Well, let's go to the market before it starts emptying.'

'Wait,' Ejiaka said. 'Perhaps what is wrong with you is *ume omumu*.'

'But that is not a disease.'

'Well, maybe the white people do not think it is a disease. At

86

home we think it is. It is not normal for a woman to keep having children who are either stillborn or die very young. We are supposed to populate the earth not the grave.'

'You are right when you say it is not normal but I still think it is not a disease, at least not one that has a cure.'

'But that is what I want to tell you. It has a cure.'

'Ejiaka, you are talking to a midwife,' Janet said moving towards the market.

'Janet, at least listen to me,' Ejiaka protested as she reluctantly followed. 'Truly, there is a cure for *ume omumu*. I mean, I know someone who has cured it before.'

'A witch-doctor?'

'He is a great medicine-man and what he does not know about herbs is not worth knowing.'

'You sound as if he had cured you,' Janet said stopping. 'Is Okechukwu awake? Turn round and let me see.'

Ejiaka turned round wishing Janet would stop her evasive tactics so that she could tell her about Dike. She was sure Dike would be able to help her.

'He is awake. Let's go. This is the right time to get into the market—before he starts crying.'

'Janet, you don't want me to tell you about Dike?' Ejiaka asked. Janet's change in attitude was surprising. It was as if she did not care at all. Yet a moment ago she had said she was prepared to do anything to have a child. Had she not meant it? 'Janet, without Dike, Nelson would have had to leave the railways.'

'Really?' she asked sarcastically.

The frivolity of the question did not stop Ejiaka from continuing. 'Nelson suffers from epileptic attacks. When he was taking the white man's medicine he had them at least once a month. They were so bad he was warned that if he did not do something about it he would be discharged from the railways. Luckily one of his co-workers took him to Dike who gave him some herbal medicine to drink twice daily for eight days whenever he has the attacks. Since then, almost eight months now, Nelson has had only two attacks. And do you know what Dike did to make things easier for us? He came to our house and taught me how to prepare Nelson's medicine and which herbs

87

to use. Now, Nelson does not even drink it as often as he is supposed to, and yet he has not had an attack.'

As though waiting for Ejiaka to stop talking, Okechukwu gave a whimper.

'Oh, poor child,' Janet exclaimed, patting him on the head. 'We have been in the sun too long. He is sweating. Let's go quickly into the market. How can I see this man?'

'You mean Dike?' Ejiaka asked.

'Is there another person?'

'I will ask Nelson when he comes home from work. I have never been to Dike's house. I am glad you want to try him.'

'I told you I will do anything, although I do not think curing epilepsy is the same as cooling down my womb.'

'Just try him. People say he is very good with female diseases. He is so famous people pay for him to travel to far away places like Okirika, Opobo and Asaba to cure women.'

'The way my things usually turn out, I wouldn't be surprised to hear he is away travelling.'

'Don't worry. People who go on journeys return. I will ask Nelson about him before chickens roost tonight.'

2 ✂ 'Beast of the forest,' Christian cursed under his breath. He made a quick mental count. 'Three weeks and the foolish man has not gone on any extended journey!'

Three weeks ago, Angela had sent him a message asking him to check at her house every other day because it was likely her husband would go on a journey lasting at least three days. The signal that the old man was away would be the shutting of all bedroom windows.

So far it did not look as if the signal would ever be forth-coming. The bedroom looked like a huge star. From his hiding-place in a thick bush across the street Christian wished he could walk boldly into the house, order the old man out and carry Angela off to bed. He sighed as he felt his penis stirring. The memory of the night of love-making they had had almost a month ago had not dimmed. In fact it often sneaked up on him at very awkward moments. He would be talking to a customer of either sex and there would be an awakening in his pants, and his heart would skip a beat as the peculiarly clean, erotic odour of Angela would be wafted to his nostrils. Yet nothing in his immediate surroundings could be said to resemble that odour.

The first time it had happened to him, less than a week after the tryst, he panicked, terminated his sales-pitch and rushed back to the store. Before he got there his penis changed its mind, so he turned back and completed the sale explaining to the customer that he was suffering from an insipient dysentery. That was more acceptable than that a man of his age could not control the huge bulge in his trousers. He took no chances after that. He wore underwear a size smaller than he usually did so that any stirring down there was countered by a sharp pain that often won out. It left him sore for the first week but he soon got used to it. It was ridiculous at forty, for his penis to suddenly have a mind of its own.

A mosquito buzzed in his ears and he was afraid to kill it. Although no house was near enough for anyone to see his attempt, he did not know who might be lurking in the bushes or passing by. It was too dark to see far and the few people who had walked down the paved street had materialized from the surrounding darkness when they were only a few feet away from him.

What would the time be now? He had left the store at seven and probably had been standing here an hour although his feet felt that it was longer. But why did he always have to stand here for hours? If the old man had gone on the journey, he would have noticed the closed bedroom windows immediately. Christian knew his waiting was ridiculous, yet he stayed hoping that the windows would suddenly start to close.

He should have made friends with the old man, then he would not have to stand in the bush like a thief waiting for the owner of the house to leave so he could sneak in. Instead he could have walked boldly into the house and, on the pretence of paying a courtesy call, found out when the old man would leave the house. But his instincts had told him from the start he could not befriend Mr. Tom Big Harry. A big and burly man with a fringe of dirty-white hair round a bald pate, he had the brusque imperiousness of a man who was used to indulging his senses to the full. With his slab-like lips and big nose standing out in an otherwise small face, Christian found him revolting and often wondered how Angela could stand the caresses of such a man.

The persistent mosquito urged Christian to move. He waved it away, but it came back. He moved a few cautious steps and stopped. The pest was gone, and before long his mind was back with Angela. It had been a lucky set of circumstances that had made their first night together possible. Could it be repeated? Pay-day was only a few days away. If only there would be another huge cash shortage. But that would be postponing things for some days. Well, it would be better than when they had grabbed it whenever and wherever they could. Oh yes, that first time. He had been taken by surprise even though from the time he first looked into her eyes, he knew that if he played his game well things might reach his expectations. That was why he did not make a big play for her. He sent out the subtlest hints with his eyes and lips. He rarely worked as hard as he did that day. Not only did he not want to lose the three-suit order Big Harry was about to place, he wanted to impress her with the fact that he would give anything, well almost anything, to have her.

For months after he received Harry's order he worried whether she had got his message. Later he realized that he need not have worried at all, for she was quite prepared to meet him more than half-way. Big Harry was so satisfied with the suits that he told Christian to help Angela choose materials to replace the heavy, gaudy furnishings of the sitting-room. Angela's tight smile showed she had had a hand in getting the new order for him.

The first couple of times they met to plan things Harry was in and the servants were all over the place. A moment after he arrived for his third visit Angela contrived to send the servants out on errands. Big Harry was not in. As Angela hurried from the kitchen located in the huge backyard, between the servant's quarters and the house, Christian knew things were going to happen at last. Angela did not give him much time to wonder how and where.

She sat him down in one of the big chairs in a corner of the room facing the open windows and the closed door. It was late morning, and the door was not locked. His heart beat so loud he felt it would be heard miles away. On his right was a pile of material they had been looking at, trying to decide which was best suited for what.

It was a reckless thing to do. She unbuttoned his fly and with her moist small hands dug out his stiff penis. Turning round quickly she lifted her *lappa* and sat on him, letting her *lappa* fall to cover her front. She was hot and wet. The thought of her ruining his trousers flashed across his mind, but did not stick. He gave himself to her. Now he knew one could get into heaven through a rear door as the very marrow of his bones shot upwards.

Then she was up in a flash, her left hand holding the back of her *lappa* to her buttocks as she walked swiftly to the door.

'Come!'

He followed and in the bathroom she quickly and expertly sponged him dry. He looked down at his trousers.

'I held it,' she said with a tight smile. 'Go back now.'

He was full of wonder at her expertise as it dawned on him that she had deliberately created the suction he felt in the heat of things.

In the sitting-room she was serene, composed and somewhat distant, as if nothing had happened. But just before the servants returned she said with her first full smile:

'We will do it again, soon.'

'We have,' Christian said to himself, coming out of his hiding-place and on to the road. 'But I want more.' It did not look as if the windows were going to be closed, not that night. So the hollowness of desire would remain unfilled for another night and day? Well, so be it. Christian walked away up the road towards his store. Senior service houses stood tall and bright over their vast grounds. In between them there was just enough light to see by, and it served as a canvas on which Christian projected Angela standing naked by the huge bed, her youthful body a copper-colour of warmth, her mound of venus a dark, jutting pout, her thighs crying to be touched.

'Hey you! Hey you! You, I say you!'

Christian turned and saw three men in shorts and short-sleeved shirts hurrying towards him. They looked tall and muscular.

'You talking to me?' he asked.

'Yes,' one of the men said. 'You, Christian?'

91

'Yes.'

'You no remember me, Mister Christian?' another man asked moving closer.

'O-oh, Jaja,' Christian said smiling with happy recognition. 'I remember you!' How could he ever forget Angela's message-bearer.

'We have message for you Mr. Christian,' Jaja said.

Christian felt a little fear. The way Jaja said that was not normal. And the two men with him were getting uncomfortably close.

Christian took a step back. 'You have a message for me, Jaja?' he asked, keeping his tone light.

'Yes, Mr. Christian,' Jaja said, his tone laugh-lined.

Laugh if you want Christian thought, poised for immediate attack or retreat, but I don't see anything amusing in the present situation. He had no doubt now that their intentions were not friendly no matter how nonchalantly Jaja played it. The youngest of the three looked more like the guide, or perhaps the Judas.

'From who?' Christian asked.

'From Big Harry!' one of the men shouted, rushing in from the right while the other rushed in from the left.

Christian jumped back lashing out with his right foot at the man on his right. He connected too solidly, close to the soft spot he had aimed at. Before he could recover from the shock of the jarring pain that shot up his leg, something heavy hit him in the stomach almost knocking his heart out of his mouth. He doubled up, his thoughts both with his suit and his pain. Then the ground came up to meet him.

A stinging, chilly wetness woke him. The thought of his suit made him sit up quickly but there was light everywhere, blinding him. Hands on his back stopped him from lying down to ease the terrible pain in his stomach. Raising his right hand to shield his eyes so that he could see through the light, he soon let it fall to the ground with a groan as a new pain shot up his upper arm.

'He wake sir,' he heard a voice say behind him.

'Good,' another voice, sounding like a white man's said. The glare dimmed and he could see the vague outlines of a car.

Was a car talking? he wondered, and then realized how ridiculous the thought was. A cold shiver reminded him he was wet.

'Can you carry him?' the voice from the car asked.

'Yes, sir,' the voice behind him said.

Christian tried to talk to the voice, to ask about Jaja and the two men, but he found his tongue would not move. He had no tongue.

'I have no tongue!' his mind shrieked and he groaned, and the hands that had moved from his back returned.

'He wound bad, sir,' the voice said.

Again there was light everywhere. The hands on his back were gone, and he was on a bed. But where? The place, wherever it was, smelt like a hospital. Yes, of course, it must be a hospital, but which one? His eyes were open but the light did not let him see. A hazy figure seemed to be bending over him from a great height.

A figure in white, with something like a white band around the head. For a short painful minute his heart gave a lurch as it beat very fast. Was he in heaven? Was that an angel? But he soon realized how ridiculous the thought was and his crazy heartbeat subsided. The haziness remained, however.

'He is awake,' the figure in white said in Igbo.

'Thanks be to God,' a voice he recognized exclaimed. 'Christian,' Janet said, looking at him from a distance also, 'what happened to you?'

'I was beaten up by some stupid men,' he tried to say but remembered he had no tongue. Again panic took hold of him and he closed his eyes to reduce its effects. So he had lost his tongue? How? He felt no pain there, so they could not have cut it off. What had they done to him?

'Christian! Christian! Christian, please wake up! Please don't die.'

He opened his eyes again to stop Janet from screaming any longer. Now she seemed closer than before.

'Thanks be to God!' she cried coming even closer. 'Thanks be to God!'

Almost every part of her face was covered with tears, and some had poured down her blouse.

93

'Where is my suit?' he asked in his mind, looking steadily at Janet. He did not feel the suit around him, not since the chilling wetness had awoken him.

'Thanks be to God,' Janet said again. 'You are still alive. Please don't die. What will I do if you die?'

Christian groaned to stop her from going on in that sentimental way of hers. He could not stand it. There were many questions he wanted answered, and he needed silence in order to figure out how to ask them.

'Oh Christian,' Janet burst out again. 'What happened to you? Were you fighting? God have mercy on me! Whoever you fought with nearly killed you. Oh God can't you talk?'

Christian shook his head slowly and was overjoyed he could do it without pain. His assumption that his neck would be stiff was wrong then. There must be other parts of his body that could move without pain. He started trying them out.

'Chukwunna,' Janet cried out anew. 'The person really wanted to kill you, but your God did not let him complete his wicked plan. It is a miracle you can see and hear. But without speech . . . oh my God, let me look at your tongue.'

Christian found that only a few parts of his body could move without pain—his left hand. Opening his mouth was excruciatingly painful; he let out a grunt of pain as Janet forced it more ajar.

'God forbid evil things,' she said softly. 'Your tongue is so swollen I can see nothing else. Christian, what did you do to the person that did this to you? And you can't even tell me. *That* is the worst thing of all!'

Christian turned his head away slowly, noticing dull grey partitions for the first time. He was glad he was to be in the open ward. It must be at one end of it. A white wall was to his left. He returned his head to its original position and Janet picked up where she had left off.

'Your face is all swollen like an overdone cassava foofoo. It is a miracle your eyes were not ruined. They are so swollen I wonder you can see with them at all. And there are big bruises on your arms, stomach and legs. Do you know I did not recognize you immediately when they called me to see you? Imagine my not recognizing you! Your suit was torn to pieces and you had blood all over you. I thought you were dead. But the white man that brought you here said you were alive. He said had he not come suddenly upon the man who was dragging you into the bush you probably would have been dead. And I thanked God that he sent a white man of all people to save you for me. The Chief Nurse on duty was very kind. He got you a bed and partitions and treated your wounds, and injected you with pain-killing medicine. You will be the first patient the doctor will see tomorrow.'

Christian was glad Janet was doing what she liked most—talking. Her emotions were drained off through her words. Already her tone had taken on the cold, distant clicking of an alarm clock, and she had stopped sniffling.

'So a white man saved my life!' He had thought so. No Igbo or *mbamiri* man would play the Good Samaritan in such a place and at such an hour. They would all pass him by, after making sure he was no relation of theirs.

Did Tom Big Harry actually find out about him and Angela? Or did she, in a moment of weakness confess to him? Angela did not seem the type that would confess voluntarily. Their moments together had been pleasurable to both of them and there were times when he thought she enjoyed it more than he did.

But everything was changed now. It was too dangerous to be seen around Angela's home or even to get in touch with her. The beating he had received meant that he might pay with his life if he were caught next time.

But what if Angela sent for him? Would he go? Not if the message came through Jaja. Did Angela know of the double role Jaja had played? What would she be doing now? Probably in bed with the gloating fat pig. How he would love to get at him with a knife, to cut off some of that fat! Would he ever have the chance? Would things ever change enough to put him in a position of power? Christian knew he had done wrong to take Angela in Big Harry's home. But that was only important in a moral tale—a tale that had to end so that the moral could be tacked on. The story of life was different. It had no ending, and no morality. It did not always have a beginning and an end, nor a progression. It picked you up and dropped you where it pleased.

So who knows? Maybe he would one day be in a position to pay Big Harry back or to once again eat the sugar on his very table. Who knows the way the story of life will go?

'How do you feel, Christian?' Janet asked suddenly.

He looked at her, trying but failing to translate into eye and head movements what his mind was screaming: 'Are you blind? Shut up and go home and stop gloating over what happened to me.'

'Do you know,' Janet said, 'it is so easy to forget that you can't talk?'

Of course, thought Christian, it is easy for you to forget. You are not the person who was hurt. My God, this must be what your hell is like—people wanting to talk but unable to do so. Oh yes, did God himself, when he could stand the silence no longer, not only talk but create things that talked? Yes, the Bible said so. And the more his creatures talked, the farther away they got from him.

'Did you tell Vitus when to close the shop?' Janet asked.

Christian groaned and closed his eyes. Oh God, let Janet find you and be silent, forever.

'*Ndo*,' Janet said. '*Ndo, ndo*, you hear?'

Christian heard and his mind screamed, 'Shut up!'

PART TWO

Chapter One

1 ✄ At last the dry, cold, dusty wind from the north had spent itself in wanton destruction, Ejiaka thought, peering out through the window as she waited for Nelson to finish eating his lunch. The white, fleecy sky was being replaced by one of lowering *icheku* charcoal. Occasionally the heavens groaned with the weight of moisture. It had been doing this for days but there was as yet no decisive sign that it would unload to slake the thirst of the caked dusty streets and give the farmers the signal to start planting maize and ọkrọ. Reading the cloud formations, the heavy whorls that were moving down to the earth, Ejiaka felt today would be different.

Nelson had almost finished eating. Ejiaka loved to watch him eat. He put so much gusto into it one felt he must be eating honey! His obvious enjoyment redeemed the smoke-filled tearful hours she spent preparing the food. The only drawback was that it made any hungry person watching him eager to try the food. Since Nelson never failed to invite friends and co-workers to share his food, there was usually a mad scramble for the last morsel on the plate. To save him from this self-destructive generosity Ejiaka often insisted he come home to eat. Too many vultures in the shed waited for him to merely glance their way to swoop down on the food.

Ejiaka smiled as Nelson caught her looking at him.

'This is wonderful stew,' he said using the last piece of yam to scoop up the remnants. 'You cook like one who was brought up in the town.' He popped the yam and stew into his mouth.

Ejiaka smiled embarrassedly at both the compliment and the way Nelson's cheeks ballooned out like those of a child blowing a fire into a blaze.

Then suddenly the sky's background groans changed to

rumbles of discontent. When these ceased, the wind died down, ushering in an oppressive silence. The sky pressed down like a black lid. Everything waited expectantly for the discordant music of the thunderstorm to begin. The Smith alarm clock went off, unnaturally loud in the silence. Perched seven feet high in a small mahogany box, it looked too small to have produced the jangling sound.

'I'm late,' exclaimed Nelson, dragging the bucket of water nearer and washing his hands quickly. 'I will try to come home for dinner, but don't worry if I don't. It just means I am too busy. Get me my raincoat and wind-cheater.'

Ejiaka soon returned with them and started clearing the table. Nelson laced up his rubber re-soled army boots, donned his raincoat, and wrapping his wind-cheater round his neck said :

'Don't forget, I may or may not come home for dinner.'

He was through the door before she could say 'Nagbo', but she said it anyway.

Taking the plates to the pantry-store, she was struck by the sudden emptiness of the house. She would never get used to Nelson's 3.00 p.m. to 11.00 p.m. shift. Just when she assumed he would be home all day, he rushed off to work. The morning shift, 7.00 a.m. to 3.00 p.m., was much better. She did not have time to don the *lappa* of aloneness after the night before, so she did not feel his absence. And when she was beginning to feel it he came home. Now, the night shift, 11.00 p.m. to 7.00 a.m., was the most welcome. It not only provided a week's respite from importunities but an easier passage through unclean periods.

Ejiaka left the plates to be washed later and started closing the windows and bringing in all the clothing she had hung out during the morning to dry. As she rushed in and out, bringing in piles of clothes without bothering to fold them neatly, it got darker and darker. She knew the ferocity of a first thunderstorm. She would fold up the clothes later in the safety of the house, although there was no guarantee the storm would not unroof the house.

Gathering up the remaining clothes she realized Onyeama should have been back from school by now. The school finished at two o'clock, and it usually took him thirty to forty minutes to walk home. Onyeama always dawdled after school, especially if Nelson was on the 3.00 p.m. to 11.00 p.m. shift. Ejiaka hoped the threatening storm would make him come home earlier. Her young uncle, an only son, had disappeared during a first storm at home, and he had only gone to the next village to cut firewood.

By the time Ejiaka got back into the house, a slight wind had sprung up. She locked the door, dumped the rest of the clothes on one of the armchairs, and went to the bedroom to see how Okechukwu was doing. He lay happily on his back, his plump legs drumming on the bed, stubby hands waving excitedly in the air and dark-pink gums displayed in a smile. Ejiaka lifted him up and with a happy laugh, threw and caught him expertly under the armpits.

'You love it, don't you?' she asked. She threw and caught him twice more. 'You wonderful bag of cassava!'

Overcome with happiness, Okechukwu made the sound of buzzing wasps.

'Let the wasp sting you,' Ejiaka said laughing.

Okechukwu made the sound even louder.

A door banged somewhere, a window rattled and the storm came down with savage fury. Ejiaka put Okechukwu back in his cot and rushed to lock the front door. She took a quick look outside hoping, as sometimes happened, to see Onyeama running home. The street was one mass of whirling dust, dotted with leaves, papers, shawls and everything that could be whipped up! Even the big mango trees bowed their heads in reverence. Only the telegraph poles stood out straight and true, the only sane things in a mad, jumbled world.

Then the first drops of rain pattered on the zinc roof and white hailstones were falling everywhere. Okechukwu's frightened cry rang out above the increasing sound. Ejiaka quickly closed the door without locking it and ran to him.

'No, no, no, *nnamu*, don't cry,' she said picking him up and rocking him. 'It is only the rain. And I am here with you so why cry?'

He stopped crying instantly. She took him to the parlour with her, worrying about Onyeama. If the boy was caught outside, the heavens would stone him to death. Hearing a timid knock on the door she opened it. No one was there. She waited, searching the slanting, taut sheet of rain, closing the door when she was convinced no one had knocked.

She had barely sat down when the knock came again. She listened intently. It was repeated, its sound more purposeful than that of the whirlwind driving the hailstones. She opened the door and Onyeama stood on the steps wet and shivering.

'Ajọ nnwa!' she said standing aside to let him in. 'What are you trying to do to me? You want me to die from shock?'

'We were not let out of school at the normal time,' Onyeama said shivering and breathing hard. 'I ran all the way but could not beat the rain.'

'Go and change before you catch cold.'

Ejiaka sat down and hugged Okechukwu to her. It was going to be a bad storm and she felt sorry for those who had to be outside. It was good Nelson did not have to work in the rain, although he did say the cold wind that blew through the open-ended shed was just as bad.

That was the main problem with this town—everything seemed so much more malevolent than at home. People were indifferent, their cruelties random and often motiveless. It made it all so frightening. And added to this was the virulence of the dogs and the bloodthirstiness of the huge mosquitoes.

Turning Okechukwu over on his stomach she searched for the angry red mosquito bites that had appeared on his back a few days ago. The swelling was down and it had formed a scab.

'Greedy things,' she said softly standing Okechukwu up. 'Biting a defenceless baby. But they won't bite you any more, eh?' she added to Okechukwu who said, 'Br-r-r-r.' 'Yes,' she agreed, 'they won't bite you. Your mosquito net stops them dead! "Halt there", it commands them, "This baby is not for eating. Go and find some other victim." And they all buzz angrily. But there is nothing they can do. So they go away disappointed. Yes, disappointed because they can see how plump you are and know how good you will taste, eh?' She tickled his stomach.

Okechukwu laughed as though he understood what had been said.

'Yes, they go away grumbling and powerless.'

Onyeama walked in dressed in his khaki jumper.

'Did you spread out your clothes to dry?' Ejiaka asked him.

'Yes.'

'You can eat now unless you want to wait for the rain to stop so you can warm the stew.'

'This rain does not look as if it will ever stop. I won't wait.'

'I didn't think you would. Take two pieces of meat.'

'Thank you,' Onyeama said grinning happily.

'Where did you leave your books?' Ejiaka asked, as he turned towards the pantry-store.

'Comfort has them. The gale caught us in front of her home.'

'Why didn't you stay there till the rain was over?'

'And let you die of shock?'

Ejiaka laughed, and Okechukwu joined in with his, 'Br-rrr-r.'

'Did you hear what he said?' she said to Okechukwu and made faces at him.

'One of these days,' Onyeama said turning away, 'he is going to answer you.'

'*Gbuwhuo asọ*!' Ejiaka said quickly. 'Don't even think of such things lest they happen. It is an abomination for a baby to talk before he grows teeth.'

'I was only joking,' Onyeama said, immediately contrite.

'Don't joke about such things. You never know who may be listening. Go and eat. I am sure you are starving.'

With bowed head Onyeama went into the pantry-store.

Ejiaka sat Okechukwu on her lap and offered him a full breast. He made a grab for it but Ejiaka pulled it back and laughed.

'Always hungry,' she said.

Okechukwu cried out his impatience.

'Here, but be sure you are hungry.'

His powerful pull showed he was. Ejiaka was filled with that feeling of tenderness and wonder that always took possession of her whole being each time she breastfed him. His sucking not only eased the pain of her overfull breast but created a pleasant sensation of warmth and peace. Let the storm have its way now, she thought.

Later that evening she and Onyeama sang and told fairy tales to each other with the rain providing the steady drumming that created a highly suggestive atmosphere. The song-tale of a young bride who could not bring herself to call her husband by name

103

until her mouth got stuck in an *udu*, brought tears to Ejiaka's eyes. It could have been herself, and she knew she could never call Nelson by name in his presence.

2 ⅍ Although it was barely two weeks since the first storm, it seemed as though the rains had started months ago. Falling with a frequency that was disheartening—rarely did a day pass without drizzle—it made Ejiaka wish she was back in her home town, where the soil invariably soaked up the rain like a sponge. Port Harcourt's soil seemed made of water, and people waded up to their waists in certain sections of Aggrey Road because the open, shallow gutters flooded easily. Quite often some of the apartments were flooded and the tenants had to bale out fast and continuously like fisherman living in boats on the River Niger.

The backyard of Ejiaka's house did not fare any better. It was now a dirty swamp she dreaded to walk through. Going to the outhouse was a carefully planned journey over treacherous swamp land. Although the kitchen was close to the house, she and Onyeama had to place stepping-stones at appropriate intervals between its door and that of the house. It made the carrying of a hot pot of soup into the house an acrobatic feat.

Ejiaka's efforts to get the yard cleaned up had failed woefully. Her neighbours said it was the landlord's duty, and the landlord who lived in a beautiful house with a cemented backyard kept promising and failing to do something about it. It frayed nerves and led easily to quarrels like the one Nelson had with the Kalus who refused to wash the general bathroom and latrine when it was their turn to do so. Although they were finally prevailed upon to do it, they stopped speaking to Nelson and Ejiaka. The yard had become a battleground and it made Ejiaka reluctant to get up this morning even though it was well past dawn. Luckily Nelson was on night duty and would not be home till eight o'clock. She had at least an hour to unwrap the layers of the night's aloneness. Leaning out of bed she looked into Okechukwu's cot where he was already wide awake and fascinated with his thumb. No wonder he had made no noise. The way time slipped by. He was already seven months old and would soon be walking.

Ejiaka snuggled back into bed. She was doing the one thing her mother hated, but she did not feel any guilt. An early riser, her mother was up and about at dawn like a hen with a large brood, and anyone who did not get up shortly after got a hand-cup full of cold water in the face. It was very effective. Her mother said female late risers were preparing for spinster-hood, or if they married would have miserable, poverty-stricken lives.

'Time to get up,' Ejiaka said to herself, and stretched. Her sadness was lifting and Okechukwu was making his preliminary noises. Before long their frequency and pitch would increase till they merged into a steady cry. Ejiaka got out of bed, went to him and wagged a finger in his face.

'Don't you start that now. I know you are awake.'

Okechukwu stopped and stared at her. From the slight odour she knew he had soiled himself, and if it was a big stool he would be getting hungry. Should she clean and feed him now?

'Don't start crying,' she told him. 'I will soon be back.'

As soon as her back was turned he started crying but she did not return. There was no urgency in the sound he made.

In the pantry-store, Onyeama lay on his back looking up at the ceiling. He was always reluctant to get up on school-days, but up earlier than the dawn for holidays and weekends. He scrambled to his stilt-like legs when he saw her.

'Why do I always have to remind you about school?' she asked him angrily. 'You have failed for two years consecutively and you still go late to school. What is the matter with you? Don't you know yet how important school is?'

Onyeama picked up his mat and started rolling it up, his eyes on his fast-moving hands.

'Onyeama,' Ejiaka said, 'why don't you want to make use of the brain God gave you? You know I am ready to help you with your problems including your school work. It is not every boy that has the chance to go to school, you know.'

Onyeama put away his mat in the far corner of the room and without turning round said, 'You know I do not like school. I have told you that many times before.'

'I know you did, but why not try and pass this class then stop?'

Onyeama turned round and said with some heat, 'I tried last year and failed. This year is not going to be any different. I feel like a fool in the school and people make a fool of me too. Look at me, I am a grown man. I want to start working or learning a trade I can do with my hands. I don't need school to learn how to become a tailor, or carpenter or mason. Please Eji, can't you convince master that I am not made for school? You know you are the person who should be in school not me.'

'Will you take care of Okechukwu and your master while I am at school?' Ejiaka now asked humorously, succeeding in bringing a smile to his face. It was not the first time they had discussed this matter, but after each talk there was a marked improvement in his attitude towards school. It was becoming a ritual.

'Do you know why your master insists you must go to school? I know you do, but I will say it again—you will learn things he couldn't because his father died early. You have heard him wish many times he could go back to school. You have also seen him practise writing and reading in the evenings. Why do you think he does all that? Don't shake your head like that, Onyeama. What I am telling you is something you will remember in your old age.'

'I won't live to be old.'

'I know you will. But listen. The world is changing and new skills are needed. Although all the things you mentioned are good, education is even better. Besides how are you going to learn about the new machines tailors will use if you don't know how to read? How will you take the measurements of your customers if you do not know how to write?'

'Eji,' Onyeama protested laughing. 'I already know how to write.'

'Yes, you know how to write like a spider! Joking aside, don't you want good pay and a house like this one?'

'No. As long as I can fill my stomach and that of my family when I have one I will be satisfied. I hate townships. I want to live at home.'

'You know your father wouldn't be happy to see you return uneducated. He wants you to be like those court people from Awka, so that all the gifts that go to the kotuma will come to your family and help towards bringing up your brothers and sisters.'

'I can help my father better by working at home. Let my younger brother be the most learned person in the world. The place for a first-born is near his father, because it is his duty to maintain the traditions, bury his father, and make sure the *umunna* do not steal all the land.'

'Where did you get all that from?' Ejiaka asked laughing. Onyeama looked so pompous he was obviously echoing someone.

'I thought of it myself,' Onyeama said, but could not keep a straight face. 'Vitus said it is what Christian says all the time.'

'Oh, yes. Christian says that because he does not want his elder brother to come here.'

'But Eji, I am serious about wanting to stop schooling and learn a trade. Do you know I am the biggest person in my class? I feel like a sick man asked to look after the children while everyone goes to the farms.'

'Did you hear a sound?'

'What?'

'No, I don't think that was Okechukwu.'

'I did not hear a thing.'

'A mother's ear picks up sounds others don't.'

'Especially new mothers!'

Ejiaka laughed. 'All right we have talked the morning away. Go and make the fire, then bring out one big yam. I will go and take care of Okechukwu. I will talk with your master sometime about your going home, but you must finish this year at school successfully. You have to show me and others that the reason you failed twice was because you do not like school and not because you are stupid. I know you are not stupid, but others don't.'

'Thank you Eji.'

'Someone is knocking.' Ejiaka tightened the top of her *lappa* over her breasts. She had no blouse on. 'Go and see who it is. Hurry.'

She went quickly to the bedroom, and lowered the top of her *lappa* to her waist. Okechukwu still lay the way she had left him, engrossed in his left thumb.

'Now, let us see what you did there,' Ejiaka said to him.

She picked him up. It was not bad. She cleaned him with the edge of the cloth on which he had been lying.

'I think you should have a bath first before you eat. Don't you agree? I knew you would.' She laughed at and with him.

'Who is it, Onyeama?' she asked as she heard the front door close.

'It is the postman.'

Ejiaka rushed out, Okechukwu on her right hip.

'What did he bring?' she asked, and then added, 'Is that all?' when Onyeama handed her a pink envelope.

'Yes,' Onyeama said.

'It is a telegram, isn't it?'

'Yes.'

'Where is it from?' She kept turning the envelope in her left hand as though she could see its contents without opening it.

'It is from home.'

'I hope nothing bad has happened.' She took a deep breath, and slowly exhaled. 'You had better go off to school or you will be so late you won't be allowed into the classroom.'

'I don't think I can learn anything today. I will spend the time thinking about what is in the telegram. Do you want me to open it?'

'No,' Ejiaka said horrified. 'Go to school. You are late.'

Although she kept very busy after Onyeama was gone, the time dragged for her. The things she had to do seemed to take up less time than they used to. Peeling and putting the yams on the fire, even with Okechukwu tied on her back, took only a few minutes. Bathing him did not drive out her inward dismay at the possible contents of the telegram, but what she worried about was a matter of degree rather than difference. She was certain the telegram contained bad news. Her conjecture ranged from the death of her mother to that of a close relative of Nelson.

If her mother had died what would she do?

She was so preoccupied with her impending grief that Okechukwu's cries now sounded far away, and she fed him automatically to stop his crying which had become merely irritating.

Telegrams were harbingers of bad news. She remembered an

aunt of hers who had received one. Everyone had started crying even before it was read. It was just as well. The telegram cryptically stated that her aunt's favourite daughter had died suddenly. In the manner of telegrams, there had been no explanation of how or what she had died of, and it was only days later they received a letter that dealt with the death in more detail.

Leaving Okechukwu to play with a small spoon and babble to himself, she went to the kitchen to warm up the stew for breakfast. Nelson would be back soon and would want breakfast immediately. Should she give him the telegram before or after breakfast? She did not want the bad news to destroy his appetite. On the other hand if she gave him the telegram after he had eaten, the food might not sit comfortably in his stomach. Perhaps it would be best to give him the thing before he ate, so that whatever he was able to eat would not turn sour.

She was about to take down the stew from the fire when Nelson's dog slunk by. The beast-of-the-forest knew precisely when Nelson was due to return and always waited at the front door for him. That dog was definitely a 'bad luck' dog. She wondered if it was not one of the things that had caused the telegram to come? The way it slunk around reminded her of the legendary dog and tortoise which human beings sent to God in order to request immortality for all humans. The greedy dog had been so busy polishing off the excreta the cunning tortoise always left for him that he got to God after the tortoise had been and gone. The tortoise having snared longevity for itself and its descendants, human beings were stuck with mortality. The dog felt so guilty he and his descendants always slunk away in the face of human anger while the tortoise withdrew into its shell afraid that it might lose the immortality it had obtained dishonestly.

It was high time that dog was sold, Ejiaka decided while carrying the cooked yams into the house. It was a reminder of Mgbeke whose existence Ejiaka would rather not think about. She had enough problems now and she did not want to start worrying about what would happen if Mgbeke recovered and came to claim her position as first wife. There was Nelson's refusal to carry out the ceremony of the eating of the new yam in the traditional way because he said he had become a Christian;

and the new Nelson which the promotion to Fitter Grade Two seemed to have let loose—a new Nelson who was as different from the one she knew as *mammy-water* was from normal women. And finally, there was her failure to help Janet. The native doctor had travelled to the north and would not be back until after the rainy season. These problems were enough to make one cry. So, she did not want the dog around to remind her of yet another. Would she be able to get Nelson to do away with the dog immediately?

✂✂✂

Nelson strode into the house whistling. Rain had fallen in the night and this morning everything looked fresh and new. Even the muddy streets looked laundered until one stepped on a soft area. Nelson had avoided them successfully, even while following with his eyes the birds that flitted by the tall shrub-bordered roadside, their many-hued wings catching and reflecting the early rays of the sun.

Laying his cap on the table, he sat in his favourite armchair to unlace his boots. He was pulling off his socks when Ejiaka walked in carrying Okechukwu.

'Welcome,' she said.

'Uh-huh,' he said. 'I thought you had all been kidnapped. Give him to me,' he added, stretching out his hands for Okechukwu who was already half-way out of Ejiaka's restraining arms. 'And how is my little man today?'

Okechukwu babbled an incoherent but apparently happy reply.

Ejiaka picked up the socks, boots and cap and took them into the bedroom.

Nelson stood Okechukwu upon his thighs, then threw him up and caught him twice.

'You love it, don't you?' he asked.

'See the telegram we got this morning,' Ejiaka said, holding it out.

'Telegram?' Nelson lifted Okechukwu off his knee. 'Carry him,' he said, taking the telegram almost at the same time Ejiaka caught Okechukwu.

Nelson's heart beat painfully as he spread out the telegram, his thoughts suspended in a void. His eyes swept over it without taking in a word, then he forced himself to read it slowly :

MGBEKE DIED YESTERDAY. NOT
WORRY HER PEOPLE BURY HER.

IBEALO

'Who died?' Ejiaka asked.

Nelson looked up at her grave face, his heartbeat subsiding. It had not been as bad as he had anticipated.

'Mgbeke is dead.'

'*Ewuo, nnemu-o!*' Ejiaka cried. Okechukwu gave her a startled look and joined in, forcing her to lower her crying one octave and rock him to and fro. He stopped crying.

Nelson sat still trying but failing to feel any grief at what he had read. Rather, he was relieved at the news. The best thing Mgbeke had ever done was to die so far away from Port Harcourt. Now, he did not have to prepare her for burial nor arrange her funeral. He did not even have to spend that much money. He would simply send a few shillings to his uncle, Ibealo, in payment for the telegram and the wine his *umunna* would have to take to Mgbeke's parents. And perhaps he would spend another few shillings to entertain those attracted by Ejiaka's crying, and the few friends who might drop in to commiserate with him.

'Ejiaka, that's enough,' Nelson said.

His remonstrance seemed to increase Ejiaka's grief. She sat down abruptly in the nearest armchair as if her legs could not support her any longer. Her tears flowed copiously, and her effortless crying bespoke total and complete loss.

Nelson did not know which made him more uneasy, the earlier keening or the present hopelessness. Although he felt guilty for his inability to shed tears his mind refused to focus on his loss. Instead it dwelt on what he had gained because of it. Now, he had *one* wife. He need no longer fear that Theodore would discover he had two. During one of their frequent discussions Theodore had told him the church was not in favour of polygamy. To marry more than one woman was a sin, since the church did not recognize the second woman as a wife. The man was therefore committing venial sin each time he had relations with her, and until he sent her away he was not allowed to have Holy Communion. As an unrepentant and unconfessed sinner his soul would be damned if he did. Nelson had asked if a man with two wives could confess his sin every Sunday, and after being absolved take Communion.

Theodore said vehemently that was a broad road to hell. The man's confession would be invalid since he did not intend to stop sinning. The essence of confession was to show that one was not only sorry for past sins but would make every effort not to commit more. To sin intentionally was to be as damned as the Devil who had purposely disobeyed God.

'And you know how awful it is to be as damned as the Devil!'

Nelson did not but was frightened at the thought of being roasted alive, *forever*. As Theodore had said, those who went to hell often wished death could put them out of their pain and misery. *That*, Nelson had thought, was the most horrible thing—for one to wish for death, even in hell, to actually prefer it to being alive.

Nelson had started wishing Mgbeke would not survive her illness. Now his wishes had been granted.

'Ejiaka, that is enough,' he said once more. 'The way you cry one would think something had happened to your mother.'

A knock at the pantry-store confirmed Nelson's worst fears.

'That is enough, Ejiaka,' he said brusquely, as someone knocked again at the door of the pantry-store. But he knew it was hopeless. Crying was one of those things that generated its own momentum once it got started.

Nelson stood up, his exasperation making it easier for him to compose his face into lines of sorrow and loss, and went to open the door.

'Good morning, ma,' he said to Mrs. Jeremiah.

'What have you done to my daughter?' she asked, and without waiting for an answer waddled past him puffing like a shunting engine.

He closed the door with a slight smile and followed her huge back into the parlour.

'Ejiaka, my child, what is the matter? Did that stupid husband of yours do something to you?'

Ejiaka shook her head, unable to speak and cry at the same

112

time. Okechukwu stared at Mrs. Jeremiah from his comfortable position on his mother's lap.

'Nelson, tell me what you have done.'

'I did not do anything, ma,' Nelson said. 'We received bad news from home today.'

'*Ewuo*, my daughter,' Mrs. Jeremiah exclaimed with quick-rushing sympathy and laid a heavy right arm on Ejiaka's shoulders. Her normally puckish face began to crumple.

'Mgbeke died at our home town yesterday,' Nelson said quickly.

'*Ewuo*, Nelson,' Mrs. Jeremiah said straightening up, her hand still on Ejiaka's shoulders. Tears streamed down her youthful-looking round cheeks. 'I knew something was wrong so I hurried over as soon as I heard Ejiaka's crying.'

For a brief moment Nelson was afraid she was coming to embrace him, to smother him with her huge chest and two slabs of breasts. He sighed with relief when she waddled over to the chair next to Ejiaka and sat down. Her tears continued to flow, her small face pretty in spite of the surrounding fat, a mask of grief.

'*Ewuo*, my children,' she said softly, 'what a big loss! What killed her?'

'We don't know,' Nelson said. 'You know telegrams don't explain things. We will know when we receive a letter from home.'

'Come, come, my child,' Mrs. Jeremiah said, turning to Ejiaka whose crying had subsided somewhat. 'Don't cry any more. Your head will start aching if you continue like that. Dry your eyes, you hear? Dry your eyes. If you cry so much now what will you do when you lose a member of *your* family.'

'I told her many times she has cried long enough,' Nelson said sitting down. 'But it is like talking to a tree.'

'Don't blame her, my child. We women are not as strong-minded as you men. What else can a woman do but cry? It eases the pain and makes it bearable. When my husband died three years ago, I cried as if I was going to die. He was such a young and handsome man too. Very much like you, Nelson. Gentle and considerate. But my crying did not bring him back. All it did was make my eyes as red as a parrot's tail. Ejiaka, that is enough. Give me Okechukwu and go and wash your face.'

'Yes, go and wash your face,' Nelson said.

Mrs. Jeremiah wiped her own eyes with the edge of her *lappa* and stretched out her arms, each as big as Nelson's thigh, to Okechukwu. 'Come, my child,' she said, smiling winningly.

Okechukwu clung to his mother as she attempted to lift him up.

'Go to mama,' Ejiaka said in between sniffles.

Okechukwu started howling, but no tears came out.

'The cunning man,' Nelson said, getting up and going to him. 'If you won't go to mama, what about coming to me?'

Okechukwu did not resist when Nelson lifted him off Ejiaka's lap.

'It is a wise child that keeps to his parents,' Mrs. Jeremiah said, lowering her arms. 'Go and wash your beautiful face my daughter,' she added. 'Mgbeke is beyond anybody's help, and the living are more important than the dead.'

'It pains me that we disturbed you ma,' Nelson said, as soon as Ejiaka left to wash her face.

'No Nelson, don't say such things. This is not the type of thing you keep quiet about, even in a town. Only animals suffer alone. You have to share your pain with people or it will be very hard to forget. You know that only those who forget survive, because if you forget the dead then you remember the living, and to be with the living is to live.'

'You are speaking the truth,' Nelson agreed. He had always respected Mrs. Jeremiah not only for her generosity but also for her experience. Of all the neighbours she had been the only one who extended a helping hand when he and Ejiaka had moved here, and her helpfulness was unique in that she did not, like other helpful people, try to run their lives. As she often said, once a child has learnt how to walk, you have to let it fall and get up on its own, or it will never learn to run.

'One thing you must never allow a bereaved to feel is alone,' Mrs. Jeremiah went on. 'When a bereaved is left alone with his grief he tends to harbour the memory too long, and it often embitters his life. As I always tell my children *life* is sharing. But you know, they never seem to understand that. All they know is *my* life, *my* life, as if they brought themselves into this world. Without the co-operation of two people, they would not have come into the world, and if when they came they had been left alone, they would not have survived. You see what I mean?'

'Yes, ma, I do. I see it clearly.'

'So when a person thinks only in terms of his life, he becomes envious and selfish. Soon he thinks his neighbours enjoy life while he suffers, or that they don't deserve to be alive at all. When someone starts thinking like that he is merely waiting for death to come and touch him between the eyes and say: "You have been waiting for me, here I am." There are so many people like that in this town—people who are just waiting for death. That is why townships are so full of wickedness. What do you expect of people who are waiting for death?'

'They act like death,' Nelson said.

'*Ehia*, my daughter,' Mrs. Jeremiah said, turning to Ejiaka who had just walked in. 'Crying does not become you. You have the face of joy and life. But it is good you cried for your dead *nwunyedi*. It shows you have feeling and compassion.' Mrs. Jeremiah struggled to her feet, puffing hard. 'I should have remembered not to sit in the armchair,' she said. 'Please stop me next time.'

'Won't you stay for breakfast?' Nelson asked. 'Ejiaka was just going to bring it in.'

'No thank you,' she said. 'My breakfast was ready before I came here. Besides you cannot satisfy me. Ejiaka, do not cry any more, you hear? What has happened cannot be undone, my daughter.'

'Thank you ma for coming,' Ejiaka said.

'It is good to visit you two,' Mrs. Jeremiah said.

Later that day, Nelson had time to think about Mrs. Jeremiah's criticism of town life. 'People who are waiting for death', she had called it, and how right she was. So far only two other neighbours had visited him, and it seemed they came only out of curiosity. In fact one of them said he thought something more catastrophic had happened, something like the death of a mother or a father. Wives, he said, were replaceable and should not be mourned with such abandon.

Nelson was glad the neighbours did not stay long. Their presence and the things they said made him uncomfortable mainly because he agreed with them yet felt it was wrong to do so. At times he even wondered if Ejiaka's grief was genuine. There was really no reason why it should not be. Although she and Mgbeke (she and her fellow spirits!) were *nwunyedi*, they had not lived together to develop any of those rivalries that were the subject of so many fairy tales.

3 ⸕ The day gave birth to a rare evening. The relief Nelson had felt at its beginning, now flowered and enveloped his whole body with soft, petals of appreciation. He felt free at last to pursue whatever he wanted, be it a new religious experience or otherwise. Previously, the remembrance of Mgbeke and her illness had acted like a brake whenever his thoughts were about to take flight. Resolutions, he thought, were better than transitions.

Aggrey Road was crowded as usual with people hurrying by, their eyes unseeing, their minds filled with whatever they pursued so avidly. Nelson followed the beautiful women that passed with his eyes till they disappeared in the distance. He loved to stand on the steps of his house and watch people go by. The sight reassured him he was in a town, an easy thing to forget stuck all day as he was in the running shed.

It was a beautiful evening, unexpected in late August. For once there were no lamp-black clouds smearing the sky. The sun, like the clayey floor of a room on which *nkpuru nkwọ* had been used to perfection, shimmered and throbbed, leaving a golden *odo* yellow splash on the western horizon. To the east there was a greyish-tinged blue, and early birds winged their way home in a leisurely fashion.

Down the street children played frenetically and noisily, their tennis ball sometimes in danger of being run over by an infrequent car. Before long, Okechukwu would be playing like that, trying to squeeze all possible daylight from the day. By then Nelson hoped Okechukwu would not be alone, because when one has more than one of a thing one can afford to let it out of sight.

'Good evening,' a voice said to his left.

'Good evening,' Nelson quickly answered, recognizing Mrs. Jeremiah's young man but for whom she would have had to leave Port Harcourt. He supported her with his earnings and she took care of him like a mother. 'How are you?'

'No trouble. What about you?'

'We thank God.'

The young man whose name Nelson did not remember disappeared into Mrs. Jeremiah's house.

Yes, there was a great deal to be thankful for. Nelson felt His presence today as he did the first time he attended high mass at St. Mary's Church with Theodore. Although self-conscious in his newly starched white shirt and trousers, Nelson was impressed by what he saw when he started looking around. Magnificent images spread down both sides of the rectangular hall, each a beautiful mixture of colours, each depicting a very lifelike scene.

The light from six candles in golden strands, increased the unearthly radiance and beauty of the altar on which also fell a soft green light from the long tapering stained glass windows.

Nelson was particularly happy about the images, for they showed that like his people, the Roman Catholics used mediums to pray to God. What he could not understand, however, was why they had to have so many of them. He remembered the names of a male and female figure—Jesus and Mary. They were said to represent the highest manifestations of the creativity of God, and Nelson felt they should have been sufficient as mediums without the myriad others. At the time he vowed he would ask Theodore about it after the service, but forgot. It is not what you see that matters, but what you remember of it, he thought ruefully.

But he did not forget the imposing figures of the priest and his retinue. Their robes of red, white and black had a glow somewhat out of this world. The priest's incantations, in a monotone sing-song infused his movements with supernatural meaning and power. Nelson felt that any prayer the priest and his acolytes offered to God would be heard. The ritual was strong, the movements precise and solemn, and the incantations a chant of immense power. The sweet sickly smell of burning incense hung in the air, an almost tangible medium for the spirit. And the spirits were out indeed, manifesting themselves in the harmonious, mesmeric chanting of the congregation, in the floating movements of the priest and his acolytes from one picture to another, in the devotional and enraptured looks of the people, and the secret language in which the service was conducted.

Nelson had taken it all in. He felt he was worshipping God and that any prayer he uttered would be answered. The realization hit him so suddenly his heartbeat accelerated and his throat felt as though a giant hand was squeezing it. He felt a slight dizziness and was frightened. Then it was time to kneel down, and he sank to his knees in relief. The giant hand released his throat and he drew a shaking hand over his sweat beaded brow. He could think coherently once more. But fear still held his tongue. He would not utter any prayer, not in the presence of God. What if it was the wrong prayer?

Nelson sneezed.

'Don't agree!' Ejiaka said behind him.

'I won't,' he replied automatically. The night was winning its daily battle with the day and there was now a chill in the air. But he did not feel like going in yet. 'Ejiaka bring my singlet.'

In the distance Janet, dressed impeccably as usual, was striding towards Nelson. 'Well, well!' he said under his breath. 'I hope she has not come to do her usual complaining.'

'Here's your singlet,' Ejiaka said.

'Do you know who is coming?' Nelson asked, obstructing Ejiaka's view as he put on his singlet.

'How can I when you won't let me see?'

'If you see the person what is the point of my asking if you know who is coming?'

'Well, since I cannot see, then I cannot say.'

'Come on, just guess.'

'All right. Is it a woman or a man?'

Nelson laughed. 'I won't tell you that. Shall I get you a husband and buy the mat too?'

'You said that wrong.'

'I know. Are you going to guess or not?'

Ejiaka's brows wrinkled in thought. 'It cannot be Theodore or I would have heard his "Bro-oh!" There is no friend who has not visited us in the past few weeks. Oh, no, there is. It must be

Janet. Now, may I see if I am right? Yes, I knew it.' Ejiaka laughed as soon as Nelson moved aside. 'My feelings are better than my eyes. Janet,' she called out, 'what river throws you up today?'

'Good evening,' Nelson said, as Janet came closer.

'Nelson, you are all well?'

'No.'

'What happened? Ejiaka, you know it did not rain today, so how can a river throw me up? Besides I am not a fish. Okechukwu my child, how are you eh? Swelling like *elekudo* I must say.' Janet poked a finger in Okechukwu's stomach making him laugh. 'You all look well,' she said. 'What did you mean when you said you are not all well? Nelson, I am asking you.'

'Let us go into the house, and I will tell you. How is Christian?'

'He was well this morning,' Janet said, sitting down. 'Ejiaka don't bring any kola. That thing should be eaten only in the mornings.'

'You are staying for supper?' Ejiaka asked, going towards the pantry-store.

'No.'

'Then you did not really come to visit us.'

'She was just passing,' Nelson said laughing. 'If we had hidden ourselves, she would have gone on to where she was really going.'

'You may all say what you like but you cannot tell me what I planned. I came here to see you not to eat. Ejiaka sit down or go out. Standing at the door will bring you unexpected guests and you will end up cooking all night.'

'The guests would not just be passing by,' Ejiaka retorted, sitting down.

'You cannot make me change my mind. When I want to eat I go to the kitchen myself and look in the pots! Nelson, we are in the house you know. Why did you say you are not all well?'

'Mgbeke died at home yesterday,' Nelson said. Yesterday, he repeated to himself. It already seemed ages ago.

'*Ewuo*! What killed her?'

'Her illness, I think.'

'She never recovered from it?'

'I don't think so. It must have been more serious than she let me know. She never did tell me what was actually wrong with her.'

'*Ewuo, she and her fellow spirits.* Will you be going home?'

'The railways won't allow me to. My leave is still ten months away. My *umunna* will act on my behalf.'

'I never did get to meet her, but from what you have told me I feel I knew her very well. She was a very unhappy woman.'

Nelson silently agreed. Mgbeke had been an unhappy and secretive woman, who had not wanted anyone, including her husband, to know what was actually wrong with her. The most she did was to assure him he would know after her death. Nelson was too impressionable to like that. With her close association with *dibias*, she could arrange for her spirit to visit him after she was dead.

'I had better see about getting myself some protection,' Nelson thought.

Perhaps the reverend fathers would have such things. He would prefer theirs to a *dibia's*, as it would be more powerful, more potent. The other day Theodore had told him a true Christian had nothing to fear from *dibias* because he was protected by the most powerful entity in the world—the creator Himself. Nelson was now determined to ask Theodore about getting a personal charm from the reverend fathers.

'Ejiaka, get me some water to drink,' Janet said.

'You are sure that is all you want?' Ejiaka asked, getting up.

'Yes. Leave Okechukwu with me. I haven't touched him in a long while. Well, my *odegwu nwoke*,' Janet said, accepting Okechukwu from Ejiaka. 'You are happy to see me? *Wai*! You are heavier than I thought. Nelson, what do you people feed him?'

'Ask Ejiaka.'

'Whatever it is, is good for him. He is twice as fat as he was a month ago.' Janet threw him up and caught him. 'My strong little man! You are not afraid of heights. Look at him laughing at me. When are you going to fill up that empty gum? Thank you,' Janet said, taking the cup from Ejiaka. As she drank she had to restrain Okechukwu from getting at the cup. 'Now you have some,' she said, after she had drunk half the contents of the cup. Okechukwu drank greedily. 'I did not know he was that thirsty.'

'He is always thirsty,' Ejiaka said.

'He works harder than all of us,' Nelson said.

'I agree,' Ejiaka said.

'That is enough my man,' said Janet, taking the cup away and giving it to Ejiaka.

'He does not know when to stop,' Ejiaka said. 'Just like his father!'

'You mean like his mother?' Nelson retorted.

'A child's bad habits are always those of the mother, right?'

'You know that.'

'Has he started crawling yet?' Janet asked.

'You mean walking?' Ejiaka said. 'These days when he crawls up to a chair he uses it to pull himself up. It is getting harder to keep him away from things, especially sand.'

'When will you start weaning him? If you plan to do it soon, you had better start giving him some grown-up food so that he will learn to like it before you breast-feed him less.'

Nelson caught Ejiaka's inquiring look. 'Are you going to eat that cup?' he asked. He smiled at the shamefaced glance she threw at him before she went to put the cup away. She was soon back and sitting down silently.

'Have you decided who is going to answer my question?' Janet asked. 'Aren't your parents funny?' she asked Okechukwu. 'At least you make an effort to answer,' she said as he smiled. 'Those people over there merely look at each other.'

'Doesn't a child have to be at least a year old before he is weaned?' Nelson asked, assuming a calculated innocent look. Trust Janet to ask about something he had not discussed with Ejiaka. He had planned to bring it up earlier but it often slipped his mind.

'No,' Janet said. 'Six months is all right.'

'Isn't that too early?' Ejiaka asked quickly.

'No. If the child has been feeding well and has not been sick, he is usually strong enough to start eating softened grown-up food.'

'That must be the European way,' Nelson said.

'It is.'

'But their grown-up food is the same as children's food.'

'How do you know?'

'My RSF, Mr Taylor, told me.'

'He told you?'

'I saw it with my own eyes one morning when I went to deliver an urgent message to him at his house. You know he likes me,' Nelson added with pride. 'He was having breakfast when I got there and as soon as he heard my voice he told his steward to bring me to him. I have never seen such a big house before, and he lives there all alone. After I gave him the message, he told his steward to bring a plate and spoon and he served me some of the food on the table. It was white and thick and you add milk and sugar to it to give it some taste. It looks like a mother's milk.'

'Did you like it?' Ejiaka asked, with rapt attention.

'I don't know,' Nelson said. 'I would have to eat it again to decide whether I liked it or not.'

'Did you ask him what it was?' Ejiaka asked again.

'You know it is not right to do that.'

'That is true.'

'So you are going to start weaning Okechukwu when he is a year old?' Janet asked.

'Yes,' Nelson answered. 'He will have some teeth to chew with then.'

'Let me go and light the lantern,' Ejiaka said, getting up.

'Where is Onyeama?' Nelson asked.

'He went to choir practice.'

'Again?'

'I told him he could. He has promised to do well in school this year.'

'I don't know what to do with that child,' Nelson complained to Janet after Ejiaka left the room. 'He prefers singing in the church to learning. He has been in the same class now for three years and there is no sign of his ever passing to the next one.'

'Perhaps he is not made for school. He is a very intelligent boy. Why don't you send him home to farm?'

'His father won't like that. One of the conditions under which he allowed me to take Onyeama was that I put him through school.'

'It is not your fault if the boy does not want to learn.'

'I keep telling myself that, but I know they won't believe it at home.'

'Have you ever asked him what he wants to do?'

'No.'

'It would be better to ask him. That way you can say *he* refused to continue schooling. His father will surely believe that. Is his father related to you?'

'Yes.'

'Now I understand your fear.'

'Ejiaka,' Nelson said, as she walked in with the light, 'do you know if Onyeama prefers learning a trade to going to school?'

'Yes.'

'When did he tell you that?'

'Last month.'

'Did he tell you the type of trade he wants to learn?'

'No. All he wants is something he can do with his hands.'

'Children of nowadays don't do what their elders want them to do. I will see if I can get him into the railways. They will be recruiting people at the end of the year.'

'I don't think he will like railway work.'

'Did he say that?'

'No, he did not. It is my feeling . . .'

'And your feeling is often more accurate?'

'Laugh at me.'

'Ejiaka take him,' Janet said, lifting Okechukwu.

'Give him to me,' Nelson said. 'Ejiaka will be seeing you off.'

'Are you driving me away?'

'No. But knowing how much you love your son you wouldn't be handing him over unless you were about to leave.'

'No wonder the white foreman likes you. Here, have him. He has been very well-behaved. With all that water he drank I thought he would bathe me with urine.'

'He does not do that to people he loves. Ejiaka get me a nappy. I won't take any chances.'

Nelson had barely sat down when he felt a growing warm wetness spread towards his inner thighs. He jumped up with a cry. Okechukwu began to cry too.

'*Ewuo-o*! What did I do to you?' he asked in dismay.

123

Ejiaka came running with the nappy.

'It is too late,' Janet said laughing. 'Nelson has been rewarded for his little faith.'

'He always does this to me,' Nelson said, handing Okechukwu over to Ejiaka. 'Where is my other *lappa*?'

'Under the pillow,' Ejiaka said. 'Shall I take him with me?' she asked, as she hushed the baby.

'No,' Nelson replied. 'It is cold outside.' He found the *lappa* where Ejiaka said it was. Drying himself with the dry part of the wet one, he felt a sudden tumescence. It was the first time he had felt it when he was not in bed. Would he be able to wait another five months or so before he could touch Ejiaka? He was not sure, but he would surely try. Would she understand if he had to have her before the year was up? Again he was not sure. He stood in the semi-darkness of the bedroom and willed his thoughts to the running shed.

'Did you find it?' Ejiaka called to him.

'Yes.'

He draped the *lappa* round him and by the time he had Okechukwu in his arms, he was all right.

Chapter Two

1 ✂ Janet hurried home in a darkness relieved here and there by points of lantern light. She should not have stayed so long with Ejiaka and Nelson, she told herself over and over again. But she needed a breath of fresh air and visiting them was the best way to get it. Besides, being with them reminded her how happy a marriage could be.

Perhaps she should take Ejiaka's suggestion and travel to Zaria to see the *dibia*. She had nothing to lose if the *dibia* turned out to be a fake since she would be visiting her parents at the same time. She had not seen them for a long time now and they would be very happy to see her. Their happiness would be somewhat reduced if they found out why she had come to Zaria. Her mother, a staunch Christian, would be particularly horrified that her daughter had travelled over five hundred miles to see a *dibia*! Her father would not mind that much. He viewed her mother's Christian fervour with some amusement. But he would pretend to be horrified if it made his wife happy. That was the danger in confiding in him. You were never sure how he would react.

It would be best to let them think she was there only to visit them. In that way if she was disappointed, no one would preach to her about the evils of what she had attempted. Not that she thought it was evil to consult a *dibia*, but often, consultation presupposed a belief in the efficacy of the thing consulted. And that Janet did not want, for she believed completely in the healing powers of modern drugs and doctors, and in the powers of Jesus Christ. She was going to Zaria mainly to satisfy her curiosity and convince herself she had tried everything. Her annual leave was due in six months. She would spend it in Zaria to see what this *dibia* could do. Should she wait till then?

Should she discuss it with Christian?

No, she would not discuss it with anyone. It would remain a secret between herself, Ejiaka and God.

The light in her home meant that Christian had returned from the store. Since they beat him up, he made sure he was home before dark. Thinking that their relationship would change as a result, Janet had tried her best to make his evenings pleasant. But she soon found out he had no intention of making her nights more meaningful. He was drunk most evenings and lay in a torpor all night, his snoring loud enough to wake up the dead.

When later she heard rumours about why he had been beaten up so badly, she was filled with disgust. But she could not revenge herself on him much as she would have loved to. She had tried, God how hard she had tried, to act towards him the way she thought she should. Each time something in his voice, face or action would stop her, and she would be flooded with a tenderness that made her body ache with longing.

She often wondered if he was aware of the effect he had on her.

'Good evening, ma,' the gate-man said.

'Good evening, Peter. What has been happening?'

'Nothing has been happening, ma.'

'That is what you always say.'

'I always say it because I have seen everything, so whatever happens is neither strange nor new.'

'How is your family?'

'They are all well.'

'Thanks be to God,' Janet said hurrying away before Peter could launch into his customary rumble about his aches and pains and the ingratitude of the members of his large family. Listening or talking to him these days reminded her of her shameful if inadvertent statement that nearly got him retired from his job. It had all started with her saying to the doctor, jokingly, that it was time Peter was retired. Unfortunately, the doctor took her seriously and would have carried it out if she had not convinced him otherwise. The incident brought home to her once more, one of her father's favourite maxims—never say in jest what you are not prepared to back up in earnest. The furore her statement raised was such that she began to feel like an outcast, a condemned criminal. She should have known! Long ago she had discovered Peter was the type that thrived and often died on the job. Retirement was a punishment to them, for they invariably died days, or at most weeks, after they were retired. What on earth would Peter do in retirement? He had started as a labourer at the General Hospital when the grounds were being cleared for the building, and risen to Senior Gate-man in charge of a staff of three! As far as he was concerned his job with the hospital was his life, and Port Harcourt his home.

One thing Janet could not understand was the greediness of the man. How could a small wage-earner like Peter accumulate three wives and twenty-four children? That type of action merited fully Christian's biting remark: 'If the old man is greedy enough to surround himself with twice the number of the disciples of Christ, then he should be twice as strong as Christ to be able to handle them.'

Of course Christian had not realized how true his remark was. Peter was greedy, greedy for life, children, wives, anything that could be owned. From asking Janet for small loans he repaid promptly, he graduated to large loans he did his best not to repay.

'Nelson said I should greet you,' Janet said to Christian, who was sprawled in an armchair, a glass of palm wine on the table in front of him.

'Why didn't he come to say so himself?' he asked, his articulation sharp and distinct.

Janet ignored the question and went into the bedroom to change her dress. His incisive and super-sober period showed he was about a third into the gallon of undiluted wine. It was the state in which he said the most hateful and painful things, his whole body gathering its leanness into a sharp instrument for hurting. Janet kept out of his way during those periods, knowing she was too vulnerable to his cutting tongue.

Taking off her *lappa* and blouse, and folding them away in the huge box, Janet put on her stay-at-home dress. Afterwards she massaged her stomach slowly, wondering if it would ever get big again, filled with the mysterious promise of life. At the moment it seemed to be getting smaller. For a while she debated whether to take off her panties and then did so. She wanted to be prepared for anything. Oh God, just one child, just one would be enough, she prayed. As she went into the sitting-room, her lips tightened involuntarily.

'It is good to come prepared,' Christian said. 'Onward Christian soldiers, marching as to war!' He laughed, drank down his glass of wine and refilled it from the jar by his side. 'God the Father!' he swore, 'they are watering the wine these days.'

He shook the jar and its loud slushing sound was of near emptiness rather than fullness.

Janet sat down in the armchair farthest from him. She hated the odour of palm wine but she always forced herself to stay whenever he drank it. If she ever let him know how much she hated it, he would add it to the things he tormented her with.

Now she realized that once again she had been wrong about the quantity she thought he had drunk. It was going to be a long night.

'What are we having for supper tonight?' Christian asked.

'Who came home first?' Janet retorted. She simply could not resist that. Something in his voice had egged her on.

Christian laughed and gulped down half the contents of his glass. 'What an answer from *the* perfect wife. You are the perfect wife aren't you? Ready to provide everything that will make your husband happy—food, church, religion, money and vagina. Yes, we must not forget the vagina . . .'

'Christian,' Janet hissed.

'Don't worry, no one will hear us. Vitus is not home yet. Yes, as I was saying, we must not forget the vagina, even if it is a bit old and suctionless, and . . . now wait . . . what was it? And, yes, stretched beyond the capacity of any penis to fill it. So what else do you provide, or rather what else are you ready to provide at the sound of the bell as they say in infant school? Oh yes, deliveries. You are good at that. Unfortunately your own children do not survive because you boil the poor things too long in your hot womb!'

'Christian! Christian are you mad?'

'Now we are getting somewhere. But isn't it funny? When I drink I do the talking and you do the keeping quiet. Isn't it funny that as soon as you see me drinking you crawl into the shell you should never have left? Do I remind you of your father, that is before your mother turned him into a woman? Tell me. Do I?'

Janet kept reminding herself that he was drunk so as not to answer. But he *was* right. He behaved as her father did when drunk—complete change in personality, uncontrollable urge to hurt or be merry, and domination of the situation. She had been the main recipient of her father's merrymaking and had not realized the extent of his behavioural changes till she was grown-up. During her childhood, therefore, she had thought her mother picked quarrels with her father for being happy. As she grew older she noticed that her father was less merry and more drunk. She began to appreciate more her mother's constant sobriety that was leavened by flashes of humour. She realized that her mother could always be counted on to solve problems and crises that would not wait for her father to be in the mood. The distance between her and her father grew as she became older.

'Good evening, ma,' Vitus said, walking in. 'Food is ready. Shall I serve it now?'

'Yes,' Janet said, barely able to contain her anger. If looks could kill, hers would shrivel Christian and his devilish smile. *Chukwunna*, why must I have to go through this? If I had known Christian would be like this! Where did I go wrong? What did I do to deserve this? He had once been loving and always ready to please, to make one smile. When and why did he change?

'I know what you are thinking,' Christian said, as soon as Vitus left the room. Refilling his glass he continued in a falsetto voice, 'My God, what did I do to deserve this? Where did I go wrong? How did this bush animal become a bush animal? Right?' Christian laughed and sipped at his drink.

Drinking like a perfect gentleman to show me he is in control, thought Janet. She was not surprised at his ability to guess her thoughts. He had demonstrated it so often she had become inured to it. At first she had thought it was a gift from the Almighty. Now, she still thought it was a gift from the Almighty, but it was being used by that archangel, the Devil! Prince of Light, Prince of Darkness; Shining star of the Heavens, Impenetrable Deep! Christian *was* once a Christian, wasn't he? How are the mighty fallen, O Israel!

'To be able to sell anything,' Christian said suddenly, refilling his cup, 'you have to know how to read the minds of your customers!' He gulped down his drink and added whimsically, 'You know why I like to drink here instead of at the bar? I enjoy it more here. At the bar everybody is drinking, I mean drinking is their business, so it is no longer enjoyable. Business is work. Here, I am the only one drinking and each time I look up I see someone who is not drinking and also dislikes palm wine. The way you wrinkle your nose, and your whole body disapproves, increases my enjoyment. It is really a pity you don't like drinking. You should try it. It might do something for you, change your view of life.'

'You only started drinking a few months ago,' Janet said.

'There you are wrong. You are so wrapped up in your work, in your search for children that you do not know what I do with my time. I used to drink in my store before, but I moved it here a few months ago. So you see, I have had some experience in the drinking department as you nurses would call it. I think I will send Vitus for another gallon, no, a half-gallon that you will share with me. All that is left of this jar is the part women don't drink.'

As he poured the remaining wine into his cup, Vitus brought in a tray of food and set it on the second small table near Janet.

'Shall I bring hot water for tea, ma?' Vitus asked.

'No,' Janet said quickly. She did not feel like drinking tea tonight. All she wanted to do was eat, if she could, and then go to bed. You make plans and someone simply tears them to pieces without so much as a by your leave.

'Vitus!'

'Sir?'

'I want you to go and get me a half-gallon of wine from the Angel Bar.'

'Yes, sir.'

'Janet, give the boy sixpence.'

Janet was about to get up and do so but then wondered why she should. It was like paying to be killed.

'No,' she said firmly.

'I knew you would refuse,' Christian said. 'I just wanted to be sure. Vitus, you know Madame Òbò's palmy bar?'

'Yes, sir.'

'Go there and get me the wine. Tell her I have run out of money right now but will come by tomorrow and pay her.'

'Yes, sir.'

'So that is the type of place you go to?' Janet asked, as soon as Vitus left. She often passed by the bar on her journeys from one ex-patient's house to another and it always had a crowd of men and painted women standing around outside.

'I cut my coat according to my size,' Christian said. 'If you refuse to loan me sixpence, ordinary sixpence, where do you think I should go?'

'Are you going to eat?' Janet asked, changing the subject.

'You sound as if you don't want me to eat.'

Janet repressed a rejoinder. She opened the plates of food—pounded yam with the blush of light yellow that dry yam often has. It would go well with the egusi soup she had prepared the day before. She washed her hands in a bowl of water which was on the food tray and began to eat. She found she was ravenously hungry and the food tasted delicious, almost unlike something she had cooked herself. The yam had a velvety feel, the consistency malleable and easy to cut.

'I am sure that food tastes better than usual,' Christian said.

Janet paused in the act of popping a ball of yam she had just dipped in the soup into her mouth. It was decidedly uncanny the way he read her mind.

'You should see your face,' Christian said laughing.

Janet put the ball of yam into her mouth. She turned it round and round with her tongue and when she finally swallowed, it went down hard. Her appetite and hunger were suddenly gone and tears of anger and frustration pricked behind her eyes. He always did it, destroyed anything she enjoyed doing. She was not going to cry for the Devil. In slow motion, afraid that any fast movement would make the tears flow, she washed her hands, covered the food, pushed and half-carried the table away from her. She leaned back in her chair blinking her eyes rapidly, and feeling relieved as each series of blinks pushed the threatening tears farther back.

Christian seemed more thoughtful than usual as he put down the empty jar and drank off the contents of his half-filled glass. He placed the empty glass gently on the table and leaned back in his chair.

'You know,' he said, 'this is the first time you have done what I wanted you to do—stopped eating.'

'I didn't do it for you,' Janet said to herself. 'I stopped because I would have thrown up if I had swallowed another ball.'

She had complete control of herself now. If only she was sleepy, she could go to bed. But she was not, and she would feel like a prisoner if she forced herself to lie in bed.

'Seriously Janet, you have never done anything I wanted you to do, not even going to bed with me. You always went to bed when *you* felt like it and if I said we should go to bed together you said you were not ready. When you felt like getting pregnant you forced me to bed to make love to you, and as soon as you knew you were, you turned your back on me, discarding me like a used tool. Let me tell you, no one likes to feel he is merely a tool to be used and tossed away afterwards. I am sure you wouldn't like it if I used you like that.'

'If you felt like that all along, why didn't you tell me?'

'Tell you?' Christian laughed. 'Yes of course, I should tell you! You can't find out for yourself, right? You are too busy, right? You have too much on your mind. Too many people depend on you. You cannot spare the time to find out how I feel. After all I am a grown-up capable of speech, right? But you forget talking does not go alone, otherwise it becomes empty sound.'

'What do you mean?'

'See? You were not even listening to me just now. Where were you?'

'Can't you see me?'

'I am not blind.'

'You talk as if you are.'

Janet could see that she had finally stung him into exasperation. She understood what he was alluding to, but he was wrong. Their problem was not lack of communication. It was much simpler, so simple he was not ready to admit it—she loved him but he no longer loved her. Why this was so, she could not say. It was a mystery she could never penetrate, and the more she dwelt on it the more confused she became. One of the things her mother had told her the first time she took Christian to meet her, was that his type was meant to be loved and not to love. She had not seen into her father's game then and thought her mother was up to her tricks again. But now she realized her mother's statement contained a great deal of truth.

To be loved and not to love. What did it really mean? Did it paint the whole picture of relationships in this world?

It is frightening to think of the whole world divided into two camps, one to love and the other to be loved. Does this explain the numerous marriages that fail? Do they fall apart because the couples were mismatched . . . loving people bound to those who were not? It all sounds too simple. Somehow there must be a more complicated explanation. There must be a permutation of 'to love' and 'to be loved' in each person so that the situation and the environment determine which is uppermost.

Janet shook her head to clear a sudden confusion in her thoughts. Thinking that pursued its own tail could make one mad.

'I have always said . . .' Christian began, and stopped.

Seeing the listening pose he maintained Janet knew he would complete the statement without prompting from her. She waited. The usual noises of the compound rode in now, emphasizing the lateness of the hour.

'I have always thought,' Christian began again, 'that God limited himself when he spoke.'

Janet sprang up. If Christian was going to go into one of his blasphemous discussions she was not staying to listen.

'What is pursuing you?' Christian asked.

Janet picked up the food tray and walked out of the room. 'What is pursuing me indeed?' she thought. 'One of these days you will come face to face with Him.'

2 ✂ 'Oh *Chukwunna*,' Christian groaned as he finally broke surface. He had been swimming up to it for days, the closer he got the harder his head pounded. Now his head felt as if it would split in half. Slowly he shifted his head on the pillow, hoping that a different position would ease the pounding. The coolness of the new part helped but the pounding soon returned before subsiding to a steady throbbing.

He should have remembered Madame Òbò added *kaikai* to her palm wine to make it potent enough for her customers who otherwise would not get drunk on palm wine alone. But he had been so high and angry by the time Vitus brought in the half-gallon that he neither smelt nor tasted the additive.

If only he could get hold of some aspirin. Where would it be now? He could not, did not want to think, lest the throbbing in his head escalate to a pounding. Even the thought of calling Vitus sent it up a notch. He just had to wait till either Vitus or Janet came in.

What time was it anyway? Today was Tuesday? Wednesday? Or? . . . yes, Tuesday. What if Janet had gone to work and Vitus to the shop? He would then lie here for hours without anyone coming in. He had better do something even if it meant intense suffering for a short time.

He opened his eyes that he had kept shut to decrease the temptation to move. After the initial glare, speeding up of the heartbeat and a number of thumping blows in the head, he

133

decided it was past nine o'clock in the morning. Strong sunshine streamed in through the window and the air held the silence of a dying morning. If he did not want to lose the whole day, he must find the aspirins, take them and get to his shop immediately.

For a while he debated whether to get up suddenly and suffer the resultant heavy dose of pain, or do so slowly and stretch it out. He chose the former. It would be swift.

Steeling himself, Christian stood up in one swift movement and ran to the small medicine chest in the far corner of the room. He opened it and grabbed the small tin of aspirin when his head threatened to explode. It was an excruciating pain that lasted an eternity. He leant against the wall and clenched his teeth to fight off a dizzy spell. He succeeded and as soon as the hammering subsided, he threw the tablets into his mouth, swallowed hard, and flung himself back on the double bed.

Perhaps he passed out. Perhaps he fell asleep. The next time he was aware of himself, the thumping had been replaced by a dull ache, and the sun no longer poured through the window. He lay still, savouring his release from the hangover, at peace with himself. The bed had never felt so comfortable. Did suffering sharpen one's appreciation and enjoyment of the good things of life? It looked like it. Was that why people like Janet liked pain? It could be, since there was no other logical explanation.

Damn, that's enough. Why should I be thinking of Janet now? To banish her from his mind he sat up slowly and listened to his head. There were no rumbles and he smiled. He dragged himself out of bed and took off the shorts he had taken to wearing in bed after he caught Janet trying to take advantage of his dream-tumescence. He would be damned if he would give her the excuse to leave him. In an unguarded moment some time ago, she had told him that she would throw him out as soon as she became pregnant again. Somehow she felt the baby would have a better chance of survival with him out of the house. It was utter nonsense but Christian was not taking it lightly.

It did not take him long to bathe, dress and be on his way to the shop. He wished he had taken an umbrella when the sun became obscured by dark clouds. Having lost one suit to Tom Big Harry's animals he had to be careful with his remaining two.

At the shop Vitus had everything under control and there

were no messages. In order to get what had happend the previous night straight in his mind, Christian asked why he had not been woken this morning as usual.

'You told me not to wake you, sir,' Vitus said.

'I told you? When?'

'Last night sir, after you started drinking the wine I brought from Madame Òbò's palmy bar.'

'Did your mistress ask you to tell me anything?'

'No, sir.'

'Did she ask you anything about Madame Òbò's bar?'

'No, sir.'

'All right. How much have you made this morning?'

'Three shillings, sir.'

'Only three shillings?'

'Yes, sir. This is the twenty-hungry of the month.'

'Give me the money.' Christian counted it—mostly farthings and pennies. 'Do you have enough change?' he asked and on Vitus replying in the affirmative he pocketed the money.

It was nearly twelve noon, yet it seemed as though it was five in the morning. He leant against the counter undecided whether to go and see Madame Òbò immediately. Her bar had few customers during the day, and one of his privileges as a self-employed man was to be able to look the girls over at leisure. Yesterday John told him two new girls had joined the establishment. One of them was no more than seventeen years old, and they were both from the hinterland.

'I am going to Madame Òbò's,' Christian said, 'but I will first visit Nelson and his family.'

'Yes, sir. *Nagbo!*'

It was pleasant to walk, the clouds dampening the heat of the sun. The few people on the streets were the most beautiful and therefore the most parasitic—young girls with large bosoms, elaborate hairdos and audacious behinds; lush women whose walk was reminiscent of bed springs and young men with the carved features of dance-masquerades and the litheness of running-masquerades.

'My gang,' Christian murmured to himself as he fielded their admiring glances and, once in a while, hauteur. He knew that only those who did not work during the day would be out on the streets now. Their exotic dress was one thing they all had in common.

Christian was in high spirits by the time he got to Nelson's house. He felt vibrant and sensual, attributes he thought he had lost when Big Harry's men warned him off Angela. He knocked at Nelson's door for a long time before it opened.

'Is everything all right?' he asked.

'Yes,' Nelson replied opening the door wider, his face clearing up a little. 'I am on night duty.'

'Oh, then I won't come in. Go back to bed.'

'How thoughtful of you. You wake me up and then say, "Go back to bed".'

'What do you want me to say? You don't seem happy to see me.'

'Please come in and stop your argument.'

Christian laughed and followed Nelson into the room. As was his wont, he looked around appreciatively before sitting in one of the armchairs.

'I like your new furniture,' he said. 'How I wish we were not living in that hospital compound so I could buy furniture like yours.'

'Truly?' Nelson smiled for the first time. 'Let me wash off the sleep in my eyes. What time is it?'

'About one o'clock.'

'The day is already divided into two. I will soon be back.'

Christian went to the door as soon as Nelson left the room. Aggrey Road was busy as usual. There were definite advantages in having a salaried job and living in town rather than a compound full of sick people and surrounded by a six-foot wall. For the first time he began to doubt if he had chosen the right occupation. His independence seemed all of a sudden to have a very high price tag and he wondered if it was worth it. He was not growing any younger, and as he grew older he would have to hustle more to make more money. Nelson, on the other hand, would automatically make more money the older he got without increased effort.

Things did not work out the way he planned. He had hoped by now to own a number of stores, with enough cash to invest in merchandise with a quick turnover. If he had succeeded, he would automatically make more the older he became. But something had gone wrong somewhere and although he could not pin-point it, it must be tied up with Janet. Perhaps it was high time he left her. He had been nicknamed 'lucky' before he met her. Now he could be called 'bad luck', and he would answer with a ringing '*Wei*.'

'What are you doing there?' Nelson asked suddenly. 'You just came in from there and you can't stay away for a minute!'

Christian went back to his chair. 'Only children stare at walls,' he said receiving the kola Nelson had brought in a small enamel plate. He blessed the kola rapidly and broke it into its four natural parts. He took one and gave the plate back.

Nelson took a piece, set the plate on the table and sat down. 'What chased you out of your shop so early?' he asked.

'I was going to settle an account with Madame Òbò, so I decided to see how you were.'

'I have heard so much about that place but haven't had the time to go there. Is it as good as they say?'

'You know I don't tell people about something unless they can see a sample of it. So, why don't you dress up and let's go there now? Is Ejiaka asleep?'

'No, she went to the market.'

'Good. Dress up, let me take you to Madame Òbò. You will like her, I will pay for everything.'

'I can't leave Okey alone in the house.'

For a while Christian did not understand whom Nelson was referring to. Then it dawned on him and he smiled. 'Ejiaka did not take him with her to the market?' he said more as a statement than a question.

'She shops faster if she does not have him with her.'

Christian nodded agreement. He was glad his children had not lived long enough to become nuisances although he did not think Janet would have made him baby-sit with any of them. She would not trust him with them, knowing how much he disliked the squalling brats. Besides, Janet in her efficient way would employ a girl baby-sitter. Children came first and no expense was spared to make them comfortable. It was one of the ironies of life that she who wanted children so badly 'cooked' them to death in her womb.

137

'Well, I will take you to Madame Òbò whenever you are free to go,' Christian said. 'I am sure you will like the place, most young men do.'

'I am not like other young men.'

'I know. That is why I said I will take you there myself.'

'Is Madame Òbò your friend?'

'Do you mean girlfriend or just friend?' Christian asked with a laugh. 'You have changed since you became a Roman Catholic. I have to be careful what I say in your presence.'

'I have not changed at all, my eyes merely were opened.'

'They were closed before?'

Christian laughed with Nelson making sure that Nelson's laughter was not a cover for a bitter or angry thought. He was always amazed at the effect Christianity, especially Roman Catholicism, had on people. Often prior to their conversion, they were transparent-faced, according every statement its value, rarely trying to dig beneath for hidden meanings unless broad hints about their existence were given. But after their conversion, their faces became either closed or fired with zeal. Innuendos, symbolism and the reading of pauses and silences became a pastime. The more they claimed 'their eyes had been opened', the deeper they pretended to probe into the other person's soul while unknowingly revealing the deviousness of their own.

'No, they were not closed,' Nelson said. 'You sound like Ejiaka when I told her my eyes were opened. What I mean is that I am like someone who is learning to read. At first, letters don't mean a thing. They are like scratches chickens make on wet soil as they forage for worms. But then, when you learn how to read, the markings become meaningful and even beautiful. That is why I say my eyes have been opened. What I did not see before, I now see. You understand me don't you?'

'Very well.'

'Then answer my question.'

'Which one?'

'You don't want to answer? Why don't you say so? You sound like some Protestants I argue with at work. They can never answer a question directly. They keep twisting here and there like a snake.'

Christian laughed. He stood up on a reflex and to cover his

restlessness, walked to the table, took a piece of kola and bit it in half. Its fresh bitter-sweet taste filled his mouth and mind. Nelson was more astute than he had thought. The best way to keep him at bay was to appear open and easy to read. 'She was my girlfriend a long time ago,' he said, after he sat down again. 'Now we are just friends.'

'But you keep holding out to her the possibility of your becoming her lover again?' Nelson asked.

Christian did not answer immediately. He concentrated on chewing the rest of his kola while he weighed Nelson's statement carefully. Nelson was right there. He often did entertain the possibility of becoming Madame Òbò's lover once again. Although his attitudes towards her changed at such moments, he could not say, as Nelson seemed to imply, that he teased her with it. After all, she had terminated their relationship.

'Is there anything wrong with that?' he asked, to put Nelson on the defensive.

'No, nothing. I only wanted to be sure. The best time for us to go to her place will be when I am on morning duty.'

'I am ready any time. I own myself.'

'It will be something to look forward to.'

Christian thought he detected a certain eagerness in Nelson's tone, and wondered how he and Ejiaka were doing. 'I guarantee you will get whatever you desire at Madame Òbò's.'

'Anything?'

'Yes, *anything*,' Christian said, smiling what he hoped was a wicked, but reassuring smile. '*Anything*,' he said again.

'I heard you the first time,' Nelson protested mildly.

'I am getting up. I must see Madame Òbò before the labourer toro-toro fill the place.'

'Like us?'

'No, you passed that stage long ago. Do you still study in the evenings?'

'Yes.'

'Remember me when you become a big man in the railways.'

'Don't worry. A chicken does not forget the man that pulled its tail feathers during the rainy season.'

'Neither does it forget the boy that wrings its neck.' Christian

139

got up. 'Tell Ejiaka I called today. She always complains I don't come often enough.'

'She is right,' Nelson said, standing up too. 'This is also your home but you treat it as if it isn't.'

'Well, if you are complaining too, I must be doing something wrong. I will change, you will see.'

'*We* will see.'

'You don't believe me?'

'Cunny-man die who go buryam?'

'Cunny-man!'

Their loud laughter was cut short by an angry cry from Okechukwu.

'Go and see what is wrong with him. I will see you another time.'

'Don't go yet, I have something to tell you,' Nelson said, runing into the bedroom.

Christian sat down wondering what Nelson had to tell him. Was he having problems at the shed, or with Ejiaka? Was Ejiaka being unfaithful to him? Christian did not think she was the type, but one was never sure with beautiful women. For every woman there was always someone somewhere for whom she would play the fool.

'Didn't Janet tell you anything?' Nelson asked, coming out of the bedroom carrying Okechukwu over his right shoulder.

'When?'

'Yesterday.'

'No, she told me nothing.'

'Hm!' Nelson grunted and sat down in the nearest chair. 'Mgbeke died two days ago.'

'Really? May her soul rest in peace. What did she die of?'

'I don't know.'

They fell silent.

The mention of death always surprised and embarrassed Christian. Somehow he felt responsible for, or at least guilty of complicity in bringing about the death of the deceased. As such, he was ashamed to look at the faces of the bereaved members of the family. It was as if death was obscene and he, having taken part in bringing it about, was also obscene. This feeling of being in league with the agents of death had started the day he discovered a small but painful swelling on his penis. Thinking it was a mosquito bite he treated it with heated coconut-oil applied with a chicken feather. It disappeared in a few days, but four new ones appeared two weeks later, one so close to the tip that it was impossible for him to touch a woman. Alarmed he went to the hospital where he met Janet for the first time. She was shy and fresh-looking and very much like a colt.

The doctor, a drunk, said he had contracted a 'female disease' that had no cure.

'Mr. Okoro,' the mustachioed, rumpled and smelly man had said, 'you are a dead man. If I were you I would try to enjoy myself as much as possible. You are living on borrowed time, so make the most of it.'

Christian did not believe the mad, red man. He went back to his warm coconut-oil treatment and the swellings finally disappeared, but he recalled the red man's diagnosis when he heard that two of his former mistresses had died after short mysterious illnesses. Had he not been responsible for their deaths? Was he a walking death dispenser? Had the doctor been right after all? If he had the 'female disease' why had he been able to perform so wonderfully on his wedding night? Those who had the disease were supposed to be unable to make love to a woman. Christian could still make love at the drop of a coin. Still, he could not help but feel he was an instrument of death.

Suddenly Okechukwu cried out and Christian looked startled.

'That is enough Okey,' Nelson said rocking the child. 'Am I not carrying you now? What more do you want? Christian don't look as if you are related to Mgbeke (she and her fellow spirits). I had been expecting her to die, so the news was not a complete surprise. It was the best thing that could have happened to her. Cheer up, you hear?'

'You are taking it like a man,' Christian said, feeling reprieved.

'It is not that. I haven't seen her in a long time and she died in such a distant place it is hard for me to feel her death. I hope I have not spoilt your day. If I knew you would take it that badly, I wouldn't have told you.'

'No, you haven't spoilt my day,' Christian lied standing up. '*Ndo*! I will see you soon. Tell Ejiaka that I came.'

Christian opened the door quickly and stepped out into the

street which seemed unchanged since he went into Nelson's house. He pulled at the bottom of his coat, ineffectually smoothed out the wrinkles, and walked diagonally across the street to the other side. Just as he got there a crying, naked little girl ran full tilt into him. His quick footwork saved them from falling and he held on to her for a second longer to regain his balance.

'My suit is soiled,' he thought, but before he could articulate it a fat woman brandishing a whip appeared from a house in front.

'Elizabeth!' the fat woman called, advancing towards Christian and growing bigger with each step.

The little girl, whom Christian realized was partly wet, burrowed herself deeper into his legs, her shrill screaming increasing the harder he tried to pull her away.

'Wetin ee do?' Christian asked. The woman did not look like an Igbo.

She towered over him, tall and huge, a monster one only encountered in dreams. All Christian could see now was her midriff, swathed in layers of cloth that almost swept the ground.

'Elizabeth!' the woman bellowed and added something in an unintelligible language.

The little girl shrilled once and stopped, but did not budge. She was shaking like one suffering from malaria, so Christian placed protective hands on her wet head and back.

People were beginning to gather, singly and in twos and threes. Christian hated to be the centre of attraction, especially in a ridiculous role, but he also felt a sense of relief that he would not have to face the mammoth woman alone. She made no threatening moves although she carried with her a promise of violence. Suddenly and quicker by far than he had thought her capable, she grabbed the girl's hand, pulled her towards and away with her, the girl's screams loud enough to wake the dead. Outraged, Christian made as if to follow but a female voice stopped him:

'No follow-am-oh! Na im pikin.'

Under the eyes of the small mostly female crowd, Christian tried to straighten out his suit. The crowd's silence made him feel as though he had perpetrated an outrage on the little girl. He

142

felt so self-conscious and inadequate that all he wanted to do was to run back to his store. He had finally lost his urge to go to Madame Òbò.

Turning, he heard one of the few men in the crowd commend his action, but he was not happy with himself. He should have gone after that brute of a woman, or better still held the child tighter. But the brute was the child's mother. Who was he to intervene? And if he had interfered, what would he have done if the woman had quite justifiably hit him? Retaliate? Not likely—the woman's size and uncanny resemblance to his late stepmother, the terror of his boyhood days at Igbo-obele, had paralysed him completely. Christian walked slower as with nagging insistence his mind went back to his youth.

His stepmother! He thought he had forgotten all about her. She made him leave home early to serve a Protestant priest, the meanest and most miserly man he had ever known. Whenever Christian heard that someone was captivated by Christianity, he wished the person had met Pastor, and later Reverend Okoli, to discover what Christianity was not. It certainly was neither brotherhood or kindness. It was mostly the taking advantage of your fellow man, the climbing on his back for the long journey through a dreary life, and the scheming to have a lien on the life hereafter.

His stepmother! Punishing him for his mother's wrong-doing. And what wrong-doing? For being his father's favourite wife and dying young?

But then the Devil had paid his stepmother back. At fourteen, Christian discovered that Christians dreaded the Devil more than God. It made perfect sense really, for did God not hand over His so-called creations to the Devil? So Christian prayed to the Devil to take away his stepmother. And the Devil answered, a thing that God rarely did. His stepmother died of the disease of the swollen stomach, an undoubted mark of the Devil.

And thinking of it all now, Christian was impressed by his early display of wisdom. If you wanted death to visit someone, who else should you pray to other than the Prince of Death and Darkness himself?

143

Chapter Three

1 ✂ Ejiaka walked down the well-beaten, central path of her mother's village, tiredness in her bones and a heaviness in her neck. The half-empty, long rectangular basket she carried seemed weighted with stones, and the small hoe with which she had been weeding her *ede* farm earlier, was heavier than a full-sized hoe.

The village was empty, but would fill up soon. Her mother's home was a couple of *ogirishi* trees away. Each time she looked up, she saw dark, wispy smoke issuing out of the rooftop into the clear evening. The setting sun glinted on the light grey thatched roof, but not in the evanescent fashion of ordinary sunlight. There was a solidity in the light, a corporeality that was as tangible as poured molten copper.

Looking up for the umpteenth time she realized she was not getting any closer to her mother's house. But her feet were moving and the ground was changing its contours and colour. So she was moving. Reassured she looked up to find that her mother's house was no longer there. A thick forest she had passed on her way from the farm was in its place. Also many people were ahead of her apparently returning from the farms. She thought she recognized them from the shape of their backs and the way they walked or held their necks, but she could not recall their names. So she did not call out to them, but hurried on as fast as she could.

Turning a corner she found herself nearer her husband's home than her mother's. Nelson was one of those ahead of her. She called out to him but not by name. He did not turn round and before she could call a second time he went into the house.

A dog started barking furiously, and she slowed down, not wanting to get to the house before Nelson had it under control. The dog did not like her.

She was a few feet from the house when the dog, still barking furiously dashed out of the house towards her, followed by Okechukwu and Nelson, each holding a club. She stopped petrified, wanting to ask what was going on and yet feeling that she knew.

When the dog got to her she saw in a sort of detached way, that its head was matted with blood. It ran round her and headed back for the house. Okechukwu and Nelson also ran round her, their faces sweating grimaces. Half the length of Okechukwu's club was covered with a bright bloody smear. There was no blood on Nelson's club. It was clean and had the whiteness of a bleached bone.

Ejiaka had not moved. She felt her position and immobility were necessary parts of the game they were playing.

The dog, Okechukwu and Nelson disappeared into the house, and re-emerged maintaining the same order and distance from each other. Again they ran round her except that Nelson seemed angry now, muttering frighteningly to himself. Now she knew something terrible would happen if they emerged a third time. She had to do something.

But she could not move! And now the dog came out of the house, silent and running very, very slowly. Okechukwu, the sun illuminating his toothless grin, was gaining on it, his raised club garishly red. Nelson was right behind him, his face a picture of determination.

Ejiaka tried to warn Okechukwu not to hit the dog, but her voice-box was stuck.

The dog suddenly stopped a few feet from her, its brown-flecked eyes dilated with pain and sorrow. Simultaneously Okechukwu hit it on the head with a force that reverberated in the entire village. The dog gave one large yelp, leapt and crumpled at Ejiaka's feet. And with a pain that threatened to burst her heart open, Ejiaka saw Nelson's big stick descend on Okechukwu's head splitting it open.

Her voice-box came unstuck and Ejiaka let out a scream that stretched taut like a twine to the sky.

The scream still rang in her ears as her eyes flew open. Her heart beat fast. Okechukwu was crying in his cot but she could not gather up enough strength to get out of bed. For a few seconds reality and dream intertwined as from outside came a dog's bark and a yelp of pain.

Then everything became clear. She got out of bed quickly and lifted Okechukwu out of his cot. Even as she rocked him back to sleep her heart continued to beat faster than normal.

'It was all a dream,' she murmured to herself as the whining and yelping of the dog outside increased. 'It was all a dream,' she murmured once more but this time to Okechukwu who was, thank God, still his ten-month-old self.

She put him back in his crib where he fell asleep. Her legs were shaky walking back to the bed. Now she realized Nelson was not in bed. She sat down to regain control of her limbs.

Where was Nelson?

The dog's barking, interspersed with men's shouting rose and ebbed outside. She heard what she thought was Nelson's voice shouting, 'It is here, it is here, bring the light!'

Then what was going on dawned on her. They were killing the dog. The butchers were killing the dog and Nelson was with them. He had lied to her. He had promised he would not be there when the butchers who had paid for the dog a week before came to do their job. He had said he had become so attached to the dog he could not stomach being there while it was killed. But now he was there, shouting with glee, directing the other men to where the dog was hiding, knowing that the dog would trust him and not run away when approached.

What were men made of?

There he was betraying his wife, and his dog, leading the killers to the poor trusting dog. Had he been lying too when he said he was attached to the dog? Had he been lying when he said he loved and cared for his family so much he would sell the dog because it did not like his family? Had he been lying all the time? Had he no feelings, no real deep feelings? What if the dog were to bite him? It would never let go. Never!

Ejiaka jumped up as the shouting and curses and the sound of the dog's pain rose to a crescendo and subsided again. Now she knew what her dream signified. She had to stop them from killing the dog. To kill it would bring bad luck to the family, particularly to Okechukwu. Dreams were messages from the ancestors who often spoke in a language all their own. Perhaps she should go to a diviner and ask him to interpret it fully. He alone could understand and interpret the language of the ancestors. But that would have to wait. Now she had to act.

Picking up the lantern and turning up the wick, she looked at Okechukwu. He slept face down undisturbed by the noise outside. She thought of turning him over on his back but changed her mind. Going through the parlour and into the pantry-store she saw that Onyeama too was fast asleep. He always slept like a log. She went back to the parlour to find out what time it was. Two o'clock! No wonder she had fallen asleep still dressed. She had been waiting for Nelson to return from work at eleven.

Had they been trying to kill that dog for two hours or more?

She went back into the bedroom and tied a small *lappa* round her waist knotting it securely in front. She tested it for tightness. It not only held her big *lappa* in place, but gave her stomach needed support. She was ready. With the lantern in her left hand, she drew back the bolt and opened the bedroom door.

'Close the door!' a voice shouted roughly.

'Who is that beast of the forest?' another asked.

'Ejiaka, close the door and stay inside the house,' Nelson cried.

Ejiaka heard them but could not respond. What she saw robbed her of all volition. The pale, wan moonlight covered the yard with a ghostly light; the yellowish bright circles of the lamplight outlined the men, making their heavy clubs heavier by merging the shadows with the substance; and in the far corner to her right, in the dark space between the toilet walls and that of the compound, a pair of baleful eyes glowed. Ejiaka was riveted by those eyes and the thought that she was actually looking into the living eyes of death did not help her.

'Is that woman mad?' the first voice shouted angrily.

And Nelson's shadow was running towards Ejiaka for he had put his lantern down before he began to run.

'Look out!' the second voice cried. 'Nelson, look out!'

Ejiaka saw it all. The glowing eyes were suddenly extinguished as their owner, now a hurtling shadow, came after Nelson. Then everything took on a timeless quality as the other two men closed in fast behind the dog as it rushed by them.

'Please don't kill it,' Ejiaka cried, but her cry died in her throat as Nelson's face, covered with a sweating oily sheen that made its anger look grotesque, became illuminated by the light of her lamp. And as the dog sprang at her, he swerved swiftly to her right and brought his club down on its head. The dog dropped at Ejiaka's feet, its head one huge mass of blood, hair, bone, brains, blood, bone, blood . . .

Ejiaka felt a stinging on her left cheek, and another, and in sharp focus she saw Nelson about to slap her again and she cried, 'Ajọ nmuọ!'

His arm stopped in mid-air.

Turning she stumbled into the bedroom and fell on the bed, her senses dissolving into hot tears. Then her stomach heaved and barely getting her head over the edge of the bed she threw up. And as her retching subsided she asked the ancestors to help her, to save her from all this foreignness that had taken her husband and was now threatening to take her child. The dog was dead, but its malevolent spirit lived on. She had seen what it did in the dream, she recalled what it did in the fairy tale and unless something was done she would see what its spirit would do in her life. But she would not allow it.

2 ✄ Women are really different creatures, thought Nelson splashing cold water on himself. Anyone who claimed to understand them was lying himself to death. Ejiaka had asked that the dog be sold and had then changed her mind at the very last minute, almost getting herself killed as a result. Had he known she would do that he would have saved himself all the trouble.

Nelson soaped his body carefully. He had not known it would be so difficult to kill a dog. The butchers had been right. As soon as the dog realized he was an enemy too, it had kept as far away from him as possible. That was when the whole thing became dangerous. It was a good thing he had warned members of the compound not to come out during the killing. The dog was ready to run into any house or attack any defenceless person.

Nelson laid down the soap and scooped up double-handfuls of

the ice-cold water from the bucket in swift bending motions. He shivered when the first one hit his shoulders and back. After that the water was luxuriously cold. The beginning of a dance is difficult . . . even more so the dance that is life.

Those butchers were not as good as they claimed to be. If they had hit the dog squarely on the forehead, between the eyes, he would not have had to get into the act. But when he saw they were not only inept but frightened, he had had to come in. This would be the last time he would get into such a thing. He would not own a dog again.

Nelson dried himself slowly. Poor Ejiaka! He was sorry he had hit her, but it was for her own good. If he had not done so, she would have stood there for ever. Would she understand he had done it for her own good? Would she bear him any grudge for it? He would talk to her before going to sleep, although he knew that talking would never make a woman change her mind. They had to see to change, not that he blamed them. With the coming of the white man, talking began to replace action instead of being just a prelude to it. Covering himself with his *lappa* Nelson put the soap-dish in the empty bucket, and walked back to the house with it. The silence of the night took possession of his thoughts and he realized what a racket they must have made when they were killing the dog. Again he was glad he had warned the neighbours beforehand.

A train returning from a long haul whistled thrice as it approached the signal point. That must be the three-thirty goods train from Makurdi. Judging by the sound, it would require fairly extensive repairs and Nelson knew his shift would start the job later that day.

In the house Onyeama had gone back to sleep after putting out the bath water. Nelson made as little noise as possible putting away the bucket and locking the door. He did not want to wake Onyeama again.

In the bedroom, Ejiaka lay in bed with Okechukwu in her arms. When Nelson saw she was still awake, he turned down the wick and was about to get into the bed when Ejiaka motioned him to stop. Moving slowly to the edge of the bed she carried Okechukwu to his crib, covered him up with his little blanket and let down the mosquito netting Nelson had made. She got back into bed without once meeting Nelson's eyes.

He could see she was annoyed with him and wondered how he was going to make her understand that he did not strike her because he merely wanted to hurt her. He lay quietly hoping she would say something, at least a goodnight, that would give him the opportunity to start a conversation. But she remained so silent and still that he became afraid she would fall asleep without his having said a thing to her. He thought of clearing his throat but that might wake Okechukwu up.

To bridge the physical, if not emotional gap between them, he shifted towards her till he felt the warmth of her long back against his chest and stomach. Tentatively, he put his right arm on her shoulder, and when she did not react passed it down to her cloth-covered breasts. He waited.

'Ejiaka,' he whispered. 'Ejiaka,' he said again, feeling somewhat foolish when she neither answered nor stirred. He tightened his hold on her chest and felt her stiffen. He relaxed his hold.

'Ejiaka,' he said softly, 'turn towards me. I want to talk to you.'

Again he waited, but not a word or sign came from her. His mind ran through the things he could do to get some reaction from her . . . hit her, hold her really tight till she begged for mercy, plead with her, or turn round and go to sleep. He discarded all of them as inadequate.

Her warmth was so comforting. He pressed himself against her stiffly contoured back. He tightened his hold and did not desist even though she strained to get away from his embrace.

'Ejiaka,' he said sharply. 'Stop behaving like a child!'

She continued silently to strain away from him. Nelson now found that to keep their bodies together he had to exert a great deal of force, more than he had planned for.

'What is this you are doing?' he asked. I should have known, he thought as her resistance continued in silence, she would be as stubborn as her mother.

It was ridiculous that a man should struggle with his wife like two adolescents in a playground. And all he was trying to do was apologize to her and explain why he had hit her. Putting his left hand under her left shoulder he enveloped her, holding her easily to himself. She now began to actually struggle, to use all her strength in an attempt to separate his interlocked arms. Each time she succeeded, he quickly relocked his arms and before long she was gasping from the effort.

Nelson was glad he was getting some form of response from her even if was not of the type he had hoped. In their struggle her *lappa* came undone and he could feel her warm, full breasts against his arms. Desire began to mount in him. For the first time he felt the movement of her buttocks against him and as his penis rose, he manoeuvred its length in between the two halves. She stiffened and he tightened his hold as she stopped tugging at his arms.

'My breasts!' she whispered fiercely.

Nelson relaxed his hold immediately and she seized the opportunity to turn on her back. She had used the oldest trick to get her buttocks away from him. His blood pounding in his head now he pulled down her loose *lappa*, her sharp intake of breath sounding harsh in his ears as he rolled over and on her. He loosened his *lappa* with one hand and pulled it aside.

'*Nnamu-ukwu!*' she cried.

'So you can talk,' Nelson said, as he tried with his right hand to open her legs which she had locked tightly. He was no longer interested in getting her to talk.

'*Nnamu-ukwu!*' Ejiaka cried again, 'you will hurt me.'

'Really?' Nelson answered, breathing hard.

Suddenly he found himself on his side of the bed again. Ejiaka's knees were raised and she was breathing heavily. He threw himself on her before she could recover her breath. It was easy to push down her knees but he could not part her legs. Each time he was about to succeed she snatched at his hand, taking him unawares, and recrossed her legs. She was stronger than he suspected. Using all his strength he inserted himself between her legs, but she made a sudden flurry of movement and he found himself alone in the middle of the bed and she in a sitting position breathing hard and watching him closely.

He lay still not only to recover his breath but to think of a new strategy. Sweat sprang out all over his body. His penis was flaccid and he wondered if it would remain so after he overpowered her. Now, he felt he had to re-establish his superiority.

He could not afford to fail. Failure would be tantamount to giving her control over the household and himself.

Swiftly he pulled away the right hand she supported herself with, and as she fell to the bed he grasped her left hand, pinned her back to the bed and straddled her. She fought back, but slowly, inexorably, he forced her weakening hands to the bed. At the same time he lowered himself on her, her cool, wet body a welcome counterpoint to his hot and sweaty one.

'*Ewuo!*' she cried out as her hands went limp.

And as though on cue Okechukwu started to cry.

'Leave me! *Nnamu-ukwu*, the baby is crying.'

'Crying never killed anyone,' Nelson said.

'Is this how you are?'

Nelson did not bother to reply. Okechukwu's crying went up an octave injecting an element of urgency into his attempt to subdue her. And victory was in sight. Her legs parted, and her heavy breathing raised and lowered him like big ripples on the surface of the sea.

'The baby will wake up the neighbours,' she said more as a statement than a complaint.

He heard her but concentrated on the points of contact of their bodies. His penis however refused to stir. Okechukwu went into a long drawn out, hiccuping, choking cry.

'The baby is choking,' Ejiaka cried and in one galvanized, swift action, was out of the bed.

Again Nelson had been taken by surprise. He lay still on the bed and watched her pick Okechukwu up and rock him to silence.

※※※

Nelson woke up to a high-pitched cry. He lay still for a moment wondering whether he had dreamt it. The cry came again unmistakably from outside, followed by the swipe of a whip.

Someone beating his wife? No, the cry was too shrill, like a child's. Nelson sat up surprised and then annoyed that it was still early morning. It had taken him a long time to fall asleep last night and he had hoped to get up only a few hours before he went to work at three. Now he had many hours to while away.

The crying and whipping did not seem to disturb Okechukwu. He slept peacefully, probably making up for all the agitation of the night before. Thinking back now, Nelson was sorry he behaved so uncouthly. But Ejiaka had provoked him beyond what he could have taken lightly. She had turned it into a confrontation, a trial of strength and, he had not really acquitted himself well. He had allowed his fatherly feelings to take an upper hand, and lost a struggle that required cold calculation and relentless pressure.

What would Ejiaka be thinking or feeling now? Realizing that his disinclination to face Ejiaka now kept him from going to the rescue of the poor child who was still being whipped, Nelson discarded his *lappa* and put on a pair of shorts.

In the backyard it was as he had expected. Okonkwo, his harsh features set in grim rigidity, was flogging the small maid he and his wife treated worse than a dog. Nelson liked the girl and had come to feel protective towards her. Emaciated-looking, her skin cracked and ashy, she seemed like one whom the gods had sent to do penance for some terrible sins committed in a previous life.

'What has she done that you want to kill her?' Nelson shouted.

'Mind your business,' Okonkwo growled in his unpleasant voice. He was almost as tall as Nelson, but being stocky looked shorter. He wore his usual dirty-brown *lappa* and loose Hausa, rubber-soled slippers. Dry-eyed, the little girl in his grasp squirmed this way and that to avoid the rhythmic fall of the whip on her scantily clad body. She might as well have tried to avoid fate itself.

'That's enough, Okonkwo,' Nelson said, walking towards him. 'That's enough my man, that's enough.'

'I told you, mind your business! She is getting the punishment she deserves. After I finish flogging her she will carry the pot of soup round the town with a rope round her waist.'

So that was it? But why did servants always steal meat from pots of soup? Of all the things that could be stolen, it was often the first to be missed. It was also the least satisfying, even if one gobbled down two potfuls of it. And Nelson knew from experience it was not even the easiest thing to steal. One was likely to choke on it if surprised, especially if one had picked out a large stringy piece, criss-crossed with many nerves or cords of muscle. The excitement and nervousness of the moment closed the gullet and forcing down the unchewed piece of meat was more painful than a whipping. Nelson remembered. He had had the same experience. He had also learnt that the worst thing in the world was to be alone and that no matter how much you were liked by your master, you were not quite human.

Okonkwo was meting out more punishment than the little girl deserved, considering the way he maltreated and starved the poor thing till she was mere skin and bones.

'Stop, Okonkwo,' Nelson said, laying a gentle hand on Okonkwo's whipping hand.

Nelson felt himself shoved back violently and but for agile footwork would have sprawled on the dirty ground.

'Nna-mu-ukwu, watch out,' cried Ejiaka, who stood at a respectful distance with the other women of the yard.

The warning incensed rather than made Nelson cautious. Since when did Ejiaka begin to feel *that* protective towards him? Moving swiftly, he plucked the cane out of Okonkwo's hand and shoved him away when he attempted to get it back.

'How long do you want to continue whipping the girl?'

'As long as I want,' Okonkwo replied. 'Give me back that cane if you don't want any trouble.'

'I won't give it back to you,' Nelson said. The little girl hid behind him. 'And there is nothing you can do about it.'

Mrs. Okonkwo's coming out of the house just then seemed to galvanize Okonkwo into greater action. He threw himself at Nelson, grappling with him in an obvious attempt to throw him rather than to recover the cane. Nelson had not been expecting the move, but soon remedied a poor wrestling stance by breaking the latter's enveloping hold and swiftly dropping to one knee. It was one of his favourite manoeuvres during his short reign as the Ndi-okoroji's wrestling champion, and it rarely failed him.

His timing was perfect. Okonkwo hit the ground with a soft thud.

Nelson stood up quickly, expecting to be rushed at, and smiled when he saw it was not going to happen. Okonkwo, dazed not only from the fall but from the derisive laughter and tittering of the women and children, sat like a child that had taken a fall while learning how to walk. Nelson felt a lightness suffuse his own body, lifting the heaviness and the anger with which he had woken up that morning. With slow deliberateness, he broke Okonkwo's cane into small pieces and then strolled back to the bedroom and on to the parlour.

'Shall I put out your bathwater?' Ejiaka asked behind him.

He turned to look at her before answering. Why had he felt threatened by her? She had not changed. Her demeanour was still deferential her stance non-threatening. She did not, and probably could not, meet his eyes no matter how long he stared provocatively at her.

But he could not wipe out the events of last night. No matter how submissive she looked, he would always remember she could resist him physically. Oh, he had always known she was strong, stronger than most women, and some men. He had also always known she could take care of herself in an emergency, resist an attack and generally acquit herself creditably in tight situations. But, he had never associated her strength with himself. He had thought that although her moral and physical strength were not exactly inferior to his, they would succumb to his if he so desired it. This was obviously no longer the case now, and the thought destroyed the feelings of omnipotence that had filled him a moment before.

'Did you bring Ida in?' he asked.

'No,' Ejiaka said.

'Come, my child,' Nelson said to Ida, who had been trying to melt into the wooden door-frame. 'Don't you have something to do in your home? Did you hear what I said? Don't you have any work to do this morning?'

'I have, sir,' Ida said, her voice whispery.

'Go and do it then. Do you want your master to come and drag you from here? I did not save you from further flogging so you could become lazy.'

Ida showed no signs of moving. And now tears, copious and crystal-clear in the morning light cut a path down her cheeks.

'*Ewuo* my child!' Ejiaka exclaimed going to her. 'You did not cry when you were being flogged, and now that you are safe you want your tears to drown us. Dry your eyes. I thought you were a grown-up. Did you hear? Dry your eyes.'

Ejiaka put her hand round the small, thin shoulders. Ida now began to shake with huge sobs that, once in a while, escaped with a whinnying sound. Nelson controlled the laughter that was building up in the pit of his stomach. Okechukwu's sudden cry came to his rescue and he rushed to pick him up before Ejiaka could.

'We know you are awake,' he said to Okechukwu who fell silent having attracted someone's attention. Nelson lifted him up gingerly expecting the worst, but Okechukwu was only wet. Putting him over his shoulder he went into the parlour and sat down.

The commotion had died down outside, its place taken by the reverberations of pestles against mortars, interlaced with shrill childish laughter or grown-up commands. It was already ten getting on for eleven o'clock. Nelson suddenly felt the urge to get out of the house.

Ida's sobbing, like the dry season thunder it was, had subsided with characteristic speed and only widely-spaced sniffs sounded now and then.

'What about the water for my bath?' Nelson asked.

'Ida doesn't want to go back to her house,' Ejiaka said.

'Where does she want to go then?'

'Where do you want to go?' Ejiaka asked Ida, and then reported back, 'She won't say.'

'Leave her. I will talk to her.'

Ejiaka walked over to Okechukwu who had been following her movements as if he understood what was going on. She touched him on the cheek and went out through the pantry-store.

'Ida, come here,' Nelson said. She shuffled over to him, her head bent low. 'Why don't you want to go back to your home?' he asked her. 'You will gain nothing by remaining silent because I will simply drag you back myself.'

'He will beat me again,' Ida managed to say finally.

'No he won't,' Nelson said, although he felt she was right. He should have thought of that before going to her rescue. To reassure himself now more than Ida, he added forcefully, 'No, he can't beat you again!'

Ida stood like one being chastised, her thin, faded gown emphasizing rather than covering her undernourished body, her bowed, close-cropped head an *uli* design of ringworm estates.

'Why did you steal meat from the pot of soup?'

'I did not steal any meat, sir.'

'So, your master stole the meat?'

'No, sir. My mistress ate the meat.'

'You know I won't beat you, so why are you telling me lies?'

'May God burn me if I am telling you a lie.'

'Shi-i. A little girl like you should not swear falsely.'

'I am telling you the truth,' Ida said strongly, looking up for the first time. Her face and the front of her dress were wet with tears. 'My mistress eats in the middle of the night when she thinks everyone is asleep. Last night I forgot to warm up the soup, and she took some of it as she always does. This morning, the soup was sour and when my master asked what happened to it—he always has pounded yam for breakfast—my mistress said I must have put my fingers in the soup.'

'Did you report your mistress to your master?'

'He won't believe me, and my mistress will starve me more than she is doing now.'

'I don't believe your fairy tale,' Nelson said, watching her closely to see her reaction to that.

She bowed her head again without saying a word.

'How old are you?' Nelson asked her. 'Ida, tell me how old you are.'

'Fifteen.'

'Ida says she is fifteen years old,' Nelson said to Ejiaka who had just walked in.

'Fifteen?' Ejiaka said, and cocked her head on one side as though to appraise Ida. 'Yes, she looks it. The water for your bath is ready,' she added, taking Okechukwu from him.

'She also says she did not steal any meat from the pot of soup,' Nelson said, standing up and stretching.

'Yes,' Ejiaka said. 'She did not.'

'How do you know?'

'Her mistress has just told me. That was why I took so long putting out your bath water. Ida, is it true your parents died when you were little?'

'Yes, ma.'

⚒⚒⚒

Nelson hoped to find Christian in the shop; he had set his mind on their going out together. It would make the three hours he had before his afternoon shift pass swiftly. Ejiaka had been about to protest when he told her he was going to see Christian and would go to work from there, but had changed her mind and asked what she was to do with Ida.

'Let her stay till her master or mistress comes for her, then we will all talk it over.'

'What if they come for her during your absence?'

'They won't. Okonkwo is on afternoon shift too, and I don't think he has recovered enough from his fall to see me so soon.'

Nelson had liked the worried look on Ejiaka's face as he left the house. It made him feel good. He hoped she would so regret her action of the night before that she would beg him to touch her tonight. And he would refuse. As he now saw it the battle for supremacy was joined and he would accept nothing short of complete capitulation.

It would help if he could keep Ida to serve him while he sorted this thing out with Ejiaka. He still found it difficult to believe the little thing was fifteen years old, an age when girls in the village began to show they *were* girls. Ida was flat as a boy and looked five years younger.

What could have caused such retarded growth? Starvation? Malnutrition? Or heredity? If she was a true *nwa olu*, it would be easy to obtain custody over her—there would be few close relatives to argue with. Besides, her village was only six miles from his.

'Her relatives would certainly prefer me to look after her,' Nelson thought. 'Okonkwo's village is more than twenty-one miles away.'

'What did the sea throw up?' Christian shouted from his shop.

Nelson laughed embarrassed. 'You tell me.'

158

'If I knew I would not have asked.'

'Do I look that strange?' Nelson asked, shaking Christian's proffered hand.

'No,' Christian said. 'It is just that seeing a night-masquerade in the daytime makes one wonder.'

'How is your market today?' Nelson asked, to change the subject.

'I will tell you when you tell me why you are here.'

'I just came to visit you. You have often asked me to visit you, so here I am. You know the type of work I do does not give me enough free time.'

'Have the white men sacked you?'

'Sacked me?' Nelson laughed nervously. That is the last thing that will ever happen to me he thought. 'I wouldn't be here if they had,' he said.

'I believe you,' Christian said. 'What shall I give you? Although this is my home, it is not meant for receiving visitors. How are Ejiaka and the child?'

'They are well. You know I did not come to get anything from you. If I want to eat, I will visit you at home. Now, if you feel I am in the way tell me and I will go back home.'

'No, no, no! Don't say that sort of thing. I just want to be sure you did not run out as a rat would when the house is on fire. Christian raised the drop-leaf door of the counter and joined him. 'Now that I know you only came to visit,' he continued, 'there is just one thing we can do.'

'Go to Madame Òbò's,' Nelson chimed in.

'It seems you have had it on your mind for some time?'

Nelson laughed. 'A man is always ready to check on a story about fertile land.'

'True. How much time do you have or aren't you going to work today?'

'I see you do not want us to go?'

'Nothing amuses you today, Nelson. Vitus will be back in a few minutes then we can leave. I sent him to collect a debt.'

'But pay-day is still a week away.'

'I know. I sent him to one of my most stubborn customers. If I don't get hold of any important thing of hers before pay-day she will forget me on that day.'

'Oh, it is a woman.'

'Who did you think it was? Only an inexperienced trader gives credit to a man. What can you do to him if he refuses to pay?'

'Beat him up.'

'That won't get you your money.'

'What can you do to a woman?'

Vitus returned just then and Christian went behind the counter with him. Nelson continued to smile inwardly at his intentionally stupid question. He had wanted to needle Christian by appearing stupid. Walking out of the shop he stood on the elevated platform that ran round the house. People scurried up and down the street like rats. With the sun near its zenith everything looked hard and bright and alien.

Is this how God sees us from up there? Nelson wondered. A few mere feet above the street I feel apart and different from these people, as if I am not as human as they are. What of Him who actually is more than human, more remote, more everything. How does He see us?

'Let's go, Nelson,' Christian said, emerging from the shop.

Nelson jumped down from the platform. 'What did Vitus bring you?'

'The usual thing—a gold necklace.'

'How much does the woman owe?'

'Two pounds.'

'Two pounds? What did she buy?'

'You don't ask what a woman spent money on, especially one in "white man's work".'

'You are right. It is said that yam is nothing to a woman from a family rich in yams.'

'You always come up with these proverbs. Where did you learn them?'

'Learn them?' Nelson laughed. 'You don't have to learn, you just pick them up. I have forgotten most of them. You should hear the head of my *umu nna*; every word he says is followed by a proverb! It is like any skill. You lose it when you stop using it. I don't have much chance to practise, and people look at you as if you are from the bush when you use proverbs.'

'That is true. Only people who have just come from the village use many proverbs. But they soon forget it all and start speaking *Onitsha* or pidgin.'

'I didn't know it would take so much time to get to Madame Òbò's.'

'It does not really. It seems that way because this is your first time.'

'How did you discover her place?'

'A friend told me about it, and when I went there I found it was all that he said—the most homely place for a man looking for good wine.'

'And other things?' Nelson added.

'If someone had told me yesterday that today we would be going to Madame Òbò's, I would have called him a false seer. And if the same person had told me we would be having this conversation, I would have accused him of eating too many Communion cakes and speaking in tongues.'

'You don't *eat* a Communion cake, you let it melt in your mouth.'

'I told myself I should be careful what I say in your presence.'

'The Father said that if you bite it, the church will be filled with blood.'

'Whose blood?'

'Christ's of course. And it will need a great deal of praying and fasting to make the blood go back to where it came from.'

'Do you believe that?'

'Yes.'

They fell silent as though by prearrangement. Nelson had not found it difficult to believe what the Father had said. *Dibias* at home had things that possessed incredible powers, and only a fool would doubt them or dare a *dibia* to a demonstration. Nelson wondered if Christian had lost his belief in the supernatural. Was that what Protestantism did to one? A man lacking in beliefs is as exposed as a plucked chicken.

'You are deeper than I thought.' Christian said suddenly.

Nelson waited for him to continue, and when he didn't asked, 'Aren't you?'

'I don't know. What do you think?'

Nelson looked him over, the well-cut dark suit, the small

figure and the walk, sure and aloof. Was there any depth? He reminded him very much of a drawing. The general outline was familiar, but the particulars were not.

'Have you become *dumb?*'

'It is hard to see into you,' Nelson said.

'Perhaps you do not know how to look. Perhaps if you rub white chalk around your eyes you will see.'

Again they fell silent. Nelson now paid exclusive attention to the street they had just turned into. Narrow, and like a dried river-bed, it gave the impression of leading to areas one did not often frequent in the daytime or during the rains. Yet, there were houses on both sides, long, low, mud-walled, with rusted corrugated-iron sheet roofing. In front of some of them, women stood or sat on wooden folding chairs. Something about them showed they were not housewives. Their body movements, gesticulation and speech sent off waves charged with their availability.

'We have arrived,' Christian said.

They entered one of the low buildings through a wide, double door and found themselves in a large, rectangular room deserted but clean, the cemented floor looking newly washed. The square tables were covered with embroidered, dark green tablecloths and the simple folding wooden chairs were set at regular intervals around them. The air had a faint odour of stale cigarette smoke and palm wine that could not be dissipated by the creek-breeze coming in through numerous narrow windows.

'Where are the owners of this place?' cried Christian, bringing the room back to life.

Nelson smiled as he began to feel his body unwind and open up. The order and cleanliness of the room did not inhibit him at all, and he felt he could really let himself go here.

'Who is making that terrible noise so early in the morning?' a querulous female voice asked from an inner room.

'Madam, it is me,' Christian cried, his voice a cheerful ring.

'George! George!' the woman shouted as though no one had spoken.

'Ma?' an adolescent male voice answered from a distance.

'Where are you, you bad child?'

'I am washing the plates, ma,' George answered.

'You have been doing that since morning! You mean you are still wasting time on it?'

'There are many plates, ma.'

'There are many plates, ma,' the female voice mimicked. 'Go and find out who does not want us to sleep today. And if you are late again in killing the goat and chickens, I will send you where you can sleep for ever.'

'Madame Òbò, is quite well,' Christian whispered to Nelson.

'Good afternoon, sir,' George said, coming into the room. A young boy of average height, his dark, lean bare body glistened with sweat that dripped down into the top of a pair of khaki shorts. His shaven head emphasized his prominent forehead, and his small eyes twinkled with suppressed merriment.

'Good afternoon, George,' Christian said. 'I am glad to know madam is quite well,' he added in Igbo.

George smiled, his teeth a flash of white. 'Yes, sir. Shall I tell her you are here?'

'Wait a minute, let me introduce my very good friend, Mr. Achu.'

'Good afternoon, sir,' George said.

'Good afternoon,' Nelson said, excitement rising in him and making him sweat.

'George, as I said, Mr. Achu is my very best friend. I want you to treat him as you would treat me. Give him anything he wants when he comes here.'

'For nothing, sir?' George asked his teeth showing.

'If he cannot pay for it,' Christian said slowly, turning to Nelson, 'I will pay. Put it on my account.'

Nelson turned away embarrassed by the conversation and Christian's look. 'I will always pay for what I take,' he said feebly.

'You can see he is new here,' Christian said. 'Now, go and tell madam I am here.'

'That is not necessary,' Madame Òbò said in Onitsha Igbo, emerging through a multicoloured curtain and shutting the door behind her. 'Christian, I knew it must be you. No other man would come shouting at this early hour. George, go back to your work, and remember what I said. Christian, who is this fine young man with you?'

'Ha, madam, you always have eyes for good things.'

'If I did not at my age, wouldn't you be ashamed to be seen in my company? Now, don't try your usual tricks. Who is the shy young man?'

'Mr. Achu.'

'Mr. Achu? Are you from Awka?'

'No,' Nelson said, his heart beating heavily. 'Awka district.'

'Where in Awka district?'

'Eziagu.'

'I don't know the place, but it does not matter. If you are Christian's good friend, you are mine too.'

Nelson hesitated only slightly before taking the proffered plump hand. It was moist and soft and smooth, like a baby's but with a knowing pressure.

'Welcome to my home,' she said and winked.

'Thank you,' Nelson said, unable to take his eyes away from her magnificent figure and chest. The cut of her gown, made of some soft material, emphasized her small waist and large bosom. A roguish smile played on well-defined lips, the upper lip curling upwards and stretching sensuously. Oftentimes Nelson had heard men talk of dancing eyes and wondered how that could be possible. Now he knew. Madame's eyes were big, and the pupils a dark molten core floating on white, twinkled and danced in their stillness. Had Nelson, staring spellbound into the pupils, not seen his reflection in them he would have said they were not steady. They were, and yet they moved.

How long they stood looking into each other's eyes Nelson could not tell. Her hand trying to pull away from his grasp brought him back to the present. Smiling sheepishly, he released her hand, and sat down. Christian soon joined him.

'You did not tell me madam was so young,' Nelson said, after she had walked back to her room.

'She is not,' Christian said curtly.

'What do you mean?' Nelson felt betrayed. He had come expecting to see a huge old woman, mustachioed and gravel-voiced, just like others in her position. But what did he find?

'That woman is old enough to be your mother,' Christian said tightly. 'You don't believe me?' he asked.

Nelson shook his head to clear it. 'How old is she?'

'Forty.'

'You sound annoyed with me,' Nelson said. 'Have I done something wrong?'

'No, it is not your fault. It is that snake. I should have known that was what she would do. A hawk can never be cured of going after chickens.'

Nelson laughed. Did Christian think he was a chicken? What an inappropriate statement. Madam was merely a woman, even if a remarkable one, and he was a man, proven beyond doubt. The statement would have been more truthful if he had been cast in the role of the hawk. Christian really looked so crestfallen that Nelson began to worry he might have to pay for his own entertainment in the end. He did not have much money on him.

'Why are we behaving like small children?' he asked.

'Watch your step with that woman,' Christian said, as though Nelson had not spoken. 'Although you are a father you are not all that experienced in the ways of the world.'

Nelson suppressed a smile. Exhilaration was beginning to replace his earlier feeling of dissociation. Something good was going to come out of this meeting with madam. He was sure of it. Now, he could feel and smell the cool, moisture-laden breeze from the creeks.

George appeared from the yard carrying a tray laden with three bottles of Beck's beer. He was still sweating, but now had on a pair of khaki trousers. He placed two bottles in front of Christian and one in front of Nelson.

'Madam said to give you,' he said, flashing his knowing smile.

Nelson was surprised. He looked at Christian to see if they should accept such largess, and saw him smile.

'Madam is *oke nwanyi*!' Christian said. 'This is the way to welcome friends.'

'Let me go and bring glasses.'

'No, wait,' Christian said, grabbing George's hand and drawing him closer. 'What of the two young girls whom I heard came three days ago?'

'They are sleeping,' George said.

'I know. What is the name of the youngest one?'

'Mary.'

'Virgin Mary,' said Christian, casting a swift smiling glance at Nelson. 'Do you think you can wake her? Here, give her this money. All I want is to see what she looks like.'

'She is not here,' George said, rejecting the coins.

'But you said they were sleeping.' Christian's voice sounded angry.

'Yes, sir,' George said, throwing backward glances at madam's door. His constant smile made his fear look comic. 'I am sure that is what Mary is doing right now after a night's hard work. She went home with a customer last night. Many men want her.'

'Then she must be pretty,' Christian said mollified. He let go of George's hand.

'Sir, I will make sure you get her whenever you want her,' George said. 'She is my sister.'

'Is she really his sister?' Nelson asked as soon as George left.

Christian laughed suddenly. 'No,' he said, 'that is how they talk here. It simply means that Mary will do whatever George says. I almost forgot you are new here and that I am responsible for you. Women are God's right hand! How much time do you have before you go to work?'

'Less than an hour, I am sure.'

'We'd better hurry. Now that you know the place and you have been welcomed by madam herself, you can come any time you feel like it. You are a lucky man. The first time I came here no one noticed me, and here you are on the verge of getting into bed with madam.'

'Our *chi* are not the same,' Nelson said, feeling very self-conscious. He wanted to say more but did not know how Christian would react. He did not care for his sudden fits of anger and laughter.

'George,' Christian called out suddenly, 'our throats will dry up by the time you get the glasses. Don't forget the opener.'

'Yes, sir,' George answered from the backyard.

Madam's angry voice burst out in a torrent of gibberish. Nelson could not believe his ears. A moment ago she had spoken impeccable Onitsha Igbo and now she sounded as foreign as the Yoruba.

'What did she say?' Nelson asked Christian.

'I don't know. She speaks Igbo, Yoruba, Hausa and Brass.'

'Where is she from?'

'Why not ask George?'

Nelson waited till George had opened the beer and filled the glasses before asking.

'Madam is my sister,' George said in faultless Igbo. 'We are from Abonnema.'

Nelson wanted to ask many more questions but did not. Later. He was not in a hurry. Whatever he would find out would not change things much. He and madam, he was now sure, had been destined to meet, and he was not one to let his *chi* down. He sipped at the beer, the second time he had ever tasted one, and its rich, bittersweet tang fitted his mood.

'It is bad to drink beer in silence,' Christian said suddenly.

Nelson looked up. Christian was still not very happy with him. But now Nelson did not care. Grown-ups should not behave like children.

'First,' Christian said, after swallowing a large draught of his beer, 'you and madam looked at each other in silence. Then, you sit there drinking in silence. Take care. Terrible events often begin with silence.'

Nelson did not agree. Terrible events began either with a bang, or with boring chatter . . . never with silence.

Chapter Four

1 ✗ For more than two months Christian had changed and started coming home very late. Janet was now determined to find out why, even though she did not know what she would do afterwards. She could never keep to a predetermined line of attack with Christian for he was wont to not only frustrate it, but counter-attack from an unexpected position. She therefore preferred to deal with him as the situation dictated. Flexibility not being one of her virtues, she did not often succeed. But the few

times she did, made up for the humiliation and anger of previous losses. At such times Christian gave her a look containing wariness, respect, surprise and fear which she loved greatly.

What fools men were! In victory, they regarded themselves as omnipotent, displaying an arrogance that could not be justified by their equipment—a dangling vulnerable piece of flesh. They forgot that victory was the other side of defeat, and assumed it was their manifest destiny to be victorious. Forgetting that one did not often do battle with an inferior, they soon came to regard their defeated opponent as one, thus setting the stage for their downfall.

But it was in defeat that their real nature was uncovered. Filled with their inborn sense of helplessness they grovelled before their conquerors in abject abasement, willing to be used, sold, traded or sacrificed. And what traitors they became then! What filthy traitors and deceivers. And to the women of the clan was left the job of maintaining the old customs and identity, as well as bolstering the fallen ego of their men. It was mostly a thankless assignment. No sooner were the men up, than they forgot in their sadistic pursuit of pleasure that those they impaled had been instrumental to their putting on for a while the cloak of the victor.

Janet sighed as she stirred the ogbono soup she was cooking. There were times she wished she was a hermaphrodite. Women's dependence on men was a cruel joke God played on them, probably to temper their strength with humility, to make them more reasonable. Or perhaps to punish them for something they had done at the beginning of time, an act of insubordination to the Almighty, a refusal to populate the earth with godlike offspring. So like a rejected suitor, God created man in His likeness and saddled woman with him forever ... I gave you gold and you refused, take brass then! He must have said.

It was in the area of creation that Janet disagreed with the Bible. God did not create man first—why should a man create man first? It did not make sense. God created woman and then made man from her weakness.

The soup was done, and Janet took it from the fire. After stirring it for the last time, she placed the spoon across the mouth of the soup-pot and rested the cover on it. This way the pot cooled gradually. It was still too early to go to Christian's shop so she decided to have a hot bath. After she had put a pot of cold water on the re-stoked fire, she went into the house. Standing irresolute in the centre of the sitting-room she stared out of the window at the sun that was going down in all its glory.

Why didn't God make us as self-sufficient and independent as the sun? she wondered. She shook her head at the hidden meaning of his design . . . let there be light, and there was light. But the light hid more than it exposed, giving us a false sense of security, and smothering us with so much gloss that we lost sight of the fundamentals. It reminded her of the story of the three blind men who tried to describe an elephant they had *seen* with their hands. Let there be light indeed! How she would love to discuss that passage with the Pastor after the service tomorrow. But she knew she would not dare. The Pastor would think she was insane.

Janet sat down in her favourite chair. If all she was going to do was think of the past it was more comfortable to do it sitting down. She loosened her *lappa* so she could breathe more easily.

'My poor Ejiaka,' she muttered under her breath, recalling Ejiaka's tear-filled face as she told her about Nelson's change of behaviour. 'My poor, poor Ejiaka. *Ewuo!* What women have to suffer.'

Seeing Onyeama at the door two nights ago had alerted her to something being amiss. And when Onyeama said Ejiaka had sent him, Janet became alarmed.

'Is Okechukwu sick?' she had asked.

'No, nobody is sick.' Onyeama replied, 'Ejiaka said I should ask if you can come to our house tomorrow night.'

'You are sure nothing terrible has happened?'

'Yes, ma, nothing.'

'All right. I will be able to come tomorrow. How is your master?'

'He is on intermediate duty.'

'*Eh-he!* I will come tomorrow night after supper.'

But Janet had had no supper before rushing off to Ejiaka. That Nelson would be at work till eleven o'clock that night told her Ejiaka wanted to talk about him.

She was sitting in front of the house with Okechukwu on her lap when Janet arrived. The day had the ephemeral coolness and beauty of dusk with the warmth of an afterglow. It affected Ejiaka's looks too, lending her the colour of copper bangles a week after they have been washed with river sand. And like the bangles, she seemed to have undergone a kind of scrubbing. Janet put on a cheerfulness far above what she actually felt when she saw that Ejiaka's face did not light up.

'The way you look, it is as if you were expecting an important person,' Janet said loudly.

Ejiaka smiled briefly. 'Are you not an important person? Welcome.'

'O-oh! No. I am not important. Am I, Okechukwu?' Janet asked, stretching her arms out to the child, who quickly came to her. 'My God!' exclaimed Janet in mock pain, as she lifted him to her left hip, 'What do you feed this man? He is as heavy as a bag of cassava. My friend, next time I stretch my arms to you remind me you are too big to be carried, do you hear?'

'Bah ba-ba,' Okechukwu replied, showing his two, small lower teeth, in a wide smile.

'Yes,' Janet said, 'you are too big to be flung around. I nearly wrenched my shoulder joints lifting you.'

Ejiaka stood up looking lean and drawn in spite of her large *lappa* and blouse. Again Janet thought of copper bangles that showed their blemishes on closer inspection.

'Shall we go inside?' Janet asked seriously. Whatever was the matter with Ejiaka would only be made worse by forced cheerfulness.

Ejiaka led the way into the house. Onyeama met them in the sitting-room with a lighted lamp that Ejiaka took and walked on to the pantry-store. To Janet's surprise the pantry-store had been converted into a bedroom.

'It looks like you have a visitor,' Janet said, looking round the room and noticing the folded clothes on a rope running from the right to the left wall. Everything in the room was squared away making it seem bigger than before.

'No,' Ejiaka said grimly. 'This is where I sleep these days.'

Shocked, Janet quickly sat down on the bed. She did not know what to say, what to ask. Her heart beat as though she was the one who had been forced out of the marriage-bed.

'What happened?' she finally asked.

'I am coming,' Ejiaka said, getting up and opening the door to the backyard. 'Onyeama! Onyeama, come and give Okechukwu a bath.'

Janet thought she detected a break in Ejiaka's voice but she was as clear-eyed as before. Unable to wait till Onyeama had taken the child, Janet asked quickly, her own voice quivering a little:

'When did this happen?'

'A week ago,' Ejiaka said, in a flat tone.

'You should have called me long ago.'

Onyeama came in and stretched his arms out to Okechukwu.

'Nna, come,' he said coaxingly. 'Come let me give you some meat, you hear? Come.'

'Nta-nta,' Okechukwu repeated as he was being carried away.

'Yes,' Onyeama reassured him, 'Meat . . . nta-nta.'

Janet closed the door after them and sat down quickly.

'What happened?' she asked softly.

Ejiaka burst into tears.

'Ewuo-o, my child,' Janet said, moving swiftly to her side and putting her arms round her. 'You shouldn't carry things on your chest all the time. It will burst one day if you don't tell some-one. Ewuo-o, you must have been deeply hurt, to cry like this. So cry. It will cool your chest down and then you can tell me all about it. It is good you remembered to send for me. It shows you are ready to deal with your problem. I will help you with all my strength, and any problem we cannot solve can only be solved by God. So cry, and afterwards we will put our heads to work. Ewuo-o, my child.'

Janet ran out of words long before Ejiaka's tears finally sub-sided. And after some time Ejiaka started talking, her voice dry and stumbling initially, becoming lubricated and smooth-flowing, but retaining a distance that Janet felt was needed to keep the tears dammed.

About three months ago, Ejiaka had said, she had refused to have sex with Nelson. They had struggled and she fought him off. Now that she thought of the struggle she was shocked she

171

had allowed it to happen. After all he *was* her husband and she was totally and completely his. But that thought had not occurred to her then. All she could think of was to stop him from doing anything to her, and he behaved like the young men she used to fight off during moonlight games.

A week after their struggle, he began to come home late from work. Or if he came home early he went out again staying away till very late. He who used to touch her whenever they were in bed, now consistently turned his back on her and fell into a deep, snoring sleep. At first she was glad of this, but when he stopped eating lunch and dinner at home she became alarmed. Then two pay-days ago he gave her the month's food money, less his 'stomach' because, he said, he rarely ate at home any more and would need the money to pay his bills where he ate. Ejiaka sent Onyeama to find out where he ate. It was at a bar called Madame Òbò's.

'Madame Òbò?' Janet did not believe she heard correctly.

'Yes,' Ejiaka said. 'Do you know the place?'

'It is Christian's second home.'

They stared at each other as they realized what was happening. Their husbands had adopted Madame Òbò and her bar and God knows what else!

'This must be Christian's work,' Janet said. 'He must have taken Nelson there. That bad man!'

'Don't blame it all on Christian,' Ejiaka said. 'A trap rarely catches a small snake. Last pay-day, after Nelson gave me an even smaller amount for food money, I told him it would be better to bring home the woman that was cooking his meals. That way Okechukwu, Onyeama and I would not starve. We would supplement our meals with their left-overs.'

'What of Ida?'

'She had gone for a week by then.'

'So what did Nelson say?'

'Nothing. One week later, he brought home this woman that was old enough to be his mother.'

'Who?'

'The woman said her name was Elizabeth although people call her Madame Òbò. Her eyes ran all over the house like a thief's.'

172

'What you are trying to tell me is that you let Nelson bring Madame Òbò into your house?'

'He is my husband, Janet, and the house is his. If I had tried to stop him he would have thrown me and the child out.'

'God forbid! Nelson is not like that.'

'He has changed. Sometimes I don't even recognize him and I start wondering if he is the same person I married. I think that woman did something to him. What can she give him that I can't?'

'But you just told me.'

'Yes, I know. That was because he tried to force me. If he had asked me beforehand I would have agreed although it would have been against our plans.'

'Ejiaka, what shall we do?'

'I don't know, Janet, that is why I sent for you. Now that I know who my rival is, now that I know Nelson wants to marry her . . .'

'Marry her?'

'Yes. He wants to make her his second wife, that is why I moved out of the bedroom for them.'

'Is she here?'

'No. She only sleeps here when my husband is on morning duty.'

'Ejiaka, do you know who Madame Òbò is?'

'*Akwunakwuna.*'

Janet was speechless at Ejiaka's calmness. 'A harlot,' she had said, in as matter-of-fact a way as if she were talking of ordinary salt. How could Nelson do this type of thing, and how could Ejiaka not only allow it, but condone it? And why had Ejiaka not told her as soon as the whole thing started? She would have thought of a way to stop it, or at least made Nelson aware of her displeasure. Now, it was too late. If she came, she would be blamed for anything that went wrong. People would say that but for her Ejiaka would not have rebelled. The last thing Janet wanted was to be called a home breaker. And as she did not have a surviving child, it would be the same as calling her a witch. And to think of the number of times she had visited Ejiaka without knowing what was happening. But how could she have guessed such a thing would happen when Nelson was a Roman Catholic?

'Eh-he!' Janet exclaimed. 'Nelson cannot take a second wife, even if she is not a prostitute. Roman Catholics are not allowed to marry more than one wife.'

'He has not been to church for the past four months. I don't think he is still a Roman Catholic.'

'Why did he stop being a Catholic?'

'He failed to pay his dues so they told him not to come to church till he was ready to do so. He told Theodore . . . he was the one that converted him . . . that since the church wanted his money more than his presence he would no longer be a Roman Catholic.'

'Nelson has changed as you said. It is hard to know how the town will affect someone. So many things go on at the same time—good and bad, full of meaning and meaningless. A man without religion is like night without light. You cannot see into him, let alone talk to him. Where does one begin? What power can one call on or use to chasten him? And in this township where everything is possible, and many people get away with anything, what examples of retributive justice can you cite to convince a wrong-doer that evil does not pay?'

'You will talk to him, won't you?' Ejiaka asked.

'I will, although I know it won't do any good. It is like trying to change a spoilt child. Ejiaka, you know you have spoilt your husband. It is not that I blame you, but I want you to know what you did. Marriage is a place for doing battle, battle for supremacy. Unless you decide to be the defeated, you do battle every day, every hour. Sometimes you lose, sometimes you win. It is necessary that you win once in a while otherwise your husband will no longer consider you human. You will become his property and he can do anything he likes with you. I am saying all this to tell you that this is your opportunity to fight back. Do not accept the position of the loser even before you have lost. You must win this particular battle or you will not be able to say anything to your husband if in the future he decides to throw you out for another woman. But if you win, next time he wants to have another woman he will at least think of you. Yes, I will talk to Nelson tomorrow. I will come in the morning

174

from work so that he will realize how important it is to me. I will stand by you in this fight because I think your future happiness depends on whether you win or lose. Imagine allowing a harlot to take over your home! You must love your husband more than you love your life.'

Janet had talked to Nelson the next day as she promised. It was stormy and inconclusive. It also showed her the side of Nelson she had not known. Instead of hearing her out, he virtually told her to go and straighten Christian out first. His statement reminded her of the one in the Bible about removing the beam in your eye before you try to remove the mote in another's eye. So, she had mentally conceded defeat even before Nelson refused to listen to her any more. For Ejiaka's sake she hoped Nelson's feelings for Madame Òbò would be temporary. What do men find in harlots anyway?

But Nelson had been right. She should have straightened Christian up before talking to him.

Janet got up from the chair, retying her *lappa* as she went to the kitchen. The bath water was boiling and it did not take her long to bathe and dress. At the gate she told the gate-man she would be returning home late.

The street was still full of people, probably because it was Saturday and the darkness was lightened by the first quarter moon. Janet was glad of the crowd. Avoiding the bands of young men intent on colliding with her kept her from dwelling on what she would say to Christian.

Christian was not at the shop when she got there.

'Where did he go?' she asked Vitus, who was flustered by her visit.

'He went to see a customer, ma.'

'Who?'

'He did not tell me, ma.'

'Bring out a chair for me. Has he been gone for long?'

'Yes, ma.'

'When did he leave?'

'I did not look at the clock when he left, ma.'

'Don't go back into the shop yet.' Janet sat down, loosened her small top *lappa* slightly, and settling into a comfortable position asked, 'Why are you lying to me, Vitus? You know you do

175

not know how to lie. Now, tell me at what time your master left.'

'Four o'clock, ma,' Vitus said reluctantly.

'What time is it now?'

'Half-past seven.'

'Three hours! What kind of customer would keep him for so long? Not even Tom Big Harry! I think you had better go home,' Janet said standing up. 'I will look after the store till your master returns. Are you sure he will come here instead of going straight to the house?'

'He will come here, ma.'

'Good. Go home. But first return the chair to the shop. And don't fall asleep before I return.'

Janet watched him leave after putting back the chair. Such a small boy and already learning to be a man. Men always protected each other. Maybe she should get a maid too young to be seduced by Christian. It would be nice to get that type of protection. What was she thinking? She didn't need it.

Janet was happy to go into the store, away from the mosquitoes that were singing to her ears, and the night air that was growing cold. The street was emptying and the men that passed by infrequently gave her peculiar looks.

This was not the first time she had minded the store alone at night. She had done so when Christian was recovering from the awful beating he had received. The store had become a familiar place to her then, except for the area filled with samples of suitings and order-books and ledgers and measurement charts. Worried about Christian's full recovery at the time, she felt that violating that area would be acknowledging he would not be back on his feet soon. Every man, and woman, needed one *lappa* of mystery to remain human. Christian was stripped of his personal mystery daily at the hospital, and needed the suitings area to keep its mystery for him.

Which was why it had hurt her when, later, he had accused her of having ransacked the store to satisfy her curiosity. But she had been so glad he had recovered fully that she did not try to defend herself. Later Vitus had told her why Christian felt she had taken the shop apart—most of the female customers had been scared away by her presence and did not return until

Christian reassured them she was no longer going to be there. It had made her wonder what special services Christian offered them that she could not? She did not however try to find out. This time she preferred her imaginings to the truth.

The store is empty, she thought, now looking round. The general goods area was depleted and she wondered why Christian had not refilled it. She peered under the bottom shelves and found a great deal of unopened stock. As she straightened up, a young girl stood at the door.

'Wetin you want?' Janet asked.

The girl stared like one who had seen a ghost up on the shelves. When Janet turned to the shelves to see what was there, the girl disappeared. Janet stretched her hand to pick up the lamp and go after her but changed her mind. The girl looked too young and innocent. Innocent? Well, maybe not, but definitely too young to have a tryst with Christian. In spite of her obvious endowments she did look like a servant girl. Christian was too proud of himself, too aware of his self-worth to go after one.

Could it be that she had come for Vitus? She had looked startled and frightened to find Janet in the shop. And she had come with the confident stealth of a resident.

Oh, come now, Janet, you are imagining things. Vitus is not like that, even though he is at the right age to explore his curiosity. But what if . . . ?

Janet lifted the drop-leaf door and passed through. At the door, the lamplight cast her shadow like that of a huge horned beast. Did I really frighten the girl, she wondered? The street was not completely deserted. Port Harcourt never really slept. But not enough people were awake to warrant the store staying open so late. Then it occurred to her that Christian probably used the store as a cover for other business. Why had she not thought of this earlier? He may never have been at the store during the past few months when he came home late, which explained why Vitus was reluctant to tell her the exact time he left. And it was also possible Vitus seized that opportunity for his own dalliance. You don't often cover up for someone unless you stand to gain.

Suddenly dogs barked furiously in the distance, and there were yelps of pain and human shouting and cursing. Janet shuddered involuntarily. She was not afraid, and yet not quite at ease. When you have seen, touched, felt and stayed around pain and death what else is there to fear? Death *is* darkness. Just as light is always surrounded by darkness, so life is sandwiched between death.

So what is there to fear? Aloneness perhaps. If a lone source of light is surrounded by darkness a mile deep there is the fear that it will eventually be snuffed out and darkness prevail for ever. But if there are pockets of light, each encircled by darkness, there is the hope that the light will grow to encompass the world. Hope springs eternal, as the holy book says. Hope! Even Job had had it.

Janet walked back to sit behind the counter. The chair was too low, so she stood up again. Yes, she had hopes that she would become pregnant again. She had hopes that Christian would relent. She had hopes that she would bring forth a little source of light that would grow and grow. One of her favourite church songs flitted into her mind and she started humming it: *Lead kindly light amidst the encircling gloom*.

She must go to church tomorrow, to shift her burden on to broader and stronger shoulders. She had not been for a month now, and she could feel life weighing down on her like a ton of wet soil. There was nothing that moved her so much as when the Pastor with his wide shoulders and out-flung arms intoned, 'Come unto me, all ye that labour and are heavy laden, and I will give you rest,' and the choir hummed one of those quick, small tunes that gave an emotional and spiritual presence to the words, and the silence afterwards, deep and more eloquent than the words, yet meaningless had the words not been spoken, filled every man, woman and child, every bench, table and chair, and the very air. Then Janet felt a great burden lift off her shoulders, like a huge black vulture, and fly with its ungainly, slow-moving wings towards the altar and disintegrate in front of the high arch with its bold red lettering: HOLY – HOLY – HOLY.

And as though the Pastor knew what wonders the words had performed, he would add that promise that tasted like the piece of meat in the soup-plate one reserved for the last:

Verily, verily, I say unto you, he that heareth my word,
and believeth on Him that sent me, hath everlasting life.

'Verily, verily, I say unto you,' Janet murmured to herself, 'in the beginning was the word . . . and the word was God.'

A knock on the wall startled her, and she looked round guiltily thinking someone had overheard her. The knock was repeated randomly and she realized it must be one of the neighbours. Her unease was replaced with impatience. Looking at the clock she was surprised that so much time had passed. Ten o'clock. Before long the neighbours would be fast asleep and she would be the only one awake in the whole building.

What was Christian doing and where? Her vigil reminded her of when her second to last child had died at the age of five, the longest any of her children had agreed to remain on earth. Actually it was wrong to say he had died. He had gone away. One moment he was there eating supper and the next he was choking and crying, and dying. And Christian was out seeing a customer from whom he hoped to get an order of two suits.

Choking, and crying, and dying! She did not know what to do, or rather she knew there was nothing she could do. Barely six months before she had buried her youngest that had gone away in his sleep without a whimper, without even saying goodbye.

So she sat where she had been knitting a sweater for him, and watched him struggle with whoever had come to take him away. He really put up a struggle, which was understandable—there was nothing she had not done to keep him, to make him happy and comfortable. Her love for him had known no bounds, and even Christian had complained it was excessive. Yet, she felt no emotion as she watched him grapple with *them*. She knew, as soon as the battle was joined, that he would lose. That hard knowledge kept her in her chair. Also, the fact that he did not look at her once, did not cry out for help as children often do, made it easier.

Choking, and crying, and dying! They took him. And he did not make one human sound. She did not touch him. She did not continue knitting. She did nothing. She sat there, staring into space, waiting for Christian. Out of the corner of her eye but in the centre of her mind's eye, she saw her child keel over on his right side, his small hands, beautiful hands, clutch at his small throat. His knees bunched up his khaki jumper to his chest, the plates of pounded yam and *ogbọnọ* soup waited with a forlorn air to be eaten.

Later, Christian had said the sight, when he walked into the room in the early hours of the morning, had bound his feet to the floor.

It took her three weeks to cry for the dead child. It took her that long because when they performed an autopsy, they found nothing in his throat. The doctor even doubted whether the boy had actually choked to death. What could she say? Death did not always knock before it entered, nor did it always leave a trail.

Steps sounded outside and Christian came in. His smile froze, then he frowned.

'Welcome,' Janet said pleasantly. 'Did you get the money from your customer?'

'What money?'

'The money Vitus said you went to collect at four o'clock. It is now half-past ten.'

'Where is Vitus?'

'I sent him home.'

'Why?'

'I wanted to look after the store till you returned.'

'What you really mean is you wanted to meet me here. Well, here I am.'

'Did you get your money?'

'Is it your money?'

'Now I can understand why you didn't want me to put any money in the store after you repaid what I loaned you.'

'Now that you understand let us go home. I am not in the mood to talk about what is not important.'

'I have something important I want us to talk about. Where have you been all this time?'

'Are you asking me?'

'Is there any other person here?'

'When did I become your slave?'

'You are my husband.'

'Truly?'

'That is why I ask where you have been tonight.'

'Those two things do not go together.'

'Christian, Nelson is in great trouble.'

Janet watched to see the effect of her change of tactics. His face did not change as he paced the small floor. Turning abruptly he asked for the chair. She passed it to him over the counter and after he had sat down she said slowly, 'Nelson is in big trouble.'

'What kind of trouble?'

'You know,' Janet said, happy she had got him to sit down. Leaning her elbows on the counter she repeated with added emphasis, '*You* know.'

'I know,' Christian said and laughed.

Janet straightened up. She wondered what game he was playing now. How could he go from perfect seriousness to laughter in a matter of seconds unless he was acting? Why must he always upstage her?

'Everything is a game to you,' Janet said bitterly. 'Can you never be serious?'

'Eh-e,' Christian said, shaking his head, 'no sermon tonight, it is not yet Sunday. One bad thing about you is that you have such a short memory. You never remember anything outside your work for long. You once told me you liked the way I didn't take life seriously and now you are annoyed because I am doing what you said you liked. It is impossible to give you joy because you do not know what you want.'

'I know what I want and it is not joy at this moment. There is a time for everything.'

'Yes, the Bible says so.'

'Christian, why do you always bring the Bible in whenever we discuss things? You know it makes me angry.'

'I bring it in because that is where most of your ideas come from, and you always forget I have studied the Bible too.'

'I don't forget, and my ideas don't come from the Bible.'

'That is what you say, but you know it is not true. Anyone whose father is an Archdeacon, anyone who was brought up on the Bible as you were, would certainly depend on it for most things. Before I met you, you took life more seriously than St. Matthew! And that is what that book does to people brought up on it; it makes them afraid of life.'

'Look at who is talking.'

'You know what I am saying is the truth. I was not brought

181

up on the Bible. I saw it in practice, which is a completely different thing. You will not deny I make you laugh at life once in a while. I showed you that life is like a moonlight game. If you are afraid of what might happen to you you would never enjoy it. What am I saying? You never went to the games.'

He was right, she never did, not even when her family went home to Ujalli on short visits. Her father was a carpenter then and she was too young to go to the games alone. When she was the right age they no longer went home regularly even though her father now earned more as an Archdeacon. He was afraid he would be passed over in promotions if he went on leave.

'Come on, let's go home,' Christian said, standing up.

'We have not discussed anything,' Janet protested.

'We will discuss things on our way home.'

'It is not the type of discussion you hold in the streets.'

'Who said so?'

Janet did not answer. She was furious with herself for having lost the initiative, but as she helped him put things away, she stole admiring glances at him. His face was closed, and she could not guess what he was thinking. Was he rejoicing at how easily he had defeated her purpose? Was he thinking of her at all? Was he with her in the shop or miles away with one of his customers?

The shop had not made much money that day, but Christian showed no sign of that being important. They took the lamp with them and locked the store with a huge key made by railway machinists.

'You did not make much money today,' Janet said.

'We don't on Saturdays.'

'You are sure you do not want to expand the shop? Christmas is here.'

'I will tell you when I do.'

'You are the only man I know who does not take his work seriously.'

'Work is not the most important thing in life.'

'What is?'

'Being alive.'

'But you have to work to be alive.'

'No. You can remain alive without working.'

'What kind of life is that? A man's work is his life.'

'Just as a woman's life is her children.'

Janet felt like striking him but instead lengthened her stride. The devil! He knew where to stab her. His blow was always unerring, and merciless. But she would not let him know how much he had hurt her. Why was she walking so fast then? That was as much as telling him she was hurt. And he had not complained but was trying to keep up with her. Because she was carrying the lamp? Not likely. He was not afraid of the dark. Then he knew he had hurt her? Would he do something about it? Years ago she would not have had to wonder. She knew then he would have been sorry if he had hurt her, she knew he would not have hurt her intentionally. But now she had to wonder. Life had become so uncertain, so pointless.

Where did it go wrong? When did it happen?

In the beginning, we did not talk much yet understood each other perfectly. Now we talk a great deal but somehow do not communicate. Maybe he was right when he said God spoke when He lost contact with human beings. The state of the world showed how well He had been communicating with us. The Germans, the British and other white people were slaughtering one another and trying to drag all black men into it too. For what?

'What type of trouble did you say Nelson was in?'

Janet slowed down. What is he trying to do now? Does he really not know the type of trouble Nelson is in?

'Did you not take him to Madame Òbò?' Janet asked.

'And so what?'

'Madam is now living in his house.'

'I don't believe you. Madam was in her house each time I went there. How can she live in her house and in Nelson's house at the same time? She is only one person.'

'Ejiaka wouldn't lie to me.'

'Ejiaka told you that madam lives in their house?'

'Yes.'

'Where does Ejiaka stay?'

'Where does Ejiaka stay? In her husband's house of course,

but she now sleeps in the pantry-store. She has left the bedroom to Nelson and madam.'

'Young men always prefer to drown when they can swim. You are sure you are not telling me a story?'

'Does it make sense?' Janet asked coldly.

'No, it doesn't. It is insane.'

'Then it is not a story.'

They were approaching the gates of the hospital now, and the night wind seemed colder. Janet hoped the gate-man was not asleep. Waking him was always a major undertaking.

'I believe you,' Christian said. 'I must talk to Nelson.'

'I have already talked to him.'

Christian stopped suddenly. 'What did he say?'

Janet stopped too. 'He said I should control you first before trying to control him.'

'You are lucky he did not slap you.'

'Nelson is not that type of person.'

'You do not know him. That man is too deep, or too cunning.'

'Do you know him?' Janet asked, as they resumed their walking.

'Now that you have danced all the sand away, I will have to be careful. I have to approach him differently.'

'When are you going to stop going to Madame Òbò's?'

Janet did not expect him to answer that, and he did not. She had lost so many confrontations that one more did not make much difference. Losing to a husband was like losing to oneself. You just learned to live with it and kept hoping that one day you would win a major one that would wipe the previous losses off your mind. Catastrophic defeats or tremendous victories were really new beginnings. We are rarely the same after they have occurred. We become new people, new-born wearing, as Jesus Christ did after finally saying 'Get thee behind me, Satan,' a new mantle from our creator.

2 ✄ 'Master! Master! Master!' Angela cried.

Christian rode harder and the louder Angela cried, the higher the power built up in him. He was not going to let it explode too soon. He was going to build it up higher and higher till she begged for mercy, till she was silenced by the sheer force of it all. And he was not going to join her in speech either. He wanted all the power channelled down to his loins. Grimly he rode on and as the flash point came nearer, exultation rose from the top of his stomach. It was going to be the greatest. He could feel it. It had been a long time. After this she would be unable to walk, at least not immediately afterwards. After this she would regret the time they had wasted staying apart, and 'Master' would not be a word but a concrete rod tearing her apart, touching her innermost being, branding her, burning out the inhuman areas.

'Master! Master! Master!'

Oh no, she has escaped! Where is she? Where did she go?

'Master!'

Christian opened his eyes realizing now what had happened. His penis was stiff and painful.

'Master!' Vitus cried again.

'What is it?' Christian shouted angrily.

'They have stolen from us! They have stolen everything!'

'What are you talking about?' Christian asked, scrambling out of bed, grabbing at his *lappa*, unbolting the door, grabbing at his *lappa* again, rushing through to the parlour. 'What are you talking about?'

Vitus stood in the centre of the room, his face one squeezed-up, wet tear.

'They have stolen everything in the shop!'

The bottom of Christian's stomach fell away. He stared at Vitus.

'You don't know what you are saying,' he mumbled, tying and untying his *lappa*. His vision shifted momentarily to Vitus' tear-gushing eyes, and then scuttled away.

'No, it cannot be. You mean they left nothing? They left me nothing? They left me nothing with Christmas only a week away?'

'They swept it,' Vitus said.

'They swept it,' Christian said to himself, but the words had no meaning now. His heartbeat raced on, making him feel half as heavy again. Suddenly anger welled up in him as his eyes came back to Vitus as though seeing him for the first time.

185

'And what are you doing standing there?' he shouted. 'If as you say they swept the place, does that mean we will not open the shop today, eh? Are we to sit at home with arms folded?'

Vitus' face tried to work out an answer but finally dissolved into bitter, shameless crying. Christian watched him turn away bellowing like a goat to be slaughtered.

Why had he said that to the boy? Christian asked himself stumbling back into the bedroom. In a dazed fashion he drew on the nearest pair of trousers, threw on a shirt, slipped his feet into a pair of sandals and walked out of the house without a backward glance.

It had rained the previous night and Christian soon regretted coming out wearing sandals. As he picked his way slowly for fear of falling or being stuck in mud-islands that filled the street, his mind raced far ahead to the shop, discovering piles of merchandise the thieves had overlooked. Once in a while he glanced up to re-establish his bearings, and each time his heart fluttered in anticipation of being surprised by a stranger laden with the stolen merchandise from his store. But at the back of his mind he knew this would never happen. 'Oh God, oh God,' he moaned to himself, 'why me? What have I done to deserve this?' And although he knew there would be no answer, there would never be an answer unless he made up one, he continued to ask the questions.

Thrill seekers stood many people deep in front of the shop when he got there—men in ragged singlets, dirty shorts and shapeless felt hats. He had to shove and shout that he was the owner of the shop before they would clear a path for him.

Yes, Vitus had been right. The thieves had swept the place, really swept it. For a fraction of a minute everything blurred and Christian supported himself on the counter-top. When he recovered, he searched every empty space slowly with unbelieving eyes.

'How did they do this?' he asked himself, and as though she was a mind-reader, a woman in the crowd asked the same question aloud.

'They dug a hole through the outside wall,' someone answered her with relish. 'Mud walls cannot stop a determined and experienced thief,' the man added after a dramatic pause.

186

'The way you said it,' another male voice said, 'one would think you knew the thieves.'

'Are you calling me a thief?' cried the first voice, creating a sudden surge and flurry in the thick of the crowd.

Christian caught a glimpse of a squat, dark man confronting a tall, thin but broad shouldered man. The crowd heaved and shut them off from sight.

'I said, are you calling me a thief?' the first man bellowed. 'Ehh, are you calling me a thief?'

'Give them space there,' several voices shouted.

'I did not call you a thief,' the second voice now said into the sudden silence, 'but if you say you are one, then you are.'

Again there was a heave in the crowd and Christian came quickly to the double-doors of the shop to see the combatants better. But he was too late. The squat man was stretched out on the muddy street, his tattered clothing merging into the dark-brown colour of wetness around him. The crowd was also dispersing, some shouting angrily, others laughing as the tall, straight back of the victor moved speedily away from the scene. No one ran after him, nor did anyone try to aid the fallen man.

Was he dead? Christian wondered, but dismissed it from his mind as the weight of what had befallen himself came down on him anew. He leaned on the counter, his back to the door, and for the first time since he could remember, shed tears, silent tears that pained his eyes as they started but which soon felt like the overflow of a full bucket. From time to time he hit the counter-top with his right fist, rhythmic little taps that were more the manifestations of helpless emotion than anger. What should he do now? he kept asking himself. Why must life always spring such beastly surprises on him? Just when he thought he was getting on his feet, he was slapped down again, brutally, mercilessly, without warning. Perhaps it was better to stay down. Damn it!

'Mr. Okoro,' a female voice exclaimed. 'Oh, Mr. Okoro, it pained us when we heard what happened. Oh those bad people!'

'Christian,' a male voice said, 'what can a person say?'

Christian felt a heavy hand clasp his right shoulder. He shook his head both to signify he did not want to be disturbed and to stem the flood of tears. Neither worked.

'Christian,' the male voice resumed, 'I do not blame you. What has happened to you is enough to make a stone cry. So do not feel ashamed that a tough man like you is crying. It shows you are human like us. That rain last night hid every sound. We did not hear a thing. Even Comfort who does not sleep, slept like a boa constrictor that has swallowed an animal. Have you been to the police?'

Christian shook his head. The rumbling in his chest that threatened to explode had subsided. But God, if he could lay his hands on the thieves, he too would be merciless. He passed a slightly shaking hand across his face, trying to stop the flow of tears. What was the use of crying anyway? It would not bring the stolen goods back. The counter-top looked as if water had spilled over it.

'Shall we go to the police with you? I am sure they will want to ask us questions.'

Again Christian shook his head. He wondered where Vitus was, and turning round saw the boy standing in the far corner of the shop trying to melt into the wall.

'Vitus, go and tell your madam what has happened,' Christian said. His voice had regained some of its timbre, but quivered slightly. It embarrassed him but he thought, 'You never know how you will react in a situation till it hits you.' He felt as if he was climbing out of a bottomless pit.

'*Ewoh*, Christian, why did they remember you?' Comfort cried.

'That is the way the world is. No one knows when he will be remembered. Vitus, aren't you the one I told to go and tell your madam what has happened? What are you waiting for?'

Vitus left silently, his body a moving picture of misery.

'Poor child,' Nwoye said. 'He feels it more than anyone else.'

'He should,' Christian said. 'It is where his daily bread comes from.'

Christian lifted the drop-leaf door and went behind the empty counter. 'Not even a single nail,' he murmured as he looked round, stopping only briefly at the jagged hole in the wall through which the thieves must have entered. His eyes checked all the shelves again with the hope of finding something, a sample maybe, or a tin of cigarettes, anything. It was a clean sweep all right. Then he began to search the drawers.

'So, none of my neighbours heard anything?' he asked.

'I told you it was raining. No one heard anything. If you ask me, I would say the thieves must have hired a rain-maker to make rain for them. The drums the rain beat on the roof were too loud for ordinary rain.'

'Joseph!' Comfort cautioned.

'I know what I am saying,' Nwoye said.

Old men are as bad as children when it comes to beliefs, Christian thought pulling open the last drawer. His heart missed a beat when he saw a piece of paper covered with writing in capital letters. Picking it up he read: YOU TAKE SO WE TAKE. What was this all about? He read it again, letting his mind take flight in free association based on each word, and then on all the words together. It was neither a statement from the Bible, nor did it have anything to do with it. The writer was not well educated—the letters were malformed, their arms and legs askew, and he must have wetted the lead pencil with spittle to write some of the letters.

'It seems they left you something,' Nwoye said.

Then it clicked. It must be Tom Big Harry's men.

Oh, my God, that man wants to destroy me because I partook of something he was careless about, something he did not need. Tom Big Harry! Yes, I must go to the police and tell them. I must! But, will they believe me? Will that not be jumping from frying pan to fire? I am in the fire already; surely it cannot be worse. Or if it does get worse, all that can happen will be for me to burn . . . or not burn, like Shadrach . . . nonsense, what am I thinking?

Christian closed the drawer, folded the paper and put it in his pocket.

'We will wait for Janet,' he said.

'Yes,' Comfort said nodding. 'Janet knows the ways of white people.'

'The police are not white people, Comfort,' Nwoye said.

'They are under white men and do white people's work, Joseph.'

'That does not make them white people.'

189

'When a man behaves and talks like a goat we call him a goat.'

'Christian, do not forget to call me when you go to the police. Come, Comfort, you have not given me any breakfast.'

'Christian, let your heart be strong,' Comfort said. 'You acquired the things you just lost, and the way you acquired the first will get the next.'

They left, two people waiting to die, yet making it seem as if they were actually living. Was life only make-believe? Life is a holiday, as the song goes, you leave at the end of it, with nothing concrete to show. If you plan it too closely, it turns into work, drudgery, and when the time comes to leave, you feel cheated. But should one just wait like the Nwoyes?

In spite of this, Christian felt the Nwoyes were lucky. They seemed to have accomplished something in life, which was probably why they could wait patiently for the end. Their children were grown up and married. Their eldest son, a teacher in the elementary school, sent the money regularly, while their eldest daughter, married to a wealthy trader, sent them dried fish and meat.

Had Comfort and Joseph planned all this? Not too rigidly, perhaps. Being essentially chaotic, a mere collection of happenstance our minds gave meaning to after the fact, life abhorred such planning. There was no guarantee that a planned future would occur on schedule. Inevitably, things happened that wrecked it and only those who could bounce back or make adjustments survived. The best way to deal with such a situation was to take it all as a game. It had to be, for after all the caring, feeding, and washing our bodies received they ended up in the mud as food for worms!

Christian sighed. But what should a man do? The mind had a built-in system and would always try to impose it on anything it wanted to understand. The problem was that the body was an ant when compared to the outside elephantine world.

The morning was far gone. Christian was beginning to feel his disaster less, if he did not look round the empty shop. As Comfort had said, he had acquired the goods and he could do it again. From the time his grandfather had bought his freedom from the Aṛọ and settled at Igbo-obele his family had fought for survival, always getting up after a fall, always continuing to fight after a defeat. So, was life merely a getting-up after a fall? Maybe. Not maybe. Yes. A pregnant woman could climb a palm-tree only after it had fallen. As long as it stood straight and tall and proud, its green arms and head in the clouds, it was immune to degradation. Getting up after a fall was life and staying in the game was living.

How should he do it again? Would Nelson lend him some money to start with? Perhaps he could collect most of his debts. That should give him something to start with. Then he would write to London to ask for new samples. The thieves could not steal his talent. It was still in him.

He walked to the side wall through which the thieves dug their way into the store. It was careful and professional work. With the heavy downpour and the wall forming one side of a dirt-strewn alley, it would have been impossible to see or hear them dig the hole and cart away the goods. They must have used a truck. They could not have carried everything by hand without arousing suspicion. By now, the goods would be at the Onitsha or Nnewi market.

And the world does not even care that I am totally dispossessed, Christian thought, walking back to the store. The sun continued to shine, people to rush to their destinations, everybody minding his own business as though nothing had happened. Except for the little, curious crowd that had gathered in the morning, he might as well not have suffered the most crushing blow in his life. Not that he was unfamiliar with the indifference of the world, but it was one thing to be mentally aware of something and another to feel it physically. No matter how much empathy one had for another being in pain, experiencing the pain oneself was often a revelation.

My next shop must be in a house built with cement blocks, that is if there is going to be another shop. Christian, don't start that. Of course there will be another shop. What else do you know how to do? You come from a long line of master traders. It is in your blood and you will be lost in any other type of business. There has to be another shop, bigger, better and more expensive. You have to counter the indifference with a positive act—the act of survival. If you let it, the world will smother and then pulverize you, scatter you everywhere, erase any traces you may have tried to leave. Not that it will not do so whether you let it or not, but it will at least take more time. Yes, it will take a little more time, which is enough tribute to your having tried.

'Christian!' a voice called from the street.

Now who is it, Christian wondered. I should really change that name . . . Does it matter?

'Christian!' the voice called again. 'Christian!'

It was Janet. Running.

✻✻✻

The police had not been helpful. They behaved as though it was a routine matter. One of them warned Christian to be careful with his allegations (based only on a piece of dirty paper filled with scrawls) that someone like Tom Big Harry could have had a hand in the theft. What would Big Harry do with all that cheap merchandise?

Christian was furious at their blatant indifference. He wanted to accuse them of having a hand in the robbery, but Janet dissuaded him from doing so. He came away from the station with the feeling that *he* was the criminal. On the way home he told Janet that he found it hard to believe the two policemen he had spoken to were Igbo.

'But they are not,' Janet had said.

'What do you mean? I don't want any of your parables.'

'Those men stopped being Igbos the day they joined the police. They are now *ndi-police*, just as we are *ndi-Igbo*.'

Now that he thought about it, Janet had been right. So had Comfort, in her own way, when she had called the policemen *white men*. Something happened to those men after they joined the force. It was the same thing that happened to new Christian converts or Roman Catholic seminarians. They became totally different people with new ties, allegiances and sympathies that cut across and very often severed old ones. Were policemen, seminarians and the like, not aliens amongst the other inhabitants of the geographical area known as Nigeria? Or perhaps they alone were the true Nigerians?

'You are not eating,' Janet said. 'You should not think too much about what happened. Before long we will have a better and bigger shop.'

'We?'

'You remember I promised to give you the money with which to start a new shop.'

'Truly?'

'Christian, you know what happened pained me too.'

'Truly?'

Christian started washing his hands.

'If there is something you want to tell me why don't you say it?' Janet said.

'You know what I am trying to tell you.' Christian left the table and went to his favourite cushion chair. He was so glad this day was finally over. It had been a long day and the last thing he wanted was to start a quarrel with Janet. It felt good to stretch out his feet, safe for the time being from the outside world and from those who had plans for life. If life was really getting from one point to another, they were going about it in a most roundabout fashion. Only a fool who intended to get somewhere continuously retraced his steps, stopping only when he fell dead. A journey had a beginning and an end. Or did it?

Christian wished he had some wine but remembered he should be saving every penny towards his new shop.

'Christian,' Janet said, settling in the next chair, 'do you hate me?'

'Hate you?'

'Yes, hate me. Sometimes I have the feeling that you do.'

'Everything of yours is always different.'

They were silent as Vitus came in and cleared the table. As soon as he left Christian said quickly:

'Janet, I do not want to quarrel tonight.'

'I do not want to quarrel either.'

'Is there anything else you want to talk to me about?'

'Yes. I would like to help you look for a new shop tomorrow.'

'That is good.'

'How much do you need to stock a new shop?'

'Why not wait till we find one?'

'You mean you will allow me to give you the money after all?'

Christian sat up. 'What do you want to do to me? Buy me?'

Janet laughed. 'There you go again. I am only begging you to let me help. You know I do not have any money. You own me and whatever I have.'

'I have never heard you say that.'

'You have never listened to me. Once I start talking, you take your ears away from what I am saying. When you married me, I promised to love, cherish and obey you. I am yours.'

Did she ever say that to me? Christian asked himself. He could not recall it, but she sounded as though she meant it. Previously, she had drawn a line between herself and her material possessions, now she was throwing everything in. Had he finally broken her armour of selfishness, fashioned in the smithy of her drunken father? Or was this another tactic in her game of usury? Well, two can play that game, can they not? When Christ threw out the money-changers from the temple, did he not then try to sell his father's house to the gullible? Did he not say to the young, rich man, 'Give up all your possessions and follow me?' What a price to pay!

'All right,' Christian said, fixing his eyes on the face he thought he knew so well. 'How much can you give me?'

'How much do you want?'

'I am going to sleep. I have no strength for your games.'

Christian stood up and stretched. He was more tired than he thought. But he was not really sleepy. The bed was cool and luxurious. As he rolled and bundled himself up, relishing the unwound feeling that permeated his body, he felt a tumescence. And he did not mind it. He welcomed it. It was the kind of arousal that did not demand a release. After a while, he took off his *lappa*.

What am I doing? he wondered. He sensed rather than knew what he was doing.

Janet soon joined him, bringing a tenseness with her. It did not bother him. It was a pleasant counterpoint to his relaxed, inner feeling. Slowly it made him poised but not alert, expectant but not anxious. He lay still on his side wondering what she would do when she discovered his naked arousal.

It took her longer than he expected. She was at first surprised, then doubting, and when certainty dawned on her, silent and oddly hesitant, like a new bride.

PART THREE

Chapter One

1 ✂ Memory has a way of retouching scenes and events, darkening here, heightening there. Remembrance is rarely total recall, no matter how deeply one has suffered or greatly rejoiced. It is often like traversing a great distance covering hills and valleys, and stopping at a certain point to look back to where one has just been. All one sees is a huge area sloping gently up or down or lost in the horizon in its flatness or cut short by a nearby steep hill that seems now not that high. And forgotten would be the sharp little stones that were strewn on the road, the sinking, dragging sensation of sun-heated sand underfoot, the hard, hot and smooth surfaces of the steep inclines and the dangerous ruts with their invisible bits of broken glass, pins, nails, and pieces of iron. So everything seems telescoped together, the pain oftentimes coming out as sweet-bitter and the ease more than it was. Then which is the more faithful record?

It is hard to say with certainty. Certain events loom higher in significance than the tall iroko tree, even *Oji Nwoke*. Sometimes, assuming an event to be the signal of a profound change in our lives, we watch the dawning of each day with trepidation and expectation, wondering, 'Is this going to be the day?' Most of the time *the* day never comes. Days dawn, rise and sink into yesterdays, which in turn become many days ago and finally long ago. Trepidation eases and we are back once more to a boring routine.

Looking back now from the vantage point of 1944, Nelson realized that Madame Òbò had come and gone like a passing light, growing fainter in the distance, turning into the faint impulse of a memory of an excitation. Was that all? Nelson did not think so. During her 'brief' illumination she left something with him—the rich taste and scent of the freedom of the senses, the liberating effect of experimentation and the joy of total abandon. They were things a wife could not give because if she did, she would cease to be a *wife*.

As an official institution, a wife was expected to follow certain accepted modes of behaviour laid down and ritualized by practice. Any deviation from this was frowned upon, and to disregard it brought condemnation.

A prostitute on the other hand was like wild yam. You could do what you liked with it, wherever and whenever you pleased. Like wild yam, you had to cultivate the taste for it. But there Nelson had failed. After a period of revelling in its newness, he had wanted to domesticate it. At the time he had thought he was only trying to keep her just for himself, but she forced him to see his intentions.

'Why are you making faces like a child who has been refused permission to play?' she had asked him the morning after another of her three days-and-nights disappearances.

He had kept tight hold of himself. There was this strong urge to grab and break her in two. No, just hit her a couple of times till she begged for mercy, till she realized she was playing with a *man's* anger not a child's.

'Are you hungry?' she asked.

He could not decide which was more annoying, her sugary sweetness or motherly concern.

'Where did you go?' he asked.

'Who is asking?'

'Shut up if you do not want to answer my question,' he suddenly shouted. 'You are a woman! A woman that has to spread her legs to urinate, not a god.'

'Be careful what you say,' she said coldly. 'You are not in your own house.'

Nelson had stood up more infuriated than before, but not enough to overlook the truth in her statement. 'I can say what I choose whether I am in my house or not,' he said.

The hands propelled him out of the room, through the large drinking-room cool with morning emptiness, and into the street. They let him go after pushing him down the street for a few yards.

'Do not look behind you if you know what is good for you,' a voice had growled in his right ear.

He had not looked back. It was not that he was afraid. It just did not seem important. He needed something strong enough to keep him away from Madame Òbò and in his mind he purposely built up horrible images of the owners of the hands that propelled him out of the house. To see their faces would let him discover how human they were, for he was not and could not be afraid of any man born of a woman. Besides he had felt his relationship with Madame Òbò was coming to an end. The feeling of an impending explosion, to which her disappearances had merely contributed, had been growing on him for months.

So he was glad to walk home in the brightly clad and fast ripening morning. Luckily Ejiaka was not home. She must have gone to the market with Okechukwu. He changed into his *lappa* and sat in his favourite armchair. With three hours to spare before going to work, he wanted to comprehend partially at least, what had just happened to him; for as Ibealọ had once said, life was like a proverb, its meaning could not be derived as a whole from the combined meaning of its elements.

First the facts. He had lost Madame Òbò. He had nearly struck her. He had been goaded on by jealousy of an unknown man, a man who had a stronger pull over her, a man she would never give up under any circumstances. Did this mean he could not share a woman? With whom? Yes, that was the real question. With whom? Of one thing he was certain, he could share a woman with the faceless crowd. It was like living in the market place. Anyone, anything was free to walk in, including the living and the dead. But he could not share a woman with *one* man, known or unknown.

Now that he had lost Madame it was time to be reconciled with Ejiaka.

※※※

But all that was more than a year ago. During that period he had become reconciled with Ejiaka, she had become pregnant, and later had had a still-birth.

The still-birth had shaken Ejiaka badly, and in looks she

changed overnight from a young wife to a mother of many children. He had comforted her and made her realize that all one could do about a broken pot was cry, then wipe away the tears and go right out and buy a new one. One must not allow fear to take hold or one would never carry another pot to the stream. That night she had lain close to him but remembering she had not menstruated he refrained from touching her.

Since meeting an Nri diviner, soon after Madame Òbò sent him away, he had been careful not to break old taboos intentionally. Okwomma was something else. Sometimes Nelson wondered if he was all human, especially when he put *nzu* round his eyes to look into the future. He had predicted the still-birth and explained that it had to occur because his ancestors were angry over the Madame Òbò escapade. He had also said that Janet would be away when it happened. At the time Nelson's scepticism did not let him tell anyone what Okwomma had *seen*. Now all his predictions had come true. It was uncanny.

And that had not been all. Okwomma had told him why Mgbeke not only lost her only pregnancy but died. Nelson remembered how he ran home afterwards and searched frantically for the letter Mgbeke had sent just before she died. How did the diviner get hold of it? he had wondered. The letter was where he had put it the day after he received it—at the bottom of his wooden trunk box. He read it again, seeing it anew, now that the blinding scales of Christianity had fallen from his eyes. Written by a schoolboy not sure of his English, the message was still clear, especially the central part which laid an egg and began to incubate it in Nelson's brain.

> It is because I see the place I lose child from my belly. Too it mean I will not get belly anymore and I will die after some months. That place is big medicine. I catch it because I see. I go church many times but it did not help . . .

Sometimes we see, and sometimes we don't, even when what we are looking for is right in front of us. At other times we hear, and then at other times we don't, even if the sound is as loud as that of the gun of the heavens. Things, words, thoughts rush in and out. We say, 'don't forget' to ourselves and yet we forget. Many times we say 'remember', but who remembers all that he

202

wants to? Days pass, we grow older, things either remain the same or become more confused. Then one day we are no more. All our plans come to nothing. The few that do are not even permanent.

Nelson had heard rumours of the powers of the creek Mgbeke had visited. They had been only two months at Port Harcourt when she told him about it. *Iyi nwa nnunu*, a bird-shaped inlet full of silt and crab holes during the fall of the tide, but filled with greenish-blue water at high tide. He dismissed it as one of those things rumours often magnified. The appearance at high tide of something like an eye where the left eye of the bird should be and a great commotion in the centre would naturally be credited with extraordinary powers. She expressed a wish to see it and he did not try to dissuade her. Once they had planned to go together but he forgot all about it. Maybe he was lucky.

The inlet was more than thirty yards wide and was bridged at its narrowest part. This bridge had a way of disappearing at six o'clock in the evening when the sun set, until sunrise the next day, and mammy wagon drivers would not go anywhere near there at those times even if it were a matter of life and death. The *mammy-water* that supposedly lived in the creek was said to lure young drivers to the water to live with her. She was able to get one man, a headstrong boastful man from Okigwe who must have had some ancestral affinity with Mgbeke.

Mgbeke should have known better. Pregnant women were forbidden to visit the inlet before the tide came in, and the *mammy-water* with it, to take the sacrifices left by her devoted worshippers. There was the fear that the hungry *mammy-water* would prefer to eat the more succulent spirit of the unborn baby to the eggs, akara balls, liver, chicken, animal hearts and wine that were offered. And as there was a bond between the spirit of the unborn and that of the mother, the mother might lose her life as well.

That was what had happened to Mgbeke. No matter how strong one was, one did not go empty-handed to work in a farm. You had to take at least a small hoe in case there were weeds that could not be pulled by hand. Mgbeke pregnant had nothing but herself.

Nelson wondered how she had felt when she learnt she was

soon to die. It was good that many things remained hidden from us. Knowledge of an impending disaster often made it worse. No, that was not exactly right. His advance knowledge that Ejiaka would have a still-birth had made its happening easier to bear. Knowledge is power, in certain cases.

Okwomma himself had commended him for leaving the Roman Catholic church when he did. He had told the great diviner, 'Once a god that is supposed to give starts taking, it is time to drive *him* away before *he* asks for your life in sacrifice.'

Nelson had never seen Okwomma laugh so hard.

'When a handshake goes up to the elbow it becomes a wrestling match,' Nelson had added. 'Have you ever heard of a man that won a wrestling match with a god?'

'Yes, a man that is backed by a greater god,' Okwomma had said. 'Your forefathers had a powerful god.'

'My forefathers?'

'Yes,' Okwomma said, nodding emphatically, 'Your forefathers. They are waiting for you to call them to your side. The time for playing with foreign gods is over.'

Nelson had fallen silent. What could he say? When he was with his master at *Ndi-ikereọnwu*, another famous diviner had also told him about the great power of his family and clan god, but he was warned at the same time not to try to communicate with the god yet:

'You are like the palm-oil at the bottom of an old *ite-nkpa*. You have to be boiled thoroughly for the good oil to surface. So, go into the world first. I see you working with and trying to live like the white man. I see you following the white man's god. I even see you trying to act like the white man and other *mbakameshi*. But after all is done you will return to the ways of your ancestors. Your heart is with them, and they will always look out for you. When you feel as if they are no longer around, when you feel alone and the wind touches the exposed and unexposed parts of your body, you will look for them through other diviners and you will find them. They will protect you.'

That great diviner had sent him to a well-known *dibia* in the town to obtain a personal amulet. When the *dibia* learnt that he was the personal servant of Mbonu Ike, he had asked him to bring only a chicken to be sacrificed in the preparation of the amulet that the *dibia* called the 'eyes' of his ancestors. That was the only fee.

It was not the first time Nelson had heard about his ancestors. They had been great men in their time, excelling in whatever they did—farming, slave-trading, music-making, travelling and the white man's work.

There was no doubt about it. Knowledge is power, whether to the front or to the back.

'How do I call my ancestors to my side?' Nelson had asked Okwomma.

His eyes, dark pools surrounded by broad white banks of *nzu*, his small face an inquisitive, pointed darkness boring into a man with the air of a 'seeing' dog, Okwomma had finally said, 'When you really want to, you will know.'

Yes, knowledge was power. But again that was more than a year ago.

※※※

There was the month in which nothing went right. First, there was the Awka man who had just been promoted to Chargeman Grade One and put in charge of Nelson's gang. He took a fancy to Nelson because, the man said, they belonged to Awka district and were brothers.

Nelson had liked the idea of being liked by an Igbo *ọga*, but soon saw it was different in practice. The man took to sending him all over the place as though he was a boy-boy. Nelson did not mind doing things for a district man, but turning him into an errand boy interfered with his job and he was invariably blamed if anything went wrong! But the one that hurt the most was the query he had to answer about the engine a driver reported as leaving the running shed with badly packed truck-boxes. The train was seven hours late. But for the diligence of the driver it would have ended with burnt-out wheels.

It was a very serious offence that normally would have earned the Fitter-in-Charge a severe reprimand. Those who had actually worked on the packing would have been demoted. Yet, the Chargeman, a brother, falsely stated that Nelson, as deputizing Fitter Grade One, was wholly responsible for the engine. The truth saved Nelson however. He had been on another job when the Chargeman had *passed* the engine, and therefore could not be held accountable for the sloppy work that was done. The Chargeman was reprimanded and posted up north to Zaria a month later. But before this happened, Nelson had had to walk around on gentle feet, afraid the Chargeman would do him harm.

A week later, a fitter who had just returned from the railway station reported that it was filled with soldiers and policemen. Three of the soldiers had boarded the engine he and the shunting driver had taken to the point, and demanded to see the driver's permit to wear new army boots. When the driver handed it over, one of them spelt out the word PERMIT printed in bold, black type across the top of the paper. Suddenly the tallest of the three popped the permit into his mouth, chewed and spat it out. They then resumed their demands for the driver's permit. The shunting driver, a big, husky man tried to argue with them but they kept asking for his permit as if he had been talking to the wall.

'Way your pamit?' one of them would ask.

'Na him I give you jus' now,' the driver would say, standing up to them while the fitter cowered in the corner.

'Way your pamit?' another one would ask.

The driver would repeat his earlier reply, and the third soldier would ask the question again. It was only when the tallest of the three, who seemed to be the leader, asked his followers, 'Abi una see am give us anything?' and the men had said 'No!' that the driver got the message.

The tall soldier turning to him said, 'You hear now? Dem say you no give us nothing. Way your pamit? Bringam quick quick.'

'Ah no get pamit,' the driver said hesitantly.

'Awright. Comot the army boot quick,' the soldier commanded. 'We take you to police.'

The driver bent down, pulled them off, then swiftly opening the blazing furnace of the boiler threw them in and clamped the door shut. With a shout the tall soldier grabbed the handle of the furnace, but his cry of pain was louder as he quickly withdrew his hand. A black welt lay across his palm like a mark. From the ground a number of armed policemen shouted,

'What matter there?'

The tall soldier glared at the driver and hissed, 'I go get you for this!' turned round and led his companions down.

The driver and the fitter were afraid to move. After a while a policeman with three stripes on his beefy shoulders climbed up the engine. Taking in the huge barefoot driver and the cowering fitter he smiled.

'Did they hurt you?' he asked the driver, in Yoruba.

The driver shook his head, smiled and said, '*Oshe-o!*' The policeman smiled and climbed down.

When he heard the story, Nelson knew he had to get to his house immediately. It was ten in the morning and he had been at work for only three hours. Deciding not to obtain permission from the Chargeman or the Time-Keeper, he told his gang he suspected that he had a running stomach, and he sneaked away over the low fence when he thought no one was looking.

He arrived home breathless, having run most of the way. Ejiaka was out. In the bedroom he stripped the bed of its old army blanket, fished under it for the new, unstudded pair of army boots, took the heavy, grey army sweater from a pile of clothes and the greatcoat from his wooden trunk box. Now that he had them in a neat pile he realized he had not thought of how to dispose of them. Then he remembered the ceiling. Would they search there? Not if he hid them above the sitting-room.

When he finally returned from work that afternoon his worst fears were realized. There was a search going on and all the people had been turned out into the yard. The searchers here appeared to be only policemen and he wondered why soldiers had taken part in the running shed. His house had been stormed through and Ejiaka was trying to put things back in their proper places. Okechukwu was giving a 'helping hand'.

'Papa, *nno*,' Okechukwu said.

'Eeya, my son,' Nelson said, lifting him off his feet. The child squealed with delight, but as soon as he caught his breath cried out,

'Put me down, put me down. Mama and I are working.'

Nelson put him down.

'You were dismissed early,' Ejiaka said.

'Yes.'

'You have seen what they did.'

'Did they find anything?' Nelson asked.

'No,' Ejiaka said. 'Where . . .' she began.

Nelson silenced her with his eyes. 'There will be no trouble,' he whispered.

Ejiaka who had been looking unhappy and apprehensive smiled, her thin fair face coming alive.

'You should have seen me rush to the bedroom when I heard the police were coming. I do not know what would have done if I had seen them there. Mrs. Jeremiah wore her blanket covered with a *lappa*.'

'She must have been triple enormous,' Nelson said laughing.

'She was and the police were not suspicious. Our back alley is full of discarded army clothing. Shall I get you your lunch?'

'After those beasts have left.'

He was about to ask for Onyeama but remembered the boy had been gone for two weeks now. First Ida, and then Onyeama. For a time they were here and now it is as if they had never been, their presence a memory.

Ejiaka was soon done with straightening things out. The noise outside had subsided. Probably the police had moved on. Nelson changed into his *lappa* and sat in the sitting-room.

'Have you heard from Anthony again?' Ejiaka asked, coming into the room.

'Yes,' Nelson said. 'I think I saw him yesterday. He was looking very well.'

'Is he still going to join the army?'

'Yes.'

'I heard at the market that all the soldiers will be sent to fight in the white man's country.'

'That will not stop Anthony. He has made friends with some of the soldiers that swarm into his shed like flies to buy fresh fish. They complain to him that their barrack-food would not keep a dog alive. Owerri-men do all the cooking there.'

'And Anthony still wants to join up? Is he quite sane?'

'He says he knows what he is doing. In a few months' time he will go to Zaria to start his training. He says he will tell them he is married and that you are his wife. They pay married men more.'

Ejiaka laughed. 'Is that how one gets married these days? Now

I see why they say that a mother whose son is a soldier really has no child.'

Okechukwu ran in from the backyard and clung to his mother's legs. 'Mama, I am hungry,' he said.

'Have you not eaten?' Nelson asked.

'The police came as we were about to eat.' Ejiaka lifted Okechukwu up to her side. '*Nna*, we will eat soon, all right?'

'I am hungry,' the child said.

'Go and get the food. We will all eat together.'

'Do you think it will be safe for Anthony to claim me as his wife?' Ejiaka asked quickly.

'He said there will be no trouble. Many soldiers do it and the white man does not check anyway. What I say is anyone who can cheat the white man and get away with it, should do so. White men are not human beings.'

The next week Nelson was suspended from the Awka District Association for conduct unbecoming a 'brother'. His Chargeman who seemed to have a strong influence in the association, had reported Nelson and made him out to be a liar in his reply to a railway query. Nelson was unhappy about his suspension because he had hoped that if the railway authorities failed to believe his statement, the members of the Association who were not only Igbos but also brothers from the same area would. Now, he knew that the only brother he had was one born of the same father and mother, or at most from the same village. As Under-Fitter Grade One Jonathan had said to him:

'Why are you shocked an Awka man got you suspended from the Association? Before the white man came an Awka man would not see you walking alone and let you go. It is the white man that is making us think we are brothers. We know within ourselves that we are not and will never be in our lifetime. You may change the *avuke* but you can't change the bird itself.'

It was the next day that Nelson received the letter that drove him to Okwomma again to find out what the gods were trying to do to him. The letter had reported that his grandfather's brother's son, Nwaolu, had died a horrible death as a result of swearing a false oath. Nelson hoped he would not have to be the one to look after Nwaolu's young family although he knew he would be the logical choice. It would not be easy to guide the children, especially if they had inherited their father's stubbornness and disrespect for elders.

Okwomma had seemed sympathetic.

'You say he died of the disease of the swollen stomach?'

'Yes,' Nelson said. 'He swore an oath that someone's land was his. So the goddess took his life.'

'Then you do not need to mourn him. His manner of death is an abomination.'

'No, I am not mourning him. I am just worried about my future. So many bad things have happened to me this month that I would like to find out the cause. If it is something that requires a sacrifice, I will make one.'

'You have done well to come.'

Okwomma got out his divining equipment, marked himself with *nzu* and did some preliminary throws, grunting after he had read each one. Nelson watched him anxiously from a low stool nearby, wishing he too could read the future.

'You know,' Okwomma suddenly said, leaning back and looking at his last throw with quizzical eyes, 'I was just thinking of you yesterday and wondering when you were going to come and see me again. If it had not been taboo for us to look into our own futures I would have done so yesterday. Something was whispering to me that a very important thing was going to happen to you that would change your life. But since you had to come and find out for yourself, all I could do was wait. And now you are here I feel my little messenger of yesterday was right.'

Okwomma stopped and for the first time looked Nelson directly in the eyes.

'Bring out all the money you have on you,' he ordered suddenly, 'and put it in this circle here.' He drew a circle with *nzu* at a half-arm's length from himself.

Nelson hesitated but did as he was told. He had two shilling pieces and three pennies.

'Ngene!' Okwomma intoned as he threw the divining seeds, repeating the action at the end of each statement, each question, nodding his head as though the answers he read did not only augur well but were precisely what he expected. 'You have seen what he did,' he went on, 'and how he did it. It is now left to you to decide if he did well. If he did well should he be charged a fee? You are the only one that sees. I am merely an interpreter and transmitter of what you say. If he is to be charged a fee, how much? Truly? No, that cannot be true. Let us do it again. But *Ngene*, your mouth-piece has to eat. All right. Do not be angry. I have heard you. All right. I will do as you say.'

Okwomma sighed and wiped the beads of sweat from his forehead. He leant back against the whitewashed wall as though worn out.

'Nelson, *ngbọ*,' he said.

Nelson did not know how to react to the praise name. 'What is it now?' he asked uncertainly.

'Nothing,' Okwomma said. 'Put your money back in your pocket. Leave only a penny. My *agwu* will not allow me to accept anything more than that.'

'Is that a good thing?' Nelson asked.

'Is that a good thing?' Okwomma repeated, resuming his divination. 'He asked if that was a good thing. You see the young man thinks we feed on the wind. He forgets that part of us is human too. Yes, I hear you. Nelson,' Okwomma said sharply, 'I said pick up all your money except a penny. It is good,' Okwomma continued, after Nelson had quickly scooped up the money. 'Now listen to me. You have nothing to worry about. As I told you before, you are very well protected. You see I cannot even charge you more than a penny. Even my *agwu* is with you. The bad things that are happening to you now are designed to remind you your ancestors are waiting. It is getting to the time when you are to call them to your side. You will know when that time comes. No man will tell you. Also, the bad happenings are to prepare you for a great and wonderful thing that will soon happen to you. Life is a string made of black and red beads. The black ones represent good things, while the red represent bad. You have just had the bad. The good will soon follow.

'I know you will ask, what good thing will happen to me? Let me see if I can tell you. Yes I can. It is . . . it is a promotion. Yes a promotion. And it will happen by the end of the month. You have had all the bad things so far—the trouble with your Chargeman, the soldiers, and the death in your family. Now it is the turn of the good. When you hear of the promotion give your ancestors a white cock. That is all. Do not come to me because I will not be here. I will be going on a long journey in two days' time. I will come back at a time when you will need me again. So do not look for me. When you need me, come and bring a new penny with you. Did you hear all that I said? Did you note all that I said? Get up and leave now. Yes, leave. Do not look back. Some of us come to this world alone. Some of us come with an invisible multitude and people wonder why things come so easy to us. Remember what I said. Do not forget. Goodbye.'

Nelson left, his thoughts suspended in space, the dusk that had now arrived hiding the face of time. His apprehension about his future had dropped away from him, and in its place was a glow of pleasant anticipation, and . . . certainty. It was curious, but watching Okwomma perform the divination took all the doubts from his mind, much more than any of the Christian services he attended had done. There was something in the ritual he had just observed that touched an atavistic chord in him and brought the sun-bred optimism up to the surface. Now, each sunrise would be the herald rather than the break of another day. Each day would bring the expected fulfilment closer.

On Monday, 1st June, 1942, Nelson was promoted to Fitter Grade One. He followed Okwomma's instructions to the letter.

It was fitting and prophetic that the promotion should come in the month of June, *mgbe nhie le ju eju*. It showed beyond doubt that the powers of old had influence over, if not control of, the new alien systems.

But that was more than a year ago. And now with 1944 rushing to a close, Christmas barely a month away, and Ejiaka due to deliver in two months, there was no doubt that the ancestors were there watching, guiding and when necessary, interceding. Did Christian join them or was he in some Christian Hell waiting for the judgement?

※※※

2 ※ She had appeared at the door on a hot afternoon like a wrinkle-necked vulture attracted by a sacrifice. Later Ejiaka would try but fail to remember the exact day and date. All she

knew for certain was that it was in April, somewhere in the middle of it, because had it been earlier she could have easily recalled how many days it had been after the April Fool's Day. Also then, she had been heavy with child as she was now. Her cracked voice had sawed through Ejiaka's drowsiness, leaving it with serrated edges of irritation. Ejiaka finally forced her eyes open and saw an old, stocky, ugly woman whose smile was an unpleasant display of *akanwu* teeth.

'Dalu nuo,' the old woman said.

Ejiaka struggled into a sitting position in the cushion-chair. Her blouse was soaking wet, and her seven-month baby inside her sat heavily in her stomach along with the lunch of pounded foofoo and bitter-leaf soup.

'Dalu,' she said to the old woman, suppressing her annoyance with an effort. 'What can I do for you?'

'Come,' the old woman said, and beckoned with a bony right hand.

Ejiaka wished now she had closed the door before she sat down. But she did not mean to doze off and it had been so hot, closing the door would have been like shutting oneself in a burning house.

'Tell me what you want,' Ejiaka said, loath to get any closer to the old woman whose *lappa* seemed dyed in dirt, her feet flaky and ashen black, and the blouse, although made of black material, looked like compounded dirt. Ejiaka was sure the woman would have an offensive odour about her.

'Are you afraid of an old woman?' the woman asked, her smile more disgusting than her tight-lipped, wrinkled grimness.

The woman had the decency to remain at the door. Ejiaka wondered where Onyeama and Okechukwu were. Probably outside. The house was too quiet. Ejiaka stood up. She was not afraid of the woman. What harm could an old Igbo woman do to her in broad daylight?

'Now I see why it took you so long to get up,' the old woman cackled. 'You are seven months pregnant.'

How uncanny! Ejiaka remembered those fairy tales often told to children in the dead of the night or at full of noon, about prescient old hags who were in reality messengers of the ancestors. Could this woman be one of them? No one, not even her close friends could have guessed so accurately how many months pregnant she was. Their guesses were often months off because she carried her baby high. Even at full term she looked only six or seven months pregnant.

'Good afternoon, ma,' Ejiaka said, ashamed of her earlier antagonism towards the woman.

'Good afternoon, my child,' the woman said, backing away a few steps. 'Do not come too close, my daughter, I do not want you to get sick. The noses of pregnant women *see* smells miles away.'

Ejiaka stopped, grateful for such consideration.

'What can I do for you?'

'Can you give me a penny, my daughter?'

'One penny?'

'Yes. You will not regret it.'

'I will be back.'

Ejiaka got the penny from her bag in the bedroom.

'May you not die early,' the old woman said, accepting it. 'May the child you are carrying be a boy. And if you already have a boy, may it be a girl. May the child grow up tall and strong and be a source of pride and happiness to you and your husband. I see you are a very good and generous woman. You do not look like those arrogant town women. May goodness and fortune follow you wherever you go. May your husband's love be like an iroko tree, strong enough to support you when you need it, and tall and leaf-laden to give you shelter from rain and sun.'

'*Ise*,' Ejiaka said.

'What is your name?'

'Mary,' Ejiaka lied. The profuse prayer had put her on her guard.

'Mary? You are a Christian?'

'No. Are Christians the only ones that answer Mary?'

'Don't you know? Mary is the mother of the Christian god.'

'My husband gave me the name. I did not know it had any meaning or that it is that of the mother of the Christian god.'

'It is good that you are not a Christian because I would not have told you what I am going to tell you now. I am Nwaigwe of Agbenu. I am one who sees. My eyes see better than those of a watchdog. I use my vision to warn people about bad things that can happen to them in the future. I warn them against the evil of some of their children who come to this world to punish their parents and plunge them into sorrow. When I was young I had many of them. They came, deceived me and ran back. I did not have the vision then. Now that I have it I can revenge all the sorrow they caused me by forcing them to stay on in this world. With my vision I can spot the evil ones before they sicken and die. I can also find where they buried their symbols. Once we dig up their symbols they are exposed and cannot run back to their playmates with whom they entered into pacts before coming to this world. You have one child, where is he?'

'Playing outside,' Ejiaka said, now mesmerized by the woman. What the woman said about ọgbanje children was true. They caused a great deal of sorrow to their parents, often dying when they were most loved, or being born and dying time and time again. Their corpses had to be mutilated to break the cycle. Ejiaka's two elder sisters had been ọgbanje till they were discovered by a woman with the vision.

'Your son is two years old now?' the woman said rather than asked.

'How did you know?' Ejiaka asked, suddenly afraid. The woman caused such varying emotions in her that she now wished to end their conversation as quickly as possible.

The old woman laughed softly, a pleasant enough laugh that seemed, however, charged with import.

'If you knew how many people have asked me the same question,' the woman said, 'you would understand why I laugh. But yours is not that of someone who does not know, but of someone who is afraid. I have already told you I will not hurt you, so why are you afraid?'

'My son is not ọgbanje,' Ejiaka said. Much as she wanted to terminate their conversation she had to be careful not to offend the old woman. Her type was often vengeful and malicious. A pregnant woman was very vulnerable and an unborn baby even more so. Intimate communication with the spirit-world makes it easier for the living to slip through the now fragile barrier into the nether world.

215

'What of you, are you?'

'Me?' Ejiaka could not snatch her eyes away from the intense, small ones in front of her. 'I am too old.'

'But very much loved. Age has nothing to do with *ogbanje*. Love is the key. It attracts them. It drives them away. But it does not change them. Only hatred can do that. Are you an *ogbanje*?'

For a second fear and nausea swept Ejiaka from her toes up to her head. She swayed and closed her eyes to steady herself. Within herself she was protesting, 'I am not. I am not.'

'You are not,' the old woman said.

Ejiaka opened her eyes, glad to find herself still standing in front of the woman. Although nothing had changed and the sun shone as bright as ever, she felt a great deal of time had elapsed since she closed her eyes. The old woman stared at her as though she would disappear or melt like oil. And she did feel queasy and oily. She wiped her face, her palm ashine with oil. The heat of the sun often had this effect on her, made her exude oil instead of sweat. What is happening to me? she asked herself. What is this horrible woman doing to me?

'Your son is coming home,' the old woman said.

Ejiaka peered out through the door hoping it was not true. In the distance Onyeama was returning home, with Okechukwu perched on his right shoulder. Should she send the old woman away? Should she go into the house? Undecided she stood where she was.

'*Ewo*,' the old woman exclaimed, 'your son is so plump and so handsome.'

'Good afternoon, ma,' Onyeama said, stopping at the door.

'Good afternoon, my child,' the old woman said. 'Turn around, let me see his face. He is sleeping so peacefully. I will not wake him.'

The old woman took Okechukwu's right hand and gently turned the palm upwards. She looked at it frowningly and then let it go.

'Go and put him to bed, my son,' she said. 'This sun is too hard for him.'

Ejiaka, her heart beating fiercely, made way for Onyeama to pass, and followed him with her eyes till he disappeared into the bedroom. Turning to the old woman she asked in a whisper, 'Is he?'

'No,' the old woman said showing her ugly teeth. 'But you must do something for him soon or he will not live to be five years old.'

Ejiaka was angry now. In order not to give voice to the many words in her chest she went back to her chair.

'You are not to blame for that,' the old woman said in an understanding tone. 'It is written in the boy's hand. You have been so nice to me I would have not told you if I did not think I was helping you. Remember what I said. Everything is in your hands. Do not depend on your husband.'

As Ejiaka sat down the old woman moved away. But her going was not soon enough for Ejiaka. Hot and nauseated again Ejiaka felt like tearing off all her clothing. She felt bound by them and there was no breath of fresh air. And the baby was kicking in her womb.

'What did that woman want?' Onyeama asked.

'She is a beggar,' Ejiaka said faintly, struggling to gain control over herself so that Onyeama would not know how badly she was feeling.

'Is there anything you want me to do?'

Ejiaka shook her head using the motion to avoid the keen look Onyeama gave her. She wanted Onyeama to leave quickly, and yet a part of her wanted him to stay just in case . . . just in case? She should go and lie down, and try to get some sleep.

'I am going to Idigo's house,' Onyeama said. 'I will return before five o'clock to start dinner.'

'Greet his mother for me,' Ejiaka said. 'And . . .' she began, but stopped. 'Don't worry. Go where you are going.'

She wanted to send for Janet but that might have told him something was wrong. As it was he hesitated before finally leaving.

Once in bed Ejiaka began to feel better. The old woman was right, Okechukwu was a beautiful child. He looked so young and helpless by Ejiaka's side she was tempted to cover him with her body, to shield him from all evil and dangers of this world. But all she did was straighten his right arm which he had characteristically bent into an awkward configuration.

What was he dreaming? His small lips were moving as though sucking the breast. He must have been tired out at play to be taking his afternoon siesta so early. It meant he would go to bed early tonight. Propping up her head with her left palm she watched his steady, rhythmic breathing with delight. His features were like his father's, especially the chin and the nose. No, he could not be an ọgbanje. Thanks to Madame Òbò he had been weaned at the right age without any misunderstanding. Nelson was not the type that could go without a woman for years, very few men were. Sex was a type of hunger to them and as soon as it was satisfied it came up again.

She was glad she had handled the Madame Òbò situation the way she did. Had she followed Janet's advice she would have lost everything. Christians always regarded having two wives as evil, but it was better than starving a wife and lavishing all the wealth on a kept woman. Even the children did not gain from such arrangements. So, let your rival into your house. Knowing her intimately would strip her of all mythic qualities, and the outcome of any competition would depend on skill and endurance. Even a dog fought better and lasted longer when its life was at stake.

Ejiaka lay back, trying to let the luxuriousness of the cool bed fill her mind, smother the thoughts that would not go away. Just as she was succeeding a cry came from the backyard, sharply drawn out, and ending in a choking sound. Who could be making a child cry in this hot sun? Only Amoge could put that knifing, heart-cutting quality into her cry. But her mother was immune to it. One could be immune to anything if one lived long enough with it.

What would Nelson say if he was told that something had to be done so that Okechukwu would not die before he was five? *Chineke ekwene ihe ọjọ!* And that old woman did not say what could be done. Perhaps a *dibia* or a diviner would know, but where could one find a good *dibia*? It was easy at home, but to find one in this township would be like looking for a black goat on a moonless night. Townships were swamps full of crocodiles, water-snakes and tigers in human form, each out for something to eat, someone to gobble up or kill for the fun of it.

Okechukwu cried out in his sleep Ejiaka turned to him

quickly and smiled. His eyes were wide open, brilliant and big.

'Mama!' he said plaintively.

'*Nna*,' Ejiaka said, tenderly placing her hand on his forehead. It was hot.

'Mama,' he said again, his eyes beginning to close.

Ejiaka said nothing this time. He was in the half-and-half world. He would soon be completely claimed by the world of sleep.

No, Okechukwu cannot be an *ogbanje*, Ejiaka thought, even though it was in her family. Ejiaka had been ten years old when the younger of her two older sisters revealed the secret pact they had made prior to being born into the world.

Her sisters had been ill for days with acute malaria when the elder confessed they were *ogbanjes* loath to leave the world because they had not known it would be so good. Under her direction the family hearth, the vegetable farm, the roots of the tallest coconut tree and the oldest iroko tree, were frantically dug up. But their symbols were not found.

Everyone had almost given up hope when the younger girl suddenly staggered to the barn, her eyes wide with fear, her flushed face wet with malarial sweat.

'She is deceiving you,' she cried, pointing wildly at her elder sister. 'She does not want us to stay. I have begged her many times to let us remain here, but she will not listen. She has no heart. But I will betray her secret. Yes, I will betray her and make her stay even if I die. It is not good for both of us to leave at the same time.'

'Mgbafor, my child,' her mother exclaimed and burst into tears.

'Do not cry, do not cry for them,' many people cried. 'That is what they want. It will certainly make them leave.'

In the meantime, Mgbafor had run into the barn and halted at the farthest end where a few heaps of *nkpuru ji* were kept. She glanced rapidly to her left and right as though searching for a missing trail and began to moan softly, then to cry and finally to shout and jump around.

'She will not let me,' she cried. 'I can go no farther. Look, she **is** sitting there holding a gun. She is pointing the gun at me.

Nkechi, please do not shoot me. I am your sister. I promise I will not reveal your secret. I promise! I promise! I promise!'

And she collapsed.

People ran to her. She was still alive but the silence in which she was carried back to the house was for the dead. Nkechi had not moved since she gave the last false direction to those searching for her symbol. Her mother sat on the floor of the hut, dry-eyed and sorrowful.

It was then that the oldest and most respected ọgbanje hunter, Egbe-ichi, arrived. She had been sent for days ago and her timely entry testified to her having supernatural powers. Lean, sharp-eyed, a burnt-black old woman with a shock of off-white hair, the skin of her face was drawn tightly over small, protruding bones. She wore a black *lappa* tied and knotted round her waist like a woman come to do battle.

'Pour cold water on her!' she ordered as soon as she saw Mgbafor who had been laid out on the mud bed. 'She is not dead yet.'

Ejiaka's blacksmith uncle was the only one who obeyed the order. The shock of the cold water jerked Mgbafor into a sputtering, sitting position but after she had wiped her face, she sank back on to the mud.

'Where is the elder?' Egbe-ichi asked.

This time there was a scramble to show her where Nkechi lay under the shade of the Ọha tree in the centre of the compound. Egbe-ichi towered over the listless girl who now began to squirm, to try to get away from the shadow that fell on her. Egbe-ichi laughed and suddenly everyone joined in, changing the atmosphere from one of grim tragedy to comedy.

'She is afraid of my shadow. She knows what she is, and what I am.'

Turning abruptly, Egbe-ichi marched back to the house, but did not enter. Standing a few feet from the entrance she shouted: 'Mgbafor! Mgbafor! Come here quickly!'

There was absolute silence. Then an audible release of many breaths as Mgbafor came slowly out of the house, and stood in front of Egbe-ichi with bowed head.

'Look at me, you wicked child,' Egbe-ichi commanded. 'Look in my face.'

Mgbafor raised her head, took one look at Egbe-ichi's face, uttered a terrified cry and ran. No one went after her. Egbe-ichi moved only her head to follow the precipitate flight.

At the gate, Mgbafor stopped abruptly as if her legs could go no farther, and slowly turned back.

'Are you done with running?' Egbe-ichi asked her. 'I said have you finished running? You people do not know there is a difference between your world and ours. You always forget that while things last forever in your world, they last for a short time in ours. In your world it is always morning, but in ours the afternoon is on the back of the morning and the night is busy digging a hole for them before they are full blown. Where did you think you were running to? Do you think you can outrun the earth? Look at me! I said, look at me! *Nhia-a*, where did you hide the symbols?'

Mgbafor led the way into the barn again and pointed to the corner formed by the junction of the rear and side thatch walls.

'Dig it,' Egbe-ichi said without hesitation.

As the men started digging, Mgbafor quietly went back to the house. There was an expectant nervousness among the waiting crowd and it filtered through to the diggers who threw the dark packed soil to the right and left as fast as the hoe bit into it.

Suddenly, a cry of pain came from the house, fixing everyone in whatever motion he or she was in, and Nkechi ran in covered from head to toe in white dust, looking like an irate wraith.

'Don't dig any more! Don't dig any more! You will break them. You will break them.'

The men moved aside and with choking sobs Nkechi removed the loose earth from the bottom of the hole and brought out something wrapped in layers of tattered rich brocade.

'Give it to me,' Egbe-ichi said sharply, pouncing on her and snatching away the wrapped object with an agility that was as frightening as Nkechi's entrance.

Nkechi fell down in a faint.

Ejiaka never saw the objects unwrapped. In fact it was never spoken of in the house. Mgbafor and Nkechi recovered fast and in a few days were their usual laughing and joking selves, full of pranks and mock fights all aimed at their forebearing mother who feared she would and could still drive them back to their world. Now, they were the mothers of two and three children respectively.

No, Okechukwu could not be an *ogbanje*. Before Egbe-ichi left that day she had read Ejiaka's palm and pronounced her free of the *ogbanje* markings. She also commended her for resisting the pressure of her elder sisters to join, to be marked as one of them. Ejiaka had not been aware of any pressure from her sisters, but after Egbe-ichi's statement she began to watch them closely, always doing the opposite of what they did, marrying a man who lived away from home because they had married stay-at-home farmers. She did not want to belong to them, to have to leave her mother, to go to *their* world no matter how good life was over there. She found the present world immensely satisfying and enjoyable. She hoped she would be able to impart this feeling to Okechukwu.

Could she? Who knows. Each *chi* was different. If she failed she had another chance growing in her womb.

And then her chance had been stillborn, strangled according to the doctor by the umbilical cord. Who put that cord around his neck? Who deprived the child of life? Why should the innocent die while the guilty, the sinner and the perpetrators of abominations live and prosper?

Why did Janet choose to go on leave a month before the baby was due? She had postponed that leave many times till it had accumulated and laid eggs.

And why did Janet's colleague and friend, who should have taken care of everything, fall ill on the very day the baby was to be born? And why was it that it was the midwife Janet distrusted most, a thin, owl-eyed Itsekiri woman, who was on duty that day?

Why did all these circumstances come together that particular day and not any other day with another woman and another baby?

Why, why, why?

From the day she lost the baby Christian had visited her almost daily. At first she thought he spent all that time with her because he had nowhere else to go. With Janet away he seemed directionless, a surprising change in a man who always knew what he wanted, and took it.

She began to *hear* him three months after she lost the baby. Everything he said now carried a special significance far and above its surface meaning. He had a depth of feeling that bordered on despair, as though there were so many wonderful things one could enjoy in this world but the creator had not found it worthwhile to teach human beings how. There was also a deep-grained goodness and understanding he spent most of his time trying to conceal. Ejiaka was pleased to discover all these hidden traits. Always Janet had given her the impression that Christian was a bundle of evil covered with black skin.

Once, in their numerous discussions about Christianity and the old way of life, he had asked her what she thought of Janet, the devoted Christian, going to Zaria to consult a *dibia*.

'I see nothing wrong in it,' she had replied.

'*Eziokwu?*'

'Yes, truly. I suggested that she go and see the *dibia*.'

'You did? When?'

'A long time ago. If she had gone when she planned to, she would have been back long ago.'

'And you would not have lost your baby!'

'Christian! That was not what I was thinking.'

'You would not be to blame, if you thought of that.'

'But it would not be right for me to think like that.'

'Who said so? You lost the baby, so only you can really say how you feel about it. And had Janet been here, the baby might have been saved.'

'It is not right to blame anyone for that type of thing.'

'Yes, it is not fair. But who else are we to blame?'

He was right. Who else are we to blame? Our *chi*? God? Ourselves? Circumstances? No matter how much we dislike it, we do end up blaming somebody.

'What shall I cook this evening?' Onyeama asked, coming in from the backyard.

'How the day runs,' Ejiaka exclaimed. 'Christian, you will eat supper with us, won't you?'

'Will there ever be a time that I will visit and not eat?'

223

Ejiaka laughed. 'Not as long as Janet is not home to cook for you.'

'Janet did not cook when she was here.'

'Who did the cooking then?'

'Vitus.'

'Yes, but it isn't the same without Janet to supervise him.'

'You are right. That is why I have most of my meals here.'

'Yes, you really do, don't you? Onyeama, do we still have soup?'

'Yes. We have only had it for one day.'

'I don't remember things these days! We will have pounded yams tonight. We still have those big yams?'

'Yes.'

'Pound just enough for the three of us. I will prepare a fresh one for your master just before he is due to return. Okechukwu is not awake yet?'

'No.'

'So you think there is nothing wrong in a Christian going to a *dibia*?' Christian asked, as soon as Onyeama went to the kitchen to begin cooking.

'What is wrong? Tell me. The *dibia* is older than Christianity and there are things he can do that a priest cannot.'

'You are right there.'

Ejiaka laughed and said, 'Now I know what you are doing. You just want me to continue talking like a fool.'

'You do not talk like a fool. Everything you say makes sense, and I like to listen to you talk. There are two types of talkers, you see, those who talk to tell you something you do not know and those who talk because they can't help it.'

'Which group do I belong to?'

'The first one.'

Ejiaka did not know what to say to that. Compliments embarrassed her and made her tongue-tied. It was true she had never enjoyed talking with anyone as much as she did with Christian, but somehow she felt she should not be enjoying it that much. It was not right for a woman to talk so much, even with a family friend.

'I should not be talking so much anyway,' Ejiaka said.

'Who should?'

'Those who know what they are talking about.'

'And who are those?'

He was always like that, turning whatever she said into a question or a compliment. He made the time pass quickly. And the way he listened to her, as though she were an elder and he a young relation seeking advice.

Sometimes she caught him looking at her, his head tilted to one side, his thin lips slightly open, speculation shining in his eyes. Yet she was the one embarrassed by the look, for he continued to stare till she was forced to look away. And throughout the rest of his visit that day his image would stay with her, and she would wonder why he had looked at her that way, why she continued to see him in her mind's eye in different postures and attired in various suits, why when she had caught him looking at her, her heart had missed a beat and she had been the one, apparently, filled with shame. She was sure he was not fascinated by her looks because she was still too thin then.

With her new-found facility of speech she had asked him. But as she should have known, he waited till she looked at him to reply.

'I always wonder at the great difference between you and Janet.'

'What difference can there be between us?' she had asked, laughing. 'We are both women. Christian, if you want to start talking like a child, it is time for you to go.'

'Now you see what I am talking about. If I had told Janet that she was different from you she would say "Of course." But you? You laugh at my saying so, because as you said you are both women. I know you are both women, but that is all you have in common.'

'Who looks after your store when you are here?'

Christian laughed as if she had said the most amusing thing. He had been laughing a great deal lately and she did not know she could be so funny.

'You think I don't know what you are trying to do?'

Ejiaka could not suppress a smile. 'What was I trying to do?'

'You don't want me to tell you the difference between you and Janet. I am going to tell you anyway . . . You did not go to school but she did.'

'Everyone knows that.'

'But everyone does not know that *you* are more intelligent than she is.'

'How can you say such a thing, Christian? Janet is my elder.'

'Yes, but intelligence and age do not go hand in hand.'

'Janet went to school and passed her exams well to become a midwife. You can't say that is not intelligence. I am sure I couldn't do as well as she did.'

'That is because you have not tried. I know you could pass anything she passed. You can't really say how good a mother a woman will be until she has had a child.'

'You are right there,' Ejiaka conceded.

'Eh-he, that is another difference between you and Janet. She would never agree that I am right. She is always the one that is right.'

'That is because she knows so much.'

'Yes, she knows a great deal.'

'You make it sound like a bad thing.'

'It is a bad thing. You have never lived with someone who knows a great deal, someone who knows everything.'

They were silent. Christian's words lay heavy in the air as if they had been condensed into something concrete. Perhaps it was the bitterness in the words that solidified them. Ejiaka had not heard him sound so bitter before. He had always been the man of the world, independent, experienced, cheerful, even tending to be wilful. But now she could see that his pride was simply sewn on to his suits.

He did not get round to telling her the other ways she differed from Janet, and she was glad. Later when she realized that she now liked him more than just a family friend she wondered if he had intentionally, and delicately, kept away from enumerating the physical differences between her and Janet. A crude and less experienced man would have shouted them out. In fact he spoke rarely of things that were too obvious. That was a mark of knowledge . . . to see things that were hidden or concealed from other eyes. In that respect, Nelson, despite his constant studies, still had a long way to go, a very long way to catch up.

It was after that day that Ejiaka entered the most emotionally trying period of her life, all because of Christian.

She began to look forward to his visits. If he came later than usual, or failed to come altogether she passed the rest of the day in gloom. The days when he did visit on time were joyful and painful at the same time. Happy that he came, she also took pains to conceal how much it meant to her. At such times her new-found facility for words failed her. When he was gone she remembered all the things she had wanted to say to him, and the answers she should have given to his questions. She would be covered then with shame at the thought of how dumb she must have seemed to him. It was terrible. She could not understand why she felt like that for someone she had known for so long.

Janet's return made matters worse. His visits became infrequent. To see him more often she visited Janet every other evening, but it did not work well. He was rarely at home in the early evenings, and when he was it would have been better if he stayed at his shop. It made her sad to see that Janet's return had made their intimacy evaporate. Although she had told herself often that she had expected it to happen, it did not make her feel better.

During one of her visits, she arranged with Janet to have Okechukwu baptized at the C.M.S. church. Nelson did not approve, but she insisted. He finally gave in after failing to get her to admit that Christian had converted her to Christianity.

'I am glad he does not come here as often as he used to,' Nelson had said in his new off-hand manner. 'Not that I mind. He is my closest friend, the only real friend I have. But people often talk when they see a man visiting another man's house at all hours.'

For weeks afterwards, Ejiaka wondered which one of her neighbours had told tales about her?

When Christian asked why she wanted to have Okechukwu baptized she told him that every child should be given a grounding of faith with which to face the world. Children should be grounded in Christianity because of its newness and general acceptance, rather than in the waning traditional religion.

'Why not bring up your children on rice alone?' he had asked her. 'Why feed them yams and cassava?'

'What do you mean?' she had asked. She wanted him to keep on talking to her.

'Rice is the new and accepted form of food; yams and cassava are the old ones.'

'You cannot compare food and religion,' she had protested.

'Well I hope you know what you are doing,' he had said and would not say another word.

He left her soon after to return to his shop. Passionate people often exaggerate things. If she had told him she baptized Okechukwu to protect him from an old woman's prediction and to get closer to Christian himself, although she now realized she had miscalculated, he would have thought she was lying. Wrapped up in himself as he was, he would not have understood. Janet's return had shown beyond doubt that his goodness was centred in himself. As long as his desires coincided with those of the people around him, he was considerate.

Okechukwu had been baptized on Christmas day. Throughout the ceremony he stared at the officiating priest and neither blinked nor cried out when the cold water was splashed on his forehead. He had already become a man at the age of three.

By March it was agreed that Janet's treatment at Zaria had not been successful. Ejiaka suggested a repeat and after some heated arguments it was accepted.

But who would have known they were all like bluebottle flies dancing on a heap of excrement?

Who would have known *they* would enter into Christian and lead him stark, raving naked to his death? A death that left him without dignity, without honour?

Who would have known what was in tomorrow's womb?

3 ⚸ No matter how much we wish it, or the passing years bring fulfilment and joy, certain periods and moments in our lives refuse to dim or be forgotten. Their memories are often fresh, as if they happened yesterday, and recalling them is made easier if they have left a legacy. For Janet, one of those periods began in late November 1942, and its legacy was her toddling son, John. In the past year, whenever she came home tired from her work in the General Hospital in Zaria, and found her parents out with John, she relived the fear bred by the incidents of that November. Those incidents had started with an empty house and

a reddish-brown telegram on the cupboard. Her heart had beat fast as she picked up the telegram expecting bad news, but not as bad as what she read:

CHRISTIAN DIED SUNDAY STOP RETURN IMMEDIATELY
DOCTOR

And the cryptic message had not changed on second reading. It only made it concrete, the pressure making her heart want to jump out of her mouth. Sitting down in the nearest chair she brought the paper to the focus of her vision once more:

CHRISTIAN DIED SUNDAY . . .

Oh God, how? Why? What killed him? Who killed him?

Her hand shook uncontrollably and the telegram blurred, seeming to melt away into black-streaked red pools. But floating on them and standing out in grey sharpness that pierced the brain and the heart and the loins and the legs were the three words:

CHRISTIAN DIED SUNDAY . . .

Janet had cried out. The sound caught her unawares and she froze expecting someone to remonstrate with her. But she was alone and the silence of the ageing morning reconstituted itself.

She was alone. Not just physically alone. If what she had read *was* true, she was now totally alone.

To make sure, she raised the telegram to her eyes again, but the lettering was now refracted into a quivering unintelligibility. However, she did not really need to see the lettering. The feel of the paper, and its colour were enough. It was true! Oh God, it *was* true. Christian died! Christian *is* dead.

And she sat in the chair while her silent tears splashed down, wetting her blouse, soaking it and spreading down towards the bottom of her belly.

Oh, Christian, it is like you to leave in my absence. Perhaps I should not have taken Vitus with me. Perhaps I should have left him with you. Perhaps you would not have died.

But you insisted on it. Did you know? Had you planned it? You always hated my being around when you were sick. You said you felt defeated when you were sick, and you did not like

229

people to see you at a time you were defenceless. You always thought people lay in wait to take advantage of you.

Christian, did you plan it this way?

Was it the next day or the day after that she had got on the train to go back to Port Harcourt? Or was it a week later?

As her father had said in his usual survival type of wisdom, it did not really matter when she went back to Port Harcourt. One did not have to hurry to see a dead man, which was the reason Peter was so tardy in going to the Son of Man's grave on the morning of resurrection.

Janet was reluctant to give up the idea of going by lorry which was the faster way. Her reluctance was overcome by her mother's cryptic statement, 'To win, it is enough to survive.'

Had Janet finally won because she had survived Christian? Was anyone supposed to win in life? Not when everyone had to die! Death negated life's victory. Besides life was not a competition in which there must be a winner and a loser. It was more than that, much more than winners and losers. Life was itself losing. All living things lost in the end. It did not matter what one did, one lost it all when one was dead. Unless one believed in life after death.

'So I have won, have I?' Janet thought. 'Finally won.'

But her tears did not cease.

For once, the train arrived and left the station on time. Also for the first time her father came to see her off. His sharp face had worn its most serious and pious mask. She caught him once without it, and the joy, pleasure and boyish excitement she saw brought tears to her eyes. Had he not said only the Devil found pleasure in this world, and that laughter was his greatest weapon? Her father had never really approved and, it was now obvious, had never reconciled himself to her marriage to Christian.

The second-class compartment was crowded. She was however

heartened to see that the other passengers, three middle-aged men, would be getting off at Kaduna. She did not want any company, neither did she want sympathy based on curiosity. To avoid unnecessary attention she dressed against her mother's wishes, in a plain *lappa* and blouse with a brightly coloured head-tie binding the long hair she would soon have to shave off. She even managed a smile at the small middle-aged man who gave up his corner-seat by the window.

'I am sure the train will leave on time,' her father had said, looking dapper in his 'Archdeacon' suit, from which the broiling sun bounced in scintillating arrows. The suit, the first and last present Christian had given him, reminded Janet so much of what she had lost that she feared for one moment she would lose control of herself.

'You should have worn a black head-tie at least,' her mother whispered. She was standing as close to the coach as possible, her broad lined face a mirror of longing, sadness and concern.

Janet shook her head both in disagreement and in an effort to hold back her tears.

A whistle shrilled and a hand-bell rang three times.

'Just as I said. The Devil's train will always leave on time. I am sure when you return the train will run late.'

'*Nnamu-ukwu*,' her mother had said.

But Janet did not mind her father's talk of the Devil. It was, in a way, the best thing to talk about under the circumstances. The all powerful Devil! The laughing being who wrested huge power from God—the power to tempt his creations as often and as much as he wanted.

Tears threatened to overwhelm her once more remembering she would never hear again Christian's criticisms of God, the church, and the priests. His terrible statements only reinforced her beliefs, and made her constantly aware of what she believed in by forcing her to re-examine, test and defend it. Her only Catholic friend once said the rosary did the same thing for her each time she told it at prayers. Belief and faith had to be reinforced by feelings. But now, she had lost that.

God, why?

The train pulled away smoothly. The crowd that filled the station dwindled into an appropriate size—that of a collection of

231

ants. The hills of Zaria soon came up and hid the station, the town, and the signs of habitation. Now it was as if the train was rushing through a wilderness of sparse grass and shrubs, scattered stones and rocks.

⊁⊁⊁

The train had come to a stop. The peculiar echoing and hollow-sounding sigh, the almost dead silence and the hawker's sudden plaintive cry of 'Olomah!' filled the night with a nostalgia that caught at Janet's throat. Just a month before she had been on her way to Zaria to see the *dibia* a second time, the only worry that of confirming if she could get pregnant. And now she was rushing back to Port Harcourt, the purpose in going to Zaria unfinished and she a widow.

Oh God, what have I done? Why should I be punished like this? Initially I could get pregnant any time, but my children preferred the other world. Then when I went to have that cured I could no longer get pregnant. When I went again to deal with the new illness you snatched Christian away from me. What have I done to deserve this?

Janet threw her window open. She was glad of the cool air that streamed in and the fact that she was now alone in the compartment. She would not have a companion till late the next day and she hoped it would be a nice middle-aged man who would respect her silence.

She leant her elbow on the window-sill, her hand supporting her head, and let her eyes roam over the lantern lights that seemed to dance to an inaudible beat.

I wonder where we are, she thought, and what time it is.

'Pah-eenapul!' a hawker shouted in the distance.

'*Ogbo-o-oh*,' cried another.

'*Oh-lomah*, orange,' a third cried suddenly, materializing behind a swinging palm-oil lamp.

Impulsively Janet called, '*Onye oh-lomah*.'

The hawker was a young boy who should be asleep and not out in the cold night trying to make a few farthings. Probably he does not have a mother, Janet thought, buying half a dozen peeled oranges although she did not really want to do so.

'What station is this?' she asked after she had paid.

'Makurdi, ma.'

Janet was surprised to have slept so long. The train usually passed Makurdi in the early hours of the morning and she was sure she had fallen asleep at around ten. She felt better that she was able to have a little rest. She bit into one of the oranges, the sweetness washing off the bad taste in her mouth.

Just when she was beginning to think the train would never continue the journey, she felt the jolt of the engine coupling with the first coach. Pleasant anticipation diffused through her body only to be swamped by the feeling of loss and emptiness waiting for her. Her stomach coiled upon itself and the orange began to taste worse than liquid quinine. She threw out the oranges including the half-eaten one, shut the window, and surrendered to sobs.

'What shall I do now? Oh my God, what shall I do?' she moaned. Why was life not like a journey by train? You knew where you started from and where your journey would end, and you knew the train would follow the tracks that led straight to your destination. Should the train be derailed you knew it was a temporary mishap, and that you would soon be on your way.

God, why did you not make life that straightforward?

※※※

There had been times when Janet had hated Christian with an intensity that was frightening. One thought had kept her from leaving him, something her father had wanted her to do a long time ago. When Christian acted in such a hateful manner to make her angry enough to leave him, she remembered their marriage vows and her determination not to allow him to make her break them. *That* was one victory she would not allow him. Hadn't he won everything else?

Another thing that kept her from leaving him was that she knew that for all his taunts and sarcasm, his inner self was still rooted in the Lord. His loud irreverence could only be a result of this unshakeable anchor. How often she had wished this could be true of his love for her!

The night before she left for the second treatment he had been unable to make love to her because he claimed he was sick. Yet when he, Ejiaka and Nelson had seen her off at the railway station he had been as fit as an *nmonwu ọma*.

'The way you are looking at me!' he had said. 'You are not thinking of selling me, are you?'

'Please don't talk like a child,' she said, suppressing with difficulty an angry curse. She hoped her hatred was not showing in her face.

But he had laughed and to anger her even further, Ejiaka had joined him, teeth flashing only for him. Janet pushed away her old suspicion that something had happened between Ejiaka and Christian. It was incredible the way girls matured and became corrupt, the way they exuded an air of moral decay. She promised herself she would cut Ejiaka off as a friend when she returned.

Nelson, too, seemed to have the same suspicions about them for he asked in his new sullen way, 'What are you laughing at?'

The laughter had died out immediately from Ejiaka's face, but it lingered on Christian's as though reluctant to leave such a familiar face. Never one to let well enough alone he had turned to Nelson and asked lazily,

'What do you want us to do? We are not mourning anyone.'

Janet, sensing Christian's intentions and not wanting to play the victim to his baiting tongue, withdrew herself from the conversation. It was easy to lose herself in the bustling crowd on the station platform, and she wondered why she did not withdraw from her marriage in the same manner. Surely she could have found someone to lose herself to, perhaps a man who would have made her forget the unchristian idea of divorce and Christian's devilish good looks.

Were some people destined to be Jobs? Or was there something in them that attracted that type of treatment, forcing them to seek out and perpetrate Job's suffering?

'They can have him now,' Janet had murmured.

'What did you say?' Christian had asked with a smile.

'Oh nothing,' Janet had said quickly.

'You have not left Port Harcourt yet and you are already talking to yourself. Nelson, Ejiaka, let us leave her and go home. She does not want us to be here.'

234

'Ejiaka don't mind him,' Janet had said laughing. 'I was just asking when the train will leave.'

'You see what I told you? She really does not want us here.'

Ejiaka, and even Nelson had joined Christian in one of those laughs that overwhelm whatever generated them.

Janet's heart was filled with hate as she levered the top half of her body through the window to be able to see as far up the length of the train as possible. The engine that had come out from the running shed long ago still stood many feet away from the first coach, a gleaming, disdainful and hissing black power.

'Janet you will fall out,' Nelson had warned.

'She is not a child,' Christian had said, 'although she sometimes behaves like one.'

Janet had drawn back into the coach. 'Is the train waiting for something?' she had asked Nelson.

'No. It is not yet time for the train to leave. I think it will leave on schedule.'

'But the engine has been out for a long time now.'

'Driver Bankole likes to come out early to the station.'

'An impatient man,' Christian had said.

'He is a good driver. His trains are never late.'

'Neither will his death be,' Christian had said laughing.

'Death is never late,' Nelson had said in the tone of instruction he now used often. 'It is on time whenever it comes.'

'How did death come into this conversation?' Ejiaka had suddenly asked. 'It is not good to talk about it when someone is going on a long journey. Janet, you will write us when you get to Zaria?'

'When I do get there.'

'What do you mean by "when you do get there"? You will get there!'

'By the power of God, not by our own power. Nelson, did you not say the coaches carrying the soldiers were coupled already?'

'Yes. You felt the coupling didn't you?'

'Then what are we waiting for? You of all people should know. This is your house.'

'It is not like that, Janet. I belong to the shed not the traffic division. My engine has been waiting for a long time now. If

Bankole had been waiting this long for the engine to be ready, he would have signed off-duty by now.'

'You mean he could go off-duty any time he felt like it?'

'No, not any time he felt like it. A driver can sign off-duty if his train is not ready a certain number of hours after he books on duty, and he will be paid as if he had been on the line. Bankole has done it once and I am sure he would love to do it again.'

'God will not permit him to do it again,' Janet had said fervently.

'God will not stop him from doing it if he wants to,' Christian had said, 'Remember we are God's children and he gave us free will. So we can do anything we like.'

'Ejiaka,' Janet had said tightly, 'come back into the coach. It does not look as if this journey is going to start soon.'

Janet had sat back in the compartment as Ejiaka started towards the nearest door. To ease her mind and dissipate the angry hatred that was beginning to make her sweat, she had run her hand over the thick leather-covered bench seat and bounced her back repeatedly against the deep-piled back rest that became a bunk bed when raised. Each bounce made her freshly aware of the luxurious feel of it, and on the fifth bounce she smiled at one of the ironies of life—that continuous contact often made one less appreciative and even unaware of luxurious surroundings.

As though for the first time, she sniffed appreciatively at the somewhat closed but expensive smell of the compartment, and her eyes lighted up at the sight of the highly-finished wood-panelling, shiny metallic hangers, runners, window frames and catches, and the clean plate-glass. The contrast between the cool interior of the compartment and the dusty, sun-drenched and shallow brightness of the station platform was so marked it took her breath away.

And Christian had said it was a waste of money for her to travel second class again! He knew how she hated the crowded, vile-smelling third class. Yet he would have her take it. Since she had helped him to open the new shop, he behaved now as though he owned her, hearth-stones and breadfruit. Janet could feel her anger stirring again, and to arrest it she bounced against the back rest again.

'*Ewu-o*,' Ejiaka had exclaimed as soon as she opened the sliding door. 'I lost my way. Everything looks the same out there.' She had sat in the opposite seat with an excited bounce and rearranged her multi-coloured *lappa* to cover her exposed legs. 'I wish I was travelling with you, Janet. I have never gone anywhere by train. I know it must be like taking your house with you on a journey.'

'You have grown into a very lovely woman, Ejiaka,' Janet had said slowly. 'I can't believe it is only three years ago that you looked like a girl who had become pregnant too young. Do you remember how you used to dress? Just one *lappa* and one *okirika* blouse for going to the market, visiting, and even going to the running shed! Now, you not only know what clothes to buy, but also how to wear them.'

'Is there something you want to tell me?'

'No,' Janet had said, shaking her head sadly. 'Nothing that you do not already know. I can see it in your face. And I do not blame you. He is a very attractive man.'

'Who?'

'Do you not know?'

Janet had waited, her eyes watching Christian and Nelson for any sign of their wanting to come into the compartment while her ears were totally attentive to Ejiaka's smallest rustle. She did not want their husbands to interrupt them, not before she had found out what had happened between Ejiaka and Christian.

'I know what you are thinking,' Ejiaka had said in a small voice. 'But nothing happened. He did not even know I was there. I know it sounds as if I am lying, but I am telling you the truth.'

'What about them? Why are they behaving like siblings?'

'You know how men behave.'

'Yes.'

Janet was not satisfied but she decided to let it go. If something had happened previously, she was sure it would not be repeated. Besides, Ejiaka had taught her that one should not always fight aggressively. Passivity was also a form of fighting. Sometimes being aggressive became an end in itself totally replacing one's real objective.

Suddenly a whistle shrilled and soon after, the whole train shuddered from the impact of the engine as it coupled. The station came alive and the flurry of goodbyes and descents from coaches began.

Yes. With the train you knew where you were starting from, why and where you were going.

♯♯♯

The loud, metallic rapping on the door dragged Janet from a deep sleep.

'Who is it?' she asked resentfully. No one answered. The train rushing through the night filled the air with its staccato music that spelt speed and certainty of destination.

'Who is it?' Janet said again, beginning to wonder if she had imagined the knocking.

'Ticket, ticket!' a gruff voice shouted.

Janet sat up and turned on the lamp. Rummaging in her handbag with sleepy hands and eyes she took out the train ticket and slowly stood up.

The knocking came again, louder and more peremptory.

'Ticket!'

'I am coming,' Janet shouted in English. She unlocked the door and opened it, but as she stretched out her hand with the ticket, she was pushed and half carried back into the compartment.

Her scream and the slamming of the door were so simultaneous that she doubted if she had screamed at all.

'Shut up!' the gruff voice ordered her, and slapped her hard on the face.

From the seat where the slap had thrown her, she looked up at the three men. *Three soldiers*. They towered over her, their faces darker than any she had seen before. She felt neither fear nor alarm. But for the pain and the ringing in her ears, and the tears rolling down her cheeks, she would have thought she was dreaming. But what did they want?

'She is old,' one of the soldiers said in Hausa.

'But she looks after herself well,' another said.

'Mrs. Okoro, do you understand Hausa?' the soldier who had slapped her asked suddenly in Igbo.

'No,' Janet lied quickly, alarm taking flight in the pit of her stomach for the first time.

238

'You know what we want?' he asked in Igbo again.

'No,' Janet said again, trying desperately to place the soldier's dialect. Somehow she did not think he was from Onitsha although he spoke Onitsha Igbo perfectly.

'You are no longer a child,' the Igbo soldier said. 'Neither are you *a maiden who does not know a man.*'

'I do not know what you want,' Janet said, and crossed her legs, first loosely and then tightly. Now she wished she had listened to her mother and worn a mourning dress.

'What did she say?' the first soldier asked in Hausa. There was no doubt he and the second one were Hausas.

'She does not want to give us what we want.' said the Igbo soldier in accented Hausa.

'Did you ask her nicely?' the second soldier asked.

'How can I after we slapped her?' the Igbo soldier said.

'*You* slapped her,' the first soldier said. 'You said you could get her to do anything since she is your countrywoman. My friend you don't beg old women for things, you tell them what you want. Ahmadu, bolt the door, then come and help me.'

The train rushed on into the night, slowing, stopping, starting again, rushing, waiting, steaming, and once or twice running with a disjointed clanging that told more about how it felt than any 'B' examination would. But that did not mean the train would not be on the tracks the next day. It would go through the same distances, the same motions, and achieve the same destinations till it was scrapped. For if the creator of the train had not built into it the power to find out the meaning of its journeys, or even to think about it and reason it all out, then the best it could do was to keep on moving.

Glossary

lit. = literary meaning.

afor: the name of one of the four market days.

agbisi: stinging ant.

agu: leopard; also a praise name.

ajọ nmuọ/ajọ nwa: bad spirit/bad child.

asha: weaver-bird.

avuke: fighting hen.

awa: yam broth.

chi: personal god.

chineke ekwene ihe ọjọ: God forbid evil.

chukwunna ọnwu gbara ndu anyi gburugburu: God the father our lives are circumscribed by death.

dibia: seer; herbal doctor; diviner; medical doctor.

egbe igwe: thunder; *lit.* the gun of the sky.

gbuwhuo asọ: a reprimand usually delivered by an older to a younger person for saying something unbecoming, reprehensible, or taboo. *lit.* spit out your saliva.

ibia kwa: there you go again! *lit.* you are coming.

igwe: sky.

imacha ọmugwọ: the Igbo version of the churching of a woman after childbirth; a mandatory period of rest—28 days—for a woman after childbirth.

isi ukwa: fruit of the breadfruit. *lit.* head of the bread fruit.

ite nkpa: old pot for storing palm oil.

kọtuma: court messenger; this is a corruption of 'court messenger'.

241

lappa: a long strip of cloth often brightly coloured and printed, wrapped around the lower part of the body, worn by both men and women.

mbakameshi: barbarians; uncivilized peoples; foreigners.

mbamiri: peoples of the Niger Delta.

mgbe nhie le ju eju: an onomatopoeic statement resulting from the resemblance between the sounds of the month *June* and the Igbo word, *iju*, which means 'to be full'. Another example is the *mber* in the months September, October, November and December; these months are known as the *mba* (meaning 'no') months. *lit.* the period when things are full.

mpoto ede: the broad leaves of the coco-yam plant.

nagbo: goodbye.

ndo: expression of apology, sympathy or commiseration under circumstances ranging from trivial accident to tragedy.

nkekwu: small rat.

nkpuru ji: small, round or oblong yam. *lit.* seed of yam.

nmanwu ọjọ/nmọnwu ọma: running masquerade/beautiful dancing masquerade. *lit.* bad masquerade/beautiful masquerade.

nnamu-ukwu: husband. *lit.* my great father.

nshi nwanyi: gonorrhoea and/or syphilis. *lit.* female poison.

nwa olu: an only child.

nwunyedi: husband's other wife.

nzu: natural chalk.

ọdunma: all right; ok.

ogwumagada: chameleon.

oke nwanyi: tough woman. *lit.* masculine female.

okwute: stone.

uli: a dye used by women for drawing patterns on the skin.

ume ọmumu: a woman is said to be suffering from this when two or more of her children die before the age of five. The children must have died in the order in which they were born.